LADY UNVEILED ~ THE CUCKOLD CONSPIRACY

BEVERLEY OAKLEY

CHAPTER 1

*L*ucinda's angry, discordant note on the piano brought Lissa's head up sharply. It seemed her disgruntled charge had finally —like Lissa—had enough of the muffled and completely inappropriate giggles of Lord Beecham's 'special' friend. For the last hour, Lissa had sat quietly sewing by the window, as well behaved as any good governess could be suffering such trials.

Meanwhile, seated on an elegant blue and silver silk-striped sofa opposite the piano, Lord Beecham seemed wholly occupied with his increasingly regular guest, Lady Julia, and until now, impervious to his ward's attempt to regain his attention.

Lissa slanted a glance at Lucinda. When Lucinda was angry, she was not a pretty girl. Her peaches and cream complexion became red and mottled; her rosebud-shaped mouth flattened into a harsh, thin line, and her normally luminous blue eyes seemed almost black beneath beetling brows. This was how she looked now as she hunched on the piano stool, glowering at Lady Julia—or Lady Ledger, wife of Sir Archie Ledger if she were happy to be properly identified, which, judging by the surreptitious fondling the pair were engaged in today, she would not.

Lady Julia, *supposedly* an earl's daughter fallen upon hard times, was purportedly Lucinda's very young godmother. She arrived at Lord Beecham's London townhouse at regular intervals, heavily veiled, to instruct Miss Lucinda Martindale in the musical arts, though she could not—as far as Lissa could tell—play a note. At least, Lissa had never heard her play a note, though she'd heard a lot of other noises emanating from Lady Julia during her visits to his Lordship's bedroom between music lessons.

Finally, it seemed, Lucinda had achieved what she'd been after—Lord Beecham's undivided attention.

"What an infernal noise!" he exclaimed, the dewy adoration as he'd gazed at Lady Julia instantly replaced by a thunderous scowl as he jerked his head around to look at Lucinda. "I spend a fortune on your musical education! Surely I should expect better than that!"

Lucinda's mobile face went through a gamut of emotions—devastation then outrage, however her mouth remained a thin, tight line. It was quite obvious the girl was desperately in love with her benefactor into whose care she'd been placed the previous year.

It was upon the death of her parents and younger brother during a scarlet fever outbreak in their village that Lucinda became a ward of Lord Beecham. But while Lucinda was obstinate and demanding of her governess, she had never, as far as Lissa knew, openly challenged Lord Beecham.

Nevertheless, there was an underlying challenge now as the girl asked, "Perhaps Lady Julia would care to demonstrate how Pachelbel's Canon in D should *really* sound."

Lady Julia, who had attempted to discreetly put at least several inches between her thigh and that of his Lordship's on the sofa, smiled sweetly. "My dear, I don't want to show you up." She patted her bright golden hair, then purred, "Please, play it again. With just a little more practise you will have mastered it, and Lord Beecham and I are quite happy for you to entertain us while I continue to outline to him my hopes on how your general carriage, demeanor and...might I add without offense...character itself might be improved sufficiently to make your come-out without undue embarrassment to either yourself or his Lordship."

Lissa was interested to see how Lucinda would take this. With her head still bowed over her embroidery frame, she didn't miss the flashing eyes above the pretty, pert nose of her young charge, and Lord Beecham's wolfish, apparent approval of Lady Julia's saccharine demeanor.

In the two months Lissa had spent in Lord Beecham's employ, she had not warmed to her charge; for all she knew she ought to pity the girl. It was true that she'd established more control over Lucinda than Lucinda's previous governess had. Lucinda no longer tried to undermine her at every opportunity or threw tantrums, and it appeared Lissa's policy of being firm but distant appeared to have worked. But there was little affection between the pair.

Lucinda was the first to drop her eyes from Lady Julia's scrutiny. Her shoulders slumped, and she turned back to her music which she started to play once again, this time softly and with no discordant notes. Lucinda was rather good at most things, if she put her mind to it.

Meanwhile, Lissa strained to hear what Lady Julia and Lord Beecham were discussing. It was one of the reasons she'd been placed in this position by her 'real' employer, Sir William Deane, late of the Foreign Office. The fact that Lissa could apparently appear as nondescript as the wallpaper was to her advantage, for she'd already gleaned several tidbits, which had been well-received as points of interest by Sir William's successor.

Her ears pricked up at a reference to Lord Silverton, not a name she'd expected to hear in this drawing room, but a name that induced mixed feelings since she'd learned her younger sister, Kitty, now a celebrated actress, had become his mistress.

For months, Lissa had been desperate to make contact with Kitty. She'd resisted because she feared Kitty's unbridled love of chatter, and her reputation for indiscretions might compromise Lissa's dangerous work in espionage and bringing to justice a very dangerous gentleman. Lissa was the responsible one, and Kitty was quite likely to inadvertently destroy the hard-won gains Lissa had painstakingly worked toward during these past few months.

Reluctantly, she'd therefore refrained from directly seeking Kitty out, though she kept as much of a sisterly eye upon her as she could from afar, informing their mother of Kitty's successes on the stage though their mother had, of all the family, been the most distraught at the scandalous life her daughter had embraced. Just as well she had no idea of the murky world of intrigue in which Lissa was involved.

In the midst of these musings, Lissa was brought up short by Lady Julia's loud whisper. "Did you know Silverton's betrothed is due to travel down from the north sometime next month? I wonder if word has reached poor Octavia that there's already a little cuckoo in the nest."

She wriggled against Lord Beecham and put her mouth to his ear as she ran her hand inside his waistcoat. "Kitty La Bijou! You did hear, didn't you, that the darling of the London stage arrived at the altar not four weeks ago, all set to marry Lord Nash?" Lady Julia was clearly enjoying the salacious details in inverse proportion to Lissa, whose very soul seemed to be in the process of being sucked through her feet. To hear the gossip-hungry Lady Julia muckraking Lissa's own sister as if the girl were society's grisly spoils was a particularly cruel piece of purgatory.

When Lord Beecham put his head on one side to indicate his interest, Lady Julia eagerly supplied the details Lissa had heard in only the sketchiest form. "Yes, Lord Nash's irate pater appeared in St Mary's in high dudgeon to announce his son wasn't permitted to wed before he was twenty-five. You won't believe what happened next! Miss La Bijou, in full wedding regalia, burst into tears and ran out into the street with Lord Silverton in hot pursuit. By the time Lord Nash caught up with his erstwhile lover and intended bride, to explain to Miss Bijou that he'd already ensured the legalities were iron-clad, and furthermore, here was his lawyer and now his father to attest to the fact, it was to discover Miss La Bijou in a state of post-coital bliss with... Lord Silverton!"

Lady Julia relaxed back against her cushions and said with self-satisfaction, "You can imagine the gossips have had a field day with all of this. The girl is quite ruined of course, and her hopes of ever being accepted into polite society completely dashed. But to think that if she *hadn't* miscalculated, she'd be lording it over the rest of us as Lady Nash," she tittered. "Designing little piece, that Kitty La Bijou, though butter wouldn't melt in her mouth. And the gossip sheets can't seem to get enough of her, forever lauding her performance as Desdemona these days." She sighed. "It becomes quite tiresome after a while when there's nothing else to read."

Lord Beecham chuckled and patted her cheek fondly. "My dear, you're among the worst! *You* simply can't get enough of such titillating gossip!"

It was, however, Lissa who couldn't get enough of what she was hearing—which indeed was news in the kind of detail she'd not heard. And not the kind of detail she wanted to hear.

She put her head down and tried to hold back her tears of shame. For months, she'd suffered the ignominy of her thankless role as Miss Lucinda's governess. When she'd been placed in this position by Sir Edward Keane of the Foreign Office, she'd been filled with hope and pride.

At last, she, the unacknowledged illegitimate daughter of Lord Partington, was going to prove her worth. She would keep her head down and her ears attuned to any suggestion of Lord Beecham's involvement in the attempted assassination of a cabinet minister several years before, and a spate of extortion attempts on members of the aristocracy. Beecham had been an associate of Viscount Debenham since their involvement in the radical underground Jacobin movement of the 1790s, a time when both men had no aspirations toward noble status.

Now with seats in the House of Lords, it was Sir Edward's belief that Beecham and Debenham had found more inventive ways to exploit their changed circumstances, using the criminal associations they'd made several decades before. There were old scores to be settled, and it seemed, forever empty pockets to line.

Political malice or criminal greed? Or had Lord Beecham shed his shady proclivities with his change in status?

Lissa no longer answered to Sir Edward, now a diplomat in

Constantinople, but to the Treasury Solicitor's Office and the shadowy Lord Carmody of the Home Office, a man who kept up Lissa's belief in her noble cause by his regular praise of her detailed drawings and observations.

One day, Lissa hoped, her work would be acknowledged as having helped flush out the profligacy, promiscuity, violence, mendacity, and outright criminality which many of those with whom Beecham and Debenham had once associated still peddled. If her observations could link Beecham either with Debenham, or just one ringleader in the underground rabble of counterfeiters, extortionists, and even murderers who plagued society, she'd consider it a job well done and herself a success.

But Lord, what would their mother say to Kitty's shocking exploits? The girl had nearly wed Lord Nash? Then she'd been caught in flagrante with Lord Silverton within half an hour of the truncated nuptials and was now his mistress?

Something inside Lissa seemed to curl up and die. Where had Lissa gone wrong? She'd tried so hard to be the mother Kitty had missed out on, reading her stories, drying her tears. Of course Lissa denied it, but even she could see that their mother seemed to have little affection for her bright and joyful youngest and had become even more distant following the unexpected birth of her last child only a few months before.

Reluctantly, Lissa accepted that Kitty had had little incentive to remain at home caring for a demanding mother and newborn sister, but her latest exploits were too much to condone.

Not only had she destroyed all claim to ever being accepted into the ranks of the respectable classes by becoming an actress, but she'd taken up with Lord Silverton who was himself looking into the affairs of Debenham and his ilk—Lord Smythe and the radical shoemaker, pamphleteer, and suspected counterfeiter, Buzby. On the surface, he appeared urbane and inclined to pleasure-seeking with dubious rascals, but he was very much committed to the same cause as Lissa. And now Lissa's sister had become the mistress of this very man.

"Are you all right, Miss Hazlett?"

Lissa hadn't realized she'd made a sound. She looked from the droplet of blood on her finger where she'd pricked herself with her embroidery needle then toward Lord Beecham.

"Quite all right, my lord. But if you'll excuse me, I think it's time I saw Miss Lucinda to bed." She rose and beckoned to her charge, who sent her a somewhat sour look as she put down the lid of the piano but rose nevertheless.

Meanwhile, Lissa's thoughts were in turmoil. It was now imperative to find Kitty and explain to her that she must end her contact with Silverton. Not only was it unseemly, it was *wrong*.

Lissa knew where to locate her. Several months before, she'd attended the theater and seen Kitty perform, dashing off a sketch because she'd been so enthralled. When Lord Ludbridge, the brother of Lissa's admirer, Ralph, had begged to acquire it, she'd torn it off the sketchbook so that it didn't identify Kitty. It had seemed somehow wrong to show her little sister dressed in man's attire and performing on stage to all the world.

What had struck Lissa, however, was how carefree and happy Kitty had appeared whenever Lissa had secretly observed her; a great contrast from the isolation and daily pressure Lissa felt.

But the idea that little Kitty was Lord Silverton's plaything, as Lady Julia had put it, and that this was public news, distressed her beyond measure.

And now Lord Silverton's *betrothed* was to arrive soon in the capital? Lord Silverton was to be married, yet was keeping Kitty as his mistress? The idea filled her with horror. What would become of Kitty? Would she be cast into the gutter? Lord Silverton might be on their side when it came to apprehending Lord Debenham, but he was an out-and-out cad to be exploiting innocent, credulous little Kitty.

Her outrage at these ponderings made her say more sharply than she intended, "Hurry now, Lucinda. There'll be no time for reading. It's far too late for that."

"I'm seventeen, not seven, in case you hadn't noticed," Lucinda muttered as she preceded Lissa up the stairs, adding as she turned, "And in four months, when I've had the most successful debut of the year and found myself a husband who will make all the other debutantes green about the gills, *you'll* be looking for a job and someone else to send to bed early."

Lissa sighed inwardly as she counseled herself not to respond. It was wisest not to when Lucinda was in low spirits as she certainly must be, seeing Lord Beecham making so much of his companion, Lady Julia. But she couldn't help herself.

Lucinda had turned upon opening her bedchamber door, and now Lissa regarded her with a look full of sympathy.

"Do not take Lord Beecham's criticism to heart. He is far too old and experienced for you. In three months, all the young men will be falling over themselves in their desire to court you."

Lucinda reddened. "How dare you suggest I have an interest in Lord Beecham!" she muttered, thrusting the door wide and stumbling over the threshold. "If you *ever* allude to this again, I will find a way to have you instantly dismissed."

It felt like a slap in the face. Lissa turned back toward her own bedchamber. "Good night, Lucinda," she said wearily. She'd been up since before six, mending a tear in a chemise which Lord Beecham intimated belonged to Lucinda, but which Lissa knew belonged to Lady Julia. How it had become torn could only be wondered at, for it was not Lissa's place to question her employer's requests. It was not her place to do anything but obey if she and her darling Ralph were to finally be together.

In dismal spirits, Lissa trailed along the passage to the small, sparsley-furnished room she inhabited, trying to bolster herself with thoughts of the young man she'd loved with quiet, frustrated passion for so long—brave and enterprising Ralph Tunley. Dear Ralph was long-suffering secretary to—of all people—Lord Debenham, the man the Foreign Office and now Home Office had in their sights; the man who was married, most inconveniently, to Lissa and Kitty's' half-sister, Araminta.

Wearily, she took out her sketchbook and flipped through the pages of drawings she'd made of Lord Beecham's various associates

8

who'd come to the house. None of them had been of any interest according to Lord Carmody, who had counseled patience.

But how patient could a girl be when weeks had stretched into months, and nothing had happened? When Lissa had first taken up residence under Lord Beecham's roof after her previous disastrous situation as governess to the social-climbing Lamonts, she'd thought a new life of excitement awaited her. Ralph and she would soon join each other as husband and wife, their reward for the success of their noble quest to establish Lord Debenham as the key architect on the attempt on Lord Castlereagh's life. Now she realized that as a mere governess, and a woman, she'd simply been relegated, once again, to dull, dusty domesticity—more a prisoner than she'd ever been.

She was about to undress when she heard a noise at the window. Instantly she flew across the room to push up the sash, and her heart swelled with joy to see the moonlight shining upon the boyish smile of her beloved Ralph angled up at her from where he stood upon the pavement.

Signaling him to wait, she ran to fetch paper, and quickly scribbled him a note that she wanted to go down and see him but when he received it, he shook his head, his expression concerned. Ralph sometimes made impromptu visits, but they rarely got closer than blowing each other goodnight kisses.

If ever Lissa needed Ralph's comforting common sense, it was now.

Ignoring him, Lissa slipped out of her room, descended four flights of back stairs and ran into the garden. When she was finally in his arms, her cheek pressed against his after he'd kissed her with great feeling, she whispered, "I'm *so* glad to see you, Ralph. I've never felt more in need of your bolstering company, for truth to tell, I really am not possessed of the good character needed to bear with my insufferable charge, much less her exacting employer and his ghastly female friend." She twined her arms about his neck and sighed, "But I know I have to."

"You don't have to do anything you don't want to, dearest girl," Ralph said with a look of the greatest consternation as he set her away from him. "You are brave and the most courageous female I have ever met, and you entered into this plan because I couldn't support you as I would wish, but also in the hope we could be together. But if that is taking longer than either of us can bear—and believe me, I can hardly get through each day without seeing you while my thoughts are of you constantly—then we will find another way, even if it means we must live in straitened circumstances until I receive the advance I know is forthcoming."

Lissa hugged him tighter. Her heart felt suddenly too big for her chest, and Lissa was not one who was prone to overwhelming feelings. Except where Ralph was concerned. "You know I would not risk the promotion we know will soon be yours, and that indeed to give into my foolish weakness might compromise—"

"Hush, we are both clever and enterprising, and for that reason, I am certain that whatever path we choose will compromise nothing." He traced her cheek with his forefinger. In the moonlight, his boyish features had never looked more manly or heroic. "Now, go back upstairs because I do worry about you. Lady Julia is too busy to come looking for you perhaps, but Miss Martindale might."

Lissa broke away and nodded sadly. "I fear I am of little use here, though one snippet that may be of interest is that Lord Beecham mentioned the Princess Caroline's name in the same breath as Debenham's, though it may be nothing. However, I learned of the terrible situation my sister is in, and I wish I could unburden my heart, Ralph, but I'll save it for another night. Suffice to say that poor Kitty has got herself into a scandalous situation. She might have been legally married to Lord Nash if not for her foolish, impulsive ways, but now she's compromised herself, forced into becoming a rich man's... mistress..." she nearly choked on the word "...to survive. There's more. *Worse.* I'll save it for later, but suffice to say that Kitty must be the most wretched, unhappy girl alive."

CHAPTER 2

*K*itty La Bijou, wearing only her stockings and the magnificent sapphire and diamond necklace her handsome lover had gifted her several weeks previously, arched her foot elegantly and placed it upon Silverton's shoulder as he drank the last of the champagne from her bellybutton.

Afternoon light flooded exuberantly into the room, and across the sumptuous four-poster where the lovers were enjoying their latest tryst, burnishing Kitty's hair like gold.

"Dear Lord, but I think I must be the happiest young woman in the entire world, Silverton darling," Kitty purred as she tickled his ears and stroked his brown curls back from his forehead with her toes. "If I were your wife I'd have to obey you, and I wouldn't have nearly such an exciting time of it. Of marriage, I mean. I certainly don't think we'd be doing what we're doing now with such abandon if I were your wife because I'd be forever worried about the servants. Ooh, yes, I like what you're doing. Just a little lower, if you please."

After another standing ovation and brilliantly received performance, Kitty had flown into the arms of her beloved Silverton, who'd been waiting backstage to escort her to the townhouse he'd leased for her, just as he had done every night for the past month since she'd fled from the altar where she'd so nearly committed herself to Nash.

She closed her eyes and gave herself up to the rapture of Silverton's languid kisses from her bellybutton to the core of her pleasure. Never had she imagined such bliss, such happiness, as she enjoyed in the company of this kind, funny, loving, charming man.

When Silverton finally emerged from between her legs, Kitty was breathless with need, pulling him up impatiently and helping to guide him inside her.

Silverton needed no urging. His own pleasure was clearly at breaking point, and in a repeat of their happy lovemaking, they sated themselves in each other's arms as they curled up beneath the covers.

"Are you going to stay the whole night?" Kitty asked sleepily in the aftermath, stroking his cheek. "Do say you will."

Silverton kissed her fingertips, and then her neck. "I shall stay the whole night tonight, tomorrow night, and every night—"

"Until Miss Mandelton arrives in London. Or, at least until you walk up the aisle with her." Kitty raised her face to the ceiling and sighed. "No, no, please don't think I'm complaining. You rescued me, and it was providence for I'm far happier as your mistress than I would have been as Nash's wife."

"Do you *truly* mean that, Kitty?" Silverton rolled onto his stomach and looked earnestly at her.

Kitty's sigh was bittersweet. Darling Silverton had the loveliest eyes of any of the stage lovers into whose rapt faces she'd gazed during her eight months as London's most celebrated actress. And he was, without doubt, the kindest and most earnest and principled man she'd ever met.

Despite her mixed feelings, she smiled. In fact, she'd barely stopped smiling this last month they'd been together. "You told me right from the time we met that men like you are not situated to choose people like me as a wife. Even my own father made clear at Nash's and my 'almost' wedding that the stain on my birth precludes me from moving in exalted circles." Kitty's greatest sadness was that her father, Lord Partington, had never acknowledged her as his daughter, though she'd grown up seeing him almost every day. Having long accepted that she could never aspire to a respectable marriage, Lord Nash's offer had seemed too good to be true. So much so that when Lord Nash's father and Kitty's own father had stomped into the church and announced that it *was* too good to be true, Kitty had crumbled with shame inside, and believed them rather than Nash's urgent declarations that he really *was* going to make an honest woman of her.

Lord, it had been a debacle, and yes, she'd thrown away her one and only chance for a respectable marriage, but she'd not trade places to be anywhere other than with her darling Silverton. She smiled again, this time even more brightly as she rolled onto her stomach and looked across at him, winding one of his brown curls about her finger. "I shall be happier moving in these circles, Silverton. You will have your wife, who has the right background and breeding and will give you children who can inherit. And you shall have me, who will bring you happiness. I understand my place, and I shan't be jealous."

She continued to smile because inside she'd never been happier and she truly believed what she told him.

And as long as Silverton loved Kitty above all others, nothing else mattered.

But as Silverton walked home to his own townhouse in the morning, he was again plagued with doubt and fear as to the path he'd inadvertently chosen. He'd rescued Kitty, but he'd not intended to make her his mistress with Miss Octavia Mandelton having accepted his marriage proposal only the week before.

Octavia was a good and virtuous young lady, a friend whom he'd known since boyhood. He'd not seen her in months when he'd written to make her an offer, believing at the time that Kitty was to marry Lord Nash. And when Octavia had written back to say she'd accept Silverton only on condition his heart was not engaged elsewhere, he'd answered her—he thought, honestly. In a few days, he thought Kitty would become Lady Nash and be lost to him forever. The only panacea was to throw himself into marriage in the hopes of establishing an honest bond with someone who would please his mother, give him children, and imbue his life with her gentle, maternal presence. That was how he saw Octavia.

Now he felt a cad on both scores. He wanted to marry Kitty, but he couldn't. He wanted to be a good husband to Octavia, but he couldn't. Not if that meant giving up Kitty, which he wasn't prepared to do. It wasn't only that he loved her, truly and deeply. He also owed her too much to ever leave her. Or maybe that was just an excuse. Still, he could never do it. Leave her. She was, simply, *part* of him. It would be like living without a limb.

The leaves were slippery beneath his feet as he passed the gated park near his townhouse.

Head bent against the late-night chill and damp, he wondered how he'd managed to get himself in so deep. It was too late to renege on his marriage offer, and it would devastate and quite possibly ruin Octavia, so respectable, so suitable, and so beloved by his mother.

Kitty was, and could never be, a suitable candidate for his wife. Especially not now after the recent scandal which even his own mother had brought up in shocked tones, not knowing of her son's fatal involvement. She'd heard only what a lucky escape Lord Nash had had from an ambitious actress with designs on his wealth and title.

As he put his hand on the latch to open the gate and two bats flew just above his head, his heart felt it was literally breaking in half. Indeed, he was a man torn in two. How could he break off his betrothal when Octavia looked to him to rescue her from spinsterhood and poverty in a rural backwater? When she was the ideal candidate for a man in his situation looking for a well-connected wife?

But how could he live with himself when the time came to divide his attention between the two women who should have his undivided loyalty? Silverton wasn't a man who'd ever dreamed of taking a mistress when he already had a wife.

But he was going to be a man who would take a wife when he already had a mistress.

It didn't sit well with him.

The truth was, he couldn't live with Kitty, but he couldn't live without her.

IN ANOTHER SALUBRIOUS PART OF TOWN, LORD PARTINGTON'S ELDEST daughter sat at her dressing table, pushing back her curtain of unbound dark hair to scan once more the contents of a letter that enraged her more than any letter she could remember receiving.

In fact, it was beyond outrageous, Araminta thought, resisting the impulse to hurl her bottle of Olympian Dew at the wall.

Everyone said Hetty was the sweeter-natured of Lord Partington's daughters—Lord knew, she was certainly the plainest!— but Araminta intended brandishing Hetty's insulting letter in front of all the family so that they could see her sister couldn't let bygones be bygones.

The fact that Hetty had suggested Araminta's husband Lord Debenham's presence for the forthcoming weekend family gathering might be 'difficult' was insulting and outrageous.

Clearly Hetty was still making a mountain over a molehill, harking back to the little incident when Debenham had threatened Hetty with a broken bottle. Well, Araminta knew that Debenham had been in his cups that fateful night at Vauxhall Gardens and one could hardly blame him for reacting as he had since Hetty had just announced her intention to expose him over that wretched and *apparently* incriminating letter Sir Aubrey's deranged wife had written, implicating Debenham in the attempt on Lord Castlereagh's life.

" Somefink wrong, m'lady?" Jane, her maid, had just entered the room and no doubt noticed that outrage was written all over Araminta's face. Since Jane was already the keeper of Araminta's most damning secrets, it was a relief to have someone on whom to vent her spleen this morning.

"Can you believe it, Jane, but Hetty has invited me to The Grange for a few days so the babies can be admired by all and sundry, but she says Debenham isn't welcome."

"That don't sound like Miss 'Etty."

"Well, she's suggested that it's too early for us all to be comfortable with each other. She *still* blames Debenham for trying to blacken Sir Aubrey's name, though I don't know how she can say that when no proof that my darling Debenham had anything to do with any bad business has ever been presented."

"That's b'cause ya burned that letter wot Sir Aubrey's wife wrote sayin' Debenham were guilty of bein' a Spencean 'n all 'em other terrible things; only Lord Debenham pretended it were the other way round 'n the real villain were Sir Aubrey. So, since yer burned the letter, o' course there ain't no evidence. Well, yer *thought* yer burned the letter only yer bin tryin' ter get that Lord Ludbridge ter get it back for yer. If 'e ain't done it yet, 'e neva will."

"Don't you be saucy with me, Jane!" Araminta snapped. She loathed Jane's references to the smoldering mistrust between the two dangerous gentlemen Araminta and her sister Hetty had married respectively.

She unscrewed the lid of the Olympian Dew and dabbed a little of the lotion beneath her eyes. "Sir Aubrey's first wife was deranged so what would she know about anything much less the truth? She killed herself." Unsteadily she tried to screw the lid back on. "And now I don't know what to do." Araminta felt increasingly panicked the more she dwelt on it. "I have to get that letter, only Teddy says his brother needs it, but he won't tell me *why*. Really, I don't know what anyone thinks Debenham is guilty of. " She took a deep breath as she rose and moved to the window to look out into the rainswept street, though she was distracted by her reflection in the glass. She smiled to force away the frown lines, and turned as she considered the latest new hopeful development. "Anyway, Lord Ludbridge promised he'd get me the letter during our last conversation, and it's not the only time he's helped me. You forget it was he who discovered that scheming Kitty La Bijou was mysteriously wearing my necklace, though I won't publicly condemn her since she *did* help me that night."

Jane looked up from where she was removing strands of Araminta's long dark hair from her hairbrush. "No, it might no' do ter sling mud at 'er, m'lady, since ya owe 'er rather more thanks, mayhap, than she's bin given."

Araminta decided to ignore the irony in her maid's words and to drop the subject. She didn't want to pry too much into how the very necklace Araminta had handed over for a service rendered—a service which no one must ever know about—had come to be in Kitty La Bijou's hands; or, rather, around her throat.

But, given half a chance, Jane was at the old topic like a dog with a bone. "P'raps it wouldn't be such a bad fing for you ta find out, m'lady. Yer know Miss Bijou were given the necklace from 'er admirer. Well, the admirer afore Lord Silverton who she's wiv now, so it might be interestin' ter know where 'e got it from. "

"Lord Nash," Araminta muttered. "What a lucky escape for Lord Nash." No, she was not going to pry too much into where he'd got it from. It had been traded in the underworld, the entrails of society, and a place Araminta wanted to put as far away from her own life as possible—like that half-sister, Lissa, she was determined she'd never recognise or acknowledge.

So she said in a bright voice with a veneer of self-justified disgust, "Can you just imagine it! A peer marrying an actress. What's the world coming to? I don't think Papa even knew about Miss Bijou's existence until I told him she'd come into possession of my necklace, and then he was very grim, and even more so when I mentioned the fact the pair were going to marry secretly.

"Apparently Mama follows the gossip sheets though, and she certainly was shocked by such an ill-matched coupling, so it would seem their feelings are entirely in accord with mine." She sent a narrow-eyed look at Jane, not sure where her maid's loyalties lay on this. "Yes indeed, they were *both* horrified to hear that a man of Lord Nash's standing would consider marrying a common piece like Miss Bijou." She trailed her hand over the surface of her dressing table as she stared out of the window, trying not to think of the night Miss Bijou came to her aid and wondering, uncomfortably, how much the girl knew or suspected. "Well, Lord Silverton can enjoy his lovely little plaything, but he'll have to pander to a wife soon enough. I've a mind to hint to his poor bride-to-be that there are hidden depths to her beloved."

"You know Miss Mandelton?"

"Not in the slightest. But I've no doubt she's a dashing piece. A man like Lord Silverton could have his pick."

Jane seemed to consider this for some time, as having finished cleaning Araminta's hairbrush, she started picking up various discarded pieces of clothing about the floor. "'Is Lordship certainly is the 'andsomest man afta me Jem I eva laid me eyes on," she said decidedly as she fixed her mistress with a challenging smile.

Araminta rolled her eyes. "Enough about your Jem when I have such troubles that need two heads, Jane. How am I going to respond with dignity to my younger sister's latest insult?"

"Dignity?"

Araminta didn't like her maid's tone but chose to let it pass for the moment. She went to her cupboard and threw open the door in a quest to decide upon the most appropriate ensemble for her intended meeting with the handsome and noble Lord Ludbridge later that afternoon. So much more noble than her own Debenham, though nobody—least of all her sister—was allowed to hint that her husband was deficient in anything, much less morals. "Yes! Hetty can't tell me Debenham isn't welcome. Besides, it's not her decision."

"So yer'd really like ter take Debenham ter The Grange 'n ter spend a few days wiv Sir Aubrey..." there was a telling pause before she added, "...'n yer sister 'n 'er new babe."

Now that it was phrased in such terms, Araminta couldn't in all truth say that the prospect was anything other than horrific. Her chagrin stemmed from the fact she just hadn't liked Hetty telling her what to do or suggesting Debenham wasn't less than perfect. It was true that they'd all managed to put on a decent public show, and appear at the theater together as two supposedly harmonious couples to stop the wagging tongues, but they'd rarely rubbed up against each other in anything nearly as intimate as one of each other's homes for any length of time.

"I have an idea!" She clapped her hands together, congratulating herself that, yet again, she'd hit upon a cunning plan to solve the problem. "It's my birthday shortly, and Papa asked only yesterday if I had any special requests. At the time, I said no, because I don't like to place burdens on other people, as you are aware, Jane. But now I know exactly what will bring us all together so that we can mend the rifts that divide us. A house party! At The Grange. Mama and Papa shan't mind, as it was always expected I'd be mistress there someday so I could have done whatever I liked. Besides, it's such a small birthday request." Yes, a lavish birthday celebration at The Grange would be just the answer. Her eyes moistened with sentiment as she stared out of the window onto the rain-darkened streets. "We used to have such wonderful house parties there."

"Yer mean like the one where Sir Archie 'n 'is good lady were tryin' to con Mr. Cranborne inter partin' wiv a few monkeys ova that spider racket wot were rigged?" Jane sniffed as she picked up a shawl that Araminta had just finished trying with her dress but had let slip to the floor. "'N where Sir Archie's lady friend fer that evenin'—Lady Julia I believe it were—went boatin' at midnight wiv poor Mr. Edgar wot yer decided yer wanted ter marry afta 'e started makin' eyes at Miss 'Etty. But then their boatin' trip went wrong 'n 'e slipped inter the water 'n drowned?" She eyed her mistress beadily. "That were the last 'ouse party at The Grange 'n I don't reckon it were such a good one."

"Then all the more reason to have another one!" Araminta responded brightly. She would not let Jane put a damper on her latest idea, which was rapidly growing into an occasion to rival any of those she'd attended in London. "A *splendid* house party this time. A house party that gathers together all the rich, handsome, and interesting people that we know. And I propose that we invite Miss Mandelton and Lord Silverton. Oh, and Lord Ludbridge, too." Excitement was nearly getting the better of her as she returned to her wardrobe to rummage through the lovely gowns she now had the figure to wear again, though, of course she'd have to get her dressmaker to concoct something entirely new and fetching for the occasion. "Then Hetty and Sir Aubrey will have lots of people to worry about other than my supposedly wicked husband, won't they, Jane?" she tossed over her shoulder.

A great sense of happiness was fast settling upon her. London had been perfectly beastly for weeks now with Debenham always telling her what she could and couldn't do. Well, he'd not go against her father, and if Lord Partington were hosting her birthday party, Debenham would have no say with regard to the guest list.

For the first time since before William was born, Araminta thought she might begin enjoying herself again.

CHAPTER 3

*K*itty felt a spring in her step to be back in the country for all that she'd considered herself a city girl long before she went to London.

She breathed deeply, enjoying the scent of familiar flowers, the call of birds from the trees, the soft flutter of their wings as they flew about the hedgerows that bordered the path she was now traversing through a small wooded area.

Agreeing to be part of Mr. Lazarus's traveling performance throughout the provinces was the change she needed. Raising her arms to the clear blue sky, she charged her lungs with fresh air and decided that although she'd never want to live anywhere other than London, right now she was enjoying the slower change of pace.

Of course, if Silverton had still been in residence in town she might have felt differently, but the fact that he was on business at his country estate, and away for nearly four weeks, meant she'd jumped at the chance to play the part of Pandora Mr. Lazarus had offered her during their progress through the villages and towns of Hertfordshire. It had been during this annual foray into the counties the previous year that Kitty had first met the flamboyant director when he'd given her the opportunity that had changed her life. What a green girl she'd been then, but how much she'd gained in freedom, wealth, and happiness. In one sense, she was her own mistress, in that she was free to make her own decisions. After a lifetime of being told what to do, this was addictive and liberating. However, she was also mistress to a man who made her happy from the tips of her toes to the end of her nose as she'd heard the saying go.

What didn't make her so happy was the fact that her darling Silverton had told her, carefully and with no great delight, that he was to meet his intended bride on his return journey from the north. He would then accompany Miss Mandelton back to London where she'd remain for the few weeks until their wedding.

Kitty knew that Silverton was in an impossible situation. He'd become affianced to Miss Mandelton a short time before Kitty had tumbled into his life needing his help, after they'd already built up a strong, satisfying friendship based on mutual respect and a lot of laughter at the cribbage table in front of the fire in his drawing room.

Even back then, Kitty had known she was not the kind of wife a man like Silverton could marry. Even when she'd nearly married Nash, her own father had declared the match unacceptable because Kitty—his own daughter—was too far beneath Lord Silverton, and he'd declared that society would never accept her.

She plucked a hedgerow leaf and tore at it. Without society's acceptance, she and any husband brave enough to attempt to challenge the prevailing forces that dictated propriety's boundaries would be bound to be unhappy. It was far better, therefore, she'd decided, to simply make the most of her position as London's darling of the stage. While she entertained high society and continued to know her place, they would shower her with tributes. If she tried to become one of them, her happy idyll might well come to an abrupt end. Yes, she'd read various commentaries in the gossip sheets following her close call at becoming Lady Nash, and there had been some harsh feeling about it all. Just as well her parentage was still a well-kept secret. Most people seemed to assume she was a daughter of the underbelly of society, if not the gutter. *After all, an actress was not that much farther up the social scale than a prostitute*, she thought with a touch of bitterness.

And that's why she was prepared to accept that she would never enjoy the wedded bliss for which she'd longed her whole life. But she was happy. Silverton was kind and loving, and honorable and noble. He had every attribute she prized in a man, and he adored her. It was the reason Kitty would put up with a less than ideal situation. She'd seen enough unhappy marriages with straying husbands ruling the roost to know she was infinitely better off as mistress to a man who respected her.

She took another deep breath of fresh air to banish the dismals. For the next three nights, Kitty would be performing at a theater ten miles from the village where she'd grown up. Each evening before the show, Mr. Lazarus would give his usual gushing summation on the 'deucedly decided delight and riotous rambunctiousness' of the adoration-filled audiences who crammed onto the benches of the often makeshift venues where they performed. It hadn't all been comfort and splendor.

But she'd enjoyed the experience, though in just a few days their tour would be at an end, and Kitty was looking forward to returning to London and Silverton's arms. The lovely little home he'd arranged for her some weeks before was now decorated just as she desired, and she looked upon it as a haven of peace and bliss; a solid affirmation of how far she'd come in life and how happy she was to remain right there, with nothing any different.

She had found her happy place.

Whenever Silverton visited, she would simply isolate her mind from the knowledge that he'd be returning to the other woman in his life—the wife she wished more than anything that she could be.

As she reached the lych-gate of the cottage where she and a number of her flamboyant fellow actresses were being housed, she met Mr. Lazarus issuing down the path. He doffed his feathered hat with a twinkle in his eye, extravagant, flamboyant, and not always truthful, she knew; but the fact that he saw to their interests so assiduously, and was essentially a man of decency with a kind heart, meant Kitty was happy to remain working for him. She wasn't about to look for brighter opportunities since the brightest was being Silverton's mistress.

One consolation to not being Silverton's legal wedded wife was that she'd have to give up her connection with the stage.

Didn't she have the best of both worlds then?

Mr. Lazarus greeted her with a smile. "Kitty, my dear! Prepare to be astonished and transported into raptures of excitement by this most wonderful and supremely grandiose opportunity I have this very morning secured for our little traveling troupe!"

Obligingly, Kitty put her head on one side and prepared to be just that as she smiled back and stroked the feathered trim of her blue pelisse. "Do tell all, Mr. Lazarus, and put me out of my suspense."

"Why, my dear, I've not only gained us admittance to the grandest of all estates! Indeed, a country house inhabited by a veritable collection of the most shining beacons of aristocracy that each and every one of us lowly and modest actors would be unutterably desirous to meet in person. No, not only gained admittance but secured us our moment of glory. Yes! We are to be performing within those hallowed precincts and will be feted and lauded by the highest in the land!"

"And what estate is this?" Kitty tried to inject suitable enthusiasm into her tone, but as her brain whirled with the cataloging of every country house in the area that might answer such a description, she was feeling increasingly ill.

And even while she willed it not to be true, Mr. Lazarus responded with all the fervor that flew in the face of her own horror. "Why, it is none other than The Grange, home of the illustrious Lord and Lady Partington, Kitty, and can you but believe it! We are the esteemed and magnificent performers requested to supply the entertainment for the birthday extravagance to honor London's most beautiful new bride and recent mother, Lady Debenham!"

CHAPTER 4

$\mathcal{N}$aturally, Araminta should have known that Hetty had nothing better to gush about than babies. Araminta would even have preferred to have gone on a country ramble with her mother than be confined to the drawing room, listening to her sister wax lyrical about the astonishing accomplishments and virtues of their respective offspring, which honestly felt the closest thing she could imagine to purgatory right now.

However, her mother had insisted on this intimate family gathering to precede the gaiety of the myriad guests inhabiting The Grange, and this was the first occasion since both Hetty and Araminta had given birth that the families were fully united; though apparently, the occasion was purely for the purpose of heaping adoration upon the squalling creatures rather than to celebrate Araminta's birthday.

She really wasn't feeling charitable toward William. Squalling was the only thing her son seemed capable of doing, and he'd been busy doing it the entire three hours since the traveling party had left London. Araminta had fully intended taking a separate carriage from William, but when Debenham had chosen to go on horseback, she'd had no choice but to share the one vehicle with Jane, and Mary the nursemaid.

Those three hours of pure torture were a reminder of why Araminta was convinced she was not of a maternal bent. William's screaming had given her quite the megrim, and all she'd wanted to do was retreat to her old bedchamber for some well-earned rest the moment she'd arrived at her old home.

Instead, Hetty had positively dragged her into the drawing room saying, "No, no, don't send William away with Mary. I'm sure he'll stop crying when he's with his cousin and our baby sister, for, of course, Mama has brought Celia down from the nursery." When Hetty gazed adoringly up at her husband, Araminta made sure to look away so as not to lock glances with Sir Aubrey. Not long ago she'd have been filled with fury. Not long before that, frustrated longing.

But Araminta was nothing if not pragmatic. How could she be ashamed of what she'd done purely for the good of the family? Yet, even as she tried to brush it off with such a justification, she still felt the cold steel of Sir Aubrey's occasional, and no doubt accidental, gaze like a rebuke, which immediately set her back up. As if their unconventional coupling had been all her fault. It made her feel quite indignant! Araminta had sacrificed her virtue to save the family fortune, and restore to Sir Aubrey the letter that would otherwise have convicted him—though, of course, when the letter had actually been located, it said the opposite, and that Debenham was the villain, which was why it was important that the letter never enter the public arena. Araminta had been sure she'd burnt it, but apparently the 'real' letter had surfaced and Mr. Tunley had it.

Turning her back to Sir Aubrey, she pretended to admire her nephew's cherubic looks, taking her cue from Hetty while she fumed over the baronet's inconstancy. How was Araminta to have known Sir Aubrey had married Hetty half an hour before Araminta had decided to take matters into her own hands, straddling the dangerous gentleman and giving him what he'd made clear for weeks was his desire?

He'd said he hadn't believed it was Araminta dancing her dance of the veils in her Spanish Dancing Girl costume, identical to Hetty's.

That he'd thought she was Hetty! Good lord, how could he not have known the difference between tall, beautiful, slender Araminta and short, dumpy, plain Hetty?

Now, amongst the various family members in the drawing room, Sir Aubrey appeared to studiously ignore Araminta, stepping away the moment she came within a few feet of him, which made Araminta increasingly uncomfortable.

Especially when Hetty picked up her squalling nephew, William, and thrust him at her husband, who was already in possession of their own bundle of joy.

A bundle of joy whose head covering was suddenly revealed to display that most indicting of Sir Aubrey's family traits—the dark locks, lustrous even at such a young age, streaked with a narrow but discernible band of white—the Banks' brand, he'd laughingly called it.

"Well, no surprises as to the identity of young Frederick's father. Every male in Aubrey's family has the same," Hetty said coyly, remarking with a frown, "but no family resemblance to his cousin, William. Not at this age, certainly."

Lady Partington swept forward after passing her own baby Celia to the closest male at hand, who happened to be Cousin Stephen, crooning, "Why, young William must take after the Debenham side of the family for none of us were so swarthy. What a fine pair of lungs. Now that does remind me of Araminta."

Araminta knew she was being lighthearted. Indeed, her mama was always surprisingly lighthearted these days, as if motherhood were the greatest joy ever conferred upon her, when she'd produced numerous times and must surely have been despairing to find herself breeding again at forty.

Araminta never intended having another child if she could help it. Debenham was a lusty husband, who'd made no secret of his pleasure at returning to Araminta's bed now that she'd regained her figure after William's birth. Well, Debenham had his heir, and as Araminta did not intend going through the ghastly process of procreating again, she'd been assiduous in using the Queen Anne's Lace seeds Jane bought her from the apothecary's to prevent conception. The only lapse had been the single occasion when Debenham had surprised her in the rotunda overlooking the river at Lady Marks's riverside entertainment a month before, just after dreadful Mr. Woking had emptied Araminta's reticule, causing the Queen Anne's Lace to disappear into the wind.

As Araminta watched the two cousins—William and Frederick—she felt Sir Aubrey's eyes upon her, sizing her up for any sign of what only the two of them knew—of the sin he considered they'd committed and for which he reviled her. She hated the uncomfortable churning this caused her inside, so she tossed her head, brushed Debenham's cheek with her hand and said with syrupy sweetness, "More like my husband's lusty lungs. Now, shall we put the babies away? I've had more than enough of William, who never ceased his infernal racket the entire time we were journeying here."

Hetty, who seemed ridiculously full of spirits, cozied up to her husband saying brightly, "I propose a walk, and the nursemaids can bring the young ones who need a breath of fresh air, despite it being so chillsome out. What do you think, Aubrey, my love?"

A walk was not what Araminta had in mind, and not with the babies either. However, salvation came in the form of a plume of dust upon the horizon. She shaded her eyes. "Why, I do believe the first guests have arrived," she murmured, though if she'd been alone she'd have whooped with joy. She'd been with her family less than an hour, and already she was feeling judged and found wanting. She also couldn't wait to see Lord Ludbridge again. "You carry on. I'm happy to do the greetings."

To her surprise, Debenham chose to accompany the others on their gentle stroll, though she did notice that was only after her mother specially requested his presence. Earlier, Mama had said she intended to make a special effort to better her acquaintance with her son-in-law, and Araminta had nearly told her not to bother, but when she recognized Teddy's carriage, she almost sang to the treetops. With the others safely out of the way, she could greet her beloved with the warmth she reserved only for him.

And, oh joy, the timing was perfect for they were safely in the park by the time she discharged this special greeting, out of view of the servants certainly, but with a press of the fingers and a fleeting caress upon his cheek, which had his eyes widening with pleasurable surprise.

"My darling Teddy, I held this party purely so I had an excuse to invite you, and now you've made my birthday wish come true by being the first and arriving when the others are down by the river." She held both his hands in hers, then raised them to kiss his fingertips as they communed by the bushes tucked away near the portico. "No, do not blush for we are unobserved. Oh, but I have missed you."

"As I have you, Lady Debenham," he murmured, and Araminta laughed, feeling happier than she could remember.

"There's no need for you to be so formal. We are well away from prying eyes."

"But your husband—"

"Is with my mother feeding the ducks, and will be only too pleased to welcome you when he returns. In the meantime, I am proxy to my parents and husband, and it is my desire that you accompany me on a short walk. I shall take you to see Papa. Very correct, yes, but we shall go via the pinery where no one will see us."

Teddy, she noticed with pleasure, seemed rather overwhelmed by the force of her reception, but he was certainly amenable when she pressed him against the glass of the hothouse and twined her arms about his neck. For they were well hidden by the leafy foliage of the greenery, and Araminta's desire was clearly matched by his own.

"Darling girl," he murmured between kisses. "I never expected to get a greeting like this."

Unfortunately, their trysting was cut short by the cries of Jane on the other side of the door, exclaiming that more guests had arrived and there was not a soul to greet them.

Reluctantly, Araminta smoothed her hair and dress and emerged onto the portico steps to do her duty, while Teddy continued into the garden where she directed him to meet with her father who was in the potting shed.

This time, it was Lord Silverton issuing out of his carriage whose arm Araminta took in coy pretense of being delighted that he'd arrived a day earlier than expected.

"My betrothed was delayed, but arrangements are that she will arrive here tomorrow in time for the ball before the theatrical entertainment." He gazed with admiration around Araminta's lovely home. "I don't wonder you chose to languish here awhile. This is a most charming neck of the woods. My ancestral seat is very cold and draughty by comparison."

"Miss Mandelton will supply the woman's touch needed, no doubt." Araminta conducted him into the drawing room while his trunk was carried upstairs. "I am so looking forward to meeting her. She must be very beautiful and accomplished to have earned your especial favor, my lord, when the debutantes were falling over themselves to be your partner in the waltz, I couldn't help noticing at Lady Garvey's ball last week."

Naturally, she wasn't going to mention the London actress with whom she'd heard he was now publicly linked, for, of course, she should know nothing about that. Actually, just the thought of Kitty La Bijou made her feel ill, reminding her again of her necklace and Debenham's angry protests that he'd get to the bottom of how it had left Araminta's possession and emerged around Miss Bijou's neck.

His words just brought back nightmarish memories of that frightful night, when she'd given birth too early after Miss Bijou had taken her to the hovel of that dreadful woman, Mrs. Mobbs. The occasion had ended as well as could be expected, and it was a huge relief to be reassured that Miss Bijou remained in ignorance of what had occurred, and for Araminta to learn that, in fact, the actress had gained possession of the necklace through other channels, though she was not exactly sure of the details. It was, however, a natural assumption that Mrs. Mobbs had sold it to obtain the funds required to see that the child Araminta had given birth to too early was brought up in comfort.

"Miss Mandelton is a very deserving and admirable young lady."

Lord Silverton had paused so long Araminta had forgotten what they were talking about. She laughed softly. "Deserving and admirable are not the epithets I would choose to be remembered by."

"You could not be more different from Miss Mandelton, I assure you," he murmured, and Araminta raised her eyebrows, surprised at his tone but leaving the subject as he appeared not to wish to dwell on the young lady.

But then her mama and the rest of that party emerged from the trees to the east of the lake where poor Edgar had drowned, and there was Cousin Stephen playing with baby Celia, throwing her up in the air while the others looked on and laughed.

Really, Araminta had no idea why people made such a fuss of babies since they didn't do anything agreeable. But it was easy to smile for she could hear Teddy conversing with her father nearby, and now they both arrived at the top of the stairs outside where she was gazing out at the others.

She smiled even more and reassured him appropriately when Teddy remarked, "It was very good of you to sacrifice the pleasure of enjoying the children with the others and instead greet the guests. Are you sure you're not cold?"

For the first time since Araminta could remember, the house was bursting with good cheer, and Araminta couldn't wait for Teddy to see her in her new silver and blue sarcenet gown with its lavishly-embroidered bodice and hem festooned with roses. The evening promised to be balmy, and she'd already decided upon a very diverting walk on which she planned to take him. The summer house would be the perfect trysting place, though it had bad memories for Hetty, who'd stood on the banks of the little lake and screamed her distress at seeing Edgar's upturned boat near the island, and then Edgar's body and a thrashing Lady Julia dragged to shore by Cousin Stephen. That was barely two years ago, yet it seemed an eternity now.

She shuddered at the memory, glad that she'd never been forced to endure, socially, dreadful Lady Julia's company since then, though she'd heard rumors that she and her husband spent increasing amounts of time apart since she'd done her duty and provided him with three sons. Araminta didn't think she'd ever met a more scheming, conniving piece of work in her life than the wife of Sir Archie Ledger.

CHAPTER 5

S ilverton was glad when Lady Debenham dropped the subject of his intended, and he was able to move on to greet the rest of the party. He wasn't at all sure it was a good idea to meet Octavia here, but apparently Lady Debenham had already invited her, and Octavia, who rarely enjoyed social invitations, had been in transports.

The normally placid Octavia seemed to be in transports over everything if her letters told the truth. When she wasn't waxing lyrical over the cheeky exploits of her beloved King Charles Spaniel, Poppet, she constantly credited Silverton with gilding her future, which made him feel ill with guilt.

"Were it not for your immense gallantry, I would have been destined to molder into an early grave through boredom and lack of appreciation, but you have given me something worthwhile to which to aspire," she had written in her last letter. "Not only will I endeavor to be the worthiest of wives, but at last I can make a difference and continue your mother's legacy of providing hope and opportunity to so many, including those who toil on your estates."

Oh, Miss Octavia was the worthiest of women and no doubt she'd be true to every word she penned. Silverton's mother was finding it physically taxing to carry out the modest charity work she had long enjoyed, but by all accounts, Octavia was with her daily to expedite the aging beauty's various whims. At least once a week Silverton received a long letter from the dowager telling him how pleasingly and modestly her future daughter-in-law conducted herself and assisted Lady Silverton in virtually every activity these days.

Octavia's pleasure and gratitude were heavy burdens for Silverton to bear, when all he could dream about was being wrapped in Kitty's loving embrace. Dear God, he didn't know a man could love so deeply.

At least he would meet Octavia on neutral ground. That was, perhaps, some solace, for if she suspected his heart was less engaged than she'd claimed she required for their marriage to take place, he could make a better show of appearing the devoted husband-to-be here than he could in the midst of London revels where he was forever in a fever of impatience to be reunited with Kitty after each Covent Garden show.

"Silverton, glad you could make it." Stephen Cranborne clapped him on the shoulder, matching his steps to his as he was ushered up the portico steps while a flurry of servants attended to his luggage. "I hope your mother is well."

Silverton nodded. Before he'd left to visit his estate in Norfolk's north, he'd mentioned to Cranborne that his mother had taken a mild turn; however, Octavia had reassured him all was well. So it was hardly surprising Cranborne directed his inquiries after his betrothed.

Upon hearing Miss Mandelton's name, Araminta's sister, Hetty— Lady Banks—removed herself from her husband's side to say, "I've heard so much about Miss Mandelton's goodness. I can't wait to meet her. She can be assured of a warm welcome here, for I believe she's very shy. You've known her forever, haven't you?"

"We grew up together, yes." Silverton hoped he'd injected sufficient warmth into his voice. "And thank you for your kind words."

As soon as Hetty moved away, Cranborne put his head close to Silverton's, pretending more small talk perhaps, when his words were full of portent. "Have you heard anything from Debenham pertaining to the Princess Caroline?"

Silverton raised his eyebrows in inquiry and Cranborne, with a glance over his shoulder to ensure the rest of the party continued somewhere behind them, went on, "Tunley tells me he's been reliably informed that Lord Beecham, a fairweather associate of Debenham's, has on several occasions mentioned the name of our Regent's most despised wife. Suspected plans are afoot to publicly discredit her, giving the Regent grounds for divorce."

"I thought she'd provided sufficient grounds without anyone's help."

Cranborne gave a short laugh. "That may be, but we have our suspicions that certain individuals may gain a great deal from ensuring that her fall from public approval is as thorough as it can possibly be. She has been living abroad, but during her next visit to London, it is thought some public humiliation is in the wind. Something to air in the newspapers to give the Regent greater grounds for following his inclination to be rid of her. It's just the sort of havey-cavey affair Debenham likes to dabble in—politics and the chance to grist the mill. Has Debenham let anything slip?"

"I've fallen out of favor with Debenham." Silverton lowered his voice even more as he passed through the opened double doors at the top of the house, flanked by two footmen. "He suspects I'm not the friend he once thought me to be. He's more than returned the favor. Though he would deny it, I know he was behind the attempt to discredit me through the reappearance of some ill-advised letters I sent to Lady Harvey some years ago. Fortunately, it came to nothing. I suspect he's behind a few other extortion attempts I've recently had wind of." He sighed. He was weary of his complicated life suddenly. A woman he was obliged through family obligation to marry, and a number of nasty blackmail cases involving high profile members of society, had sapped his energy. "Perhaps this weekend will go some way toward restoring the dubious trust we once shared. Sufficiently, at least, for us to go gaming." He gave a significant nod. Gaming was one activity where Debenham was guaranteed to let his guard down.

"Just as it will be a wonderful opportunity for you and Miss Mandelton to be reunited after so many months apart. How many has it been since you last saw her?" Cranborne raised his voice so that their conversation floated convivially in the air.

"Six." *Six months*, Silverton thought after Cranborne had left his side and he was ushered into the drawing room to take refreshment with the rest of the family. Those six months had been the happiest of his life as he'd become entranced by the playful, flirtatious Miss Kitty La Bijou whose rescue had become a surprising addendum to the sober life he'd planned following his formal offer of marriage to Miss Mandelton.

Duty and doubt swirled through his head as he sipped the amber liquid Lord Partington pressed into his hand. Then Kitty's lovely, smiling face seemed to coalesce as he held his glass up to the light in contemplation of the future and of Octavia's arrival in the morning.

His heart hitched, and his groin ached as desire coursed through him. However much he tried to be honorable, he knew he could never give up the delightful, charming, and utterly enchanting Miss Kitty La Bijou.

THE FOLLOWING TOMORNING, NOT FAR AWAY, AND UNBEKNOWNST TO Kitty and Silverton how close they were to one another, Kitty clutched her shawl more closely at her throat and put her head down as she hurried through the small country town's market square. She wasn't sure whether the churning in her belly was due to nerves at the possibility of being recognized by her father or someone else she knew, or possibly running into her mother.

Why, oh why, was she feeling so afraid? She could get through her lines on stage without being recognized, surely? She'd be taking on the role of another person. Tonight's performance should be no different to performing on a London stage in front of thousands. She swallowed, and her palms felt clammy as she acknowledged that tonight's audience would include her father. Her knees literally buckled with fear.

In London, she was never fearful. She marched about with her head held high, proud to be recognized and acknowledged with a nod or a flourishing bow. So many in London knew her face and her name. She was London's most celebrated actress.

But here?

Why should she suddenly be reduced once again to the frightened, downtrodden village child she'd always felt herself in the shadows of these very elms? Shouldn't she be lording it over those who might have once shunned her but who would now see her as she now was— the celebrated actress Kitty La Bijou?

It was an irony that shame had driven her to London. She'd left her village a pure and virtuous young woman— but reviled because of her illegitimacy— however, only after she'd actually committed the so-called crimes of becoming an actress and a kept woman, had she received the adulation that was continually leveled at her these days.

Well, she would do it all again, she decided, raising her head and clenching her teeth with determination. And even though she was within walking distance of the house at the end of the bridge where she'd grown up, she would *not* go and see her mother. She doubted her mother would want to see her either.

She was crossing the village green, when a burst of frenzied yapping caused her to stop and turn to see a young woman standing by a stagecoach by the local tavern, holding a small dog in her arms. Kitty, who loved animals, was just contemplating whether to go over when the little creature sprang out of its mistress's arms and bolted across the village green. It brushed past Kitty's ankles and disappeared through the hedgerows. Impulsively, Kitty hurried after it, finding a break in the hedge, while the young lady's plaintive cries could be heard in the distance entreating "Poppet" to "come back!"

As Kitty drew closer, she could see the small dog in the distance, dancing about some ducks by the edge of a small pond. She picked up her skirts and increased her pace.

It was a sweet little King Charles Spaniel she saw upon coming closer, with devilry in its large, chocolate brown eyes. Of course, the ducks had the advantage of being able to swim, much to the frustration of their would-be playmate.

Kitty had always wanted a pet dog. Lord Nash had never particularly liked them, but Silverton was very fond of dogs and had promised they would have one, together.

Kitty realized that the young lady who'd lost her traveling companion was in a difficult position in an unfamiliar town. She'd not been dressed for a country ramble, whereas Kitty didn't mind risking a bit of mud on her skirts if it meant doing a good turn. Especially one that involved a puppy.

When the ducks had progressed far out of reach, the spaniel finally started paying attention to Kitty, who'd reached within a few feet of it, and when Kitty proffered the piece of bun she'd kept from her lunch for the purpose of feeding the ducks, it was easy to entice the puppy into her arms.

"Here's your little friend," she said with a smile as she returned the runaway to the young lady who looked like she'd been crying. "A little muddy, I'm afraid, so perhaps I should put him straight into your carriage."

"If he's muddy Aunt Bertha will be most put out!" The young lady appeared positively anguished at such a scenario. "I can't possibly do that. She didn't want me to travel with Poppet, but as she goes everywhere with me, I couldn't possibly have left her on such a journey as this one."

Kitty saw her jump as a gravelly voice full of disapproval could be heard from the waiting carriage. "Octavia! What are you doing? Come here, now! I'm tired and hungry, and we haven't all day."

Clearly, the young lady was in terror of her guardian, so Kitty went up to the window and said sweetly, "It's my fault I'm holding her up, ma'am. I fear I frightened the little dog out of the young lady's arms and it ran into the mud."

"For heaven's sake, Octavia, girl! I said you weren't to bring that creature in the first place, and if it's covered with mud it will have to stay behind."

Kitty took up a position of solidarity with her new friend. She looked into the window again and said quickly, "It won't take a moment to get the puppy cleaned up, and then I know where the nicest Eccles tarts in the whole district can be found. Do let me fetch you a couple."

Before the young lady had time to object, Kitty hurried past her, indicating for her to follow her to the water trough in front of *The Black Swan*. The young lady's Aunt Bertha had looked formidable and, given her girth, would probably be ameliorated by a couple of nice tarts, which really were acclaimed in the area.

"Let me do that," she said, taking back the muddy little creature and swishing its feet in the pool of water. The young lady really looked as if she didn't quite know what to do. Clearly, traveling with that old tartar was a terrifying business.

"But your dress."

"It's in need of a launder, and it's an old one. I'm sorry; I haven't introduced myself. I'm Miss Bijou."

"And I'm Miss— Oh!" Her cry of dismay was occasioned by the fact that the wriggling bundle had slipped out of her hands and was now completely immersed in the water. "What am I going to do?" she wailed. "Aunt Bertha will never forgive me!"

Kitty wrinkled her nose. She wasn't too enamored of the idea of picking up a sopping wet puppy and taking it anywhere, so she was relieved when the young lady scooped up her beloved with no similar qualms. Kitty turned and beckoned over her shoulder. "There's nothing for it. We'll see the publican who's en route to Mrs. Lynn's Tea Rooms. That's where I can get the tarts I promised your aunt."

Of course, Mrs. Lynn's eyes nearly bulged out of her head when she recognized Kitty. "Lordy, yer've come back 'ome!" she cried. "Run away ter London, I 'eard, 'n makin' yer ma cry like that. 'Ow could yer, Kitty love?"

The young lady whose name Kitty still hadn't ascertained, looked at her wide-eyed when they came out into the sunshine on their next mission, which was to rub the dog dry.

Kitty shrugged, feeling embarrassed for the first time. "I suppose I should explain. I've shamed my family. Actually, you probably should not be seen with me for I'm not respectable at all anymore. Well, that's if I ever was."

"Not respectable?" If possible, even more color leached from the young lady's pale face, and she looked for a moment as if she might faint clean away from shock. So Kitty added hastily, in case she might think Kitty worse than she was, "I've become an actress, you see."

"An actress!"

"And I've never been happier." Kitty squared her shoulders. "I was a prisoner here in this town where I grew up, but now I can do what I want to. I love what I do, and no one can tell me I ought to do this, and I can't do that. I'm just back for a short visit, though." As her companion continued to stare, goggle-eyed at her, Kitty quickly changed the subject. "And what brings you to these parts?"

"I'm coming to stay with some people my aunt knows. And...and to meet the man I'm to marry."

"Goodness! How exciting!"

Kitty was determined that this is how she would feel—glad for anyone venturing upon the path she'd have loved more than any other. Though not if that meant she couldn't be with Lord Silverton. No, having love was definitely more important than having a ring on her finger and the respectability she craved.

"Yes."

She was surprised by the young lady's lackluster response and determined to bolster her, though perhaps her real motive was curiosity. "Is your young man dashing and handsome and worthy of you?" Kitty loved that having declared herself an actress, and therefore on a far inferior social footing, she could ask the kind of questions no proper young lady would dream of asking.

They were in possession of some linen now for which Kitty had offered the innkeeper's daughter some coins and were drying the puppy on the back step in the gentle midday sun.

"He's very handsome and dashing, and we've been friends forever. He's the most noble gentleman I've ever known. He's kind and ever thoughtful of me, which of course makes me the luckiest young lady in the world. We're getting married in a few weeks."

"Goodness! And do you have all your wedding things...your dress? Or is that the reason you're traveling with your aunt? To make arrangements?" Kitty could have kept asking wedding-related questions forever. She remembered the excitement of finding just the right ensemble for her intended nuptials to Lord Nash. Her failure to believe he hadn't tricked her was a lucky accident which had saved her from a life of being with the wrong man.

"I'm on my way to London, but I'll be meeting my intended tonight. I haven't seen him for a few months."

"How exciting! I'm sure he can't wait to see you again."

The young lady nodded, again without a great deal of enthusiasm. The sun on her sandy eyelashes emphasized the pink rims of her eyes. She seemed suddenly close to tears, perhaps overwhelmingly affected by emotion. She certainly wasn't a pretty girl, but there was a softness and sincerity about her that appealed to Kitty's protective instincts. The girl bit her lip. "I don't know where I'd be if he hadn't offered for me like he did."

"Really?" This sounded intriguing. Kitty put her head closer, inviting greater disclosure which the young lady seemed ready to give, perhaps as much for the reason that Kitty was a complete stranger as much as anything else.

"When my father died last year he left the family in a rather...difficult situation with creditors who—" She broke off, coloring as if she realized she might be divulging too much. "Fortunately, my Aunt Bertha agreed to provide me with a dowry if I made a good marriage." She shrugged, "Though that really meant provided she was satisfied with the match."

"I'd have thought it would be as important that you were satisfied," Kitty clarified.

At this, the young lady brightened. "Oh yes! He is the most wonderful of men. I've grown up in the village near his family home and known him my whole life. His mother has taken me under her wing and is delighted. Indeed, no bride-to-be could be more fortunate than I."

Yet, to Kitty's concern, she still looked as if she were trying to convince herself of the fact, and as Kitty could hear her Aunt Bertha's shouts for her niece from where they were, she decided it would be best if she shepherded her rather indecisive companion back toward where she must continue her journey.

Though if Aunt Bertha were her aunt, and Kitty was utterly dependent on doing what she wanted, she supposed she'd not want to hurry back to be cocooned for another eternity.

Which only went to show what a good decision Kitty had made to be mistress of her own destiny.

And mistress to the most wonderfully noble and dashing man on the planet, she decided with a surge of love.

CHAPTER 6

*L*ucinda was pale at the best of times but, now, traveling through a small beech wood she looked like a ghost as she clutched her stomach and wailed, "I'm going to be ill!"

Lissa eyed her young charge warily from the farthest corner of the carriage. Was it just a ruse? Lucinda had not been easy company during this tedious journey through Hertfordshire after Lady Julia had persuaded Lord Beecham to accompany them to a weekend house party. Now they were returning to London in the same carriage, and the last three hours of traveling had never been so taxing.

"Stop!" It was Lady Julia, rapping on the ceiling; her nose curled up in disgust as she cast a baleful look at the gray-faced Lucinda.

Lissa was, in fact, glad of the reprieve. It would be nice to step out and stretch her legs. The long confinement had done her mood no favors. Lady Julia and Lord Beecham had both seemed a little out of sorts while Lucinda had sulked the entire way.

With clear relief, Lucinda clambered out of the carriage and collapsed against a tree, her hands at her forehead. Lissa supposed she should feel sorry for her. At the very least, she should go to her charge and offer her services, but her inclination was to walk a little, breathe in the mild country air, and mentally prepare herself for another two to three hours of further torture. For her own part, she couldn't wait to reach London again. She knew this wood. She'd gathered berries here every summer until she'd taken up her position as a governess in London, first to the Lamonts and now to Lord Beecham's ward. She really did not wish to be recognized by any of the local villagers who might pass this way.

Conscience, of course, prevailed and she was about to go to Lucinda when Lady Julia's thin voice carried over the short distance that separated them, though a large rock physically cut them off from each other.

"The Grange is just over the rise. Lord Partington's country seat. I believe a cozy little gathering is taking place as we speak." Her tone was conversational, but the words had a chilling effect on Lissa.

"Indeed, my love?" Lissa knew by Lord Beecham's tone he was humoring her.

"Lady Debenham has chosen to celebrate her birthday with a large gathering. Silverton is on the guest list, I'm told."

"Indeed, my love?"

Lissa tensed. Was that particular interest she noted in his tone? To date, she'd found none of the evidence Sir Edward had hoped she'd dig up to suggest a collusion between Lord Beecham and Debenham. And this house party Lady Julia spoke of? Lissa knew she should move closer but her entire being screamed silently in horror at listening to something regarding her own family.

Lady Julia, she knew, must harbor unpleasant associations with The Grange. Under its roof, she'd cuckolded her husband with her father's bacon-brained nephew Edgar before the young heir had drowned. Well, perhaps not cuckolded but they'd certainly been indiscreet. Lissa had heard of the unedifying spectacle of Lady Julia's dawn departure at the side of her silent and shocked husband, Sir Archie, while poor Edgar's waterlogged body had been laid out on a door. The gossip afterward had been lurid.

Lissa wondered what Lady Julia would think if she knew how informed Lissa was on these sordid events. Surely Lady Julia would want to give The Grange a wide berth. She was certainly surprised when Lady Julia now said in a cajoling tone, "Beechy darling, I think it would be perfectly lovely to surprise Lady Debenham with a visit to celebrate her birthday. Why, I have such fond memories of making her acquaintance during her first London debut." After a short pause, she amended this more spitefully to, "Or was it her second. Her first ended somewhat under a cloud after that poor young man blew his brains out when she reneged on his marriage offer."

"My dear Julia…" clearly, Lord Beacham had no idea Lissa was in earshot else he'd not have addressed her with such familiarity, "…we haven't received an invitation."

Her tinkling laugh greeted this, followed up with, "My dear Beechy, you are somewhat lacking in imagination at times. Why, we'll invent a reason for being invited. A broken carriage axle just outside their entrance should do nicely."

KITTY TOOK A DEEP BREATH AND KEPT HER HEAD DOWN AS SHE AND THE rest of the theater troupe were shown the stables after Mr. Lazarus had asked where they should leave their props and costumes. Puddles, The Grange butler, had looked down his nose at the gathering as if he thought himself superior to the lot of them, which riled Kitty no end. She remembered the pompous and overbearing Mr. Puddles from her childhood growing up in the village.

Although she'd been determined since her London success never to feel shame again, the truth was that it was potentially too dangerous to be recognized—certainly at this stage—so she'd kept her face averted each time she passed any of the staff.

The truth was that these last twenty-four hours the theater troupe had been staying in the village had been the most terrifying of her entire life. Fortunately, neither the tavern keeper, the draper nor the blacksmith had drawn the correlation between the drably-garbed village lass they remembered with Kitty La Bijou, celebrated London actress.

Well, it was one thing to avoid detection by the servants but what about tonight? Her father, for one, would die of apoplexy when he saw her on stage, and she doubted Araminta would be impressed, though it was fortunate Araminta remained in ignorance of her true identity and the fact they shared a father.

That's when she simply pushed her shoulders back and once again reminded herself that *she* wasn't the one who ought to feel shame. Nor fear of exposure. It was hardly as if her father would acknowledge her —the man who'd put her in this position. He'd be only too horrified at the sight of his illegitimate daughter on stage in his drawing room, contaminating the rest of his precious family.

Araminta would not acknowledge her either. She'd not want it known that she'd been aided by Kitty La Bijou the night she nearly lost her babe, when clearly she should not have been gallivanting alone in such an advanced state of pregnancy.

So that meant Kitty might well simply go through the motions of performing her role before she returned to London with the rest of the actors and actresses the following day, after which she hoped Silverton wouldn't be too long in getting back from his estates.

She couldn't wait to see the gorgeous man. He'd written to her every day, and somehow all his letters had reached her. Every time she recalled his words she felt warmed right through, and it was quite hard to concentrate; such as now when Jennie obviously felt aggrieved at having to utter something a second time since she felt it incumbent to jab Kitty in the ribs.

"I said, ain't this the grandest 'ouse yer ever saw, though yer'd reckon we'd a bin 'oused inside instead o' the stables."

Kitty agreed, removing her mantle and untying her bonnet as she gazed at the piles of hay stacked about the walls. "The butler doesn't know what to do with us. Did you see his face when Lydia smiled at him?"

"You mean pouted at him, all sultry-like?" Jennie giggled. "Yes, he went crimson to the tips of his ears."

The ten members of the troupe had certainly attracted considerable interest from the staff at The Grange. Jennie had no compunction in revealing more than a respectable quantity of creamy-white shoulder and thigh to the goggle-eyed stable boys, as she immodestly slipped off her tawdry crimson and green silk day dress before wriggling into the scanty attire required for her role as a storm-tossed village maiden. Kitty, however, had no intention of being so immodest. She was always careful to ensure no male members of the company glimpsed her in any state of undress. No, Kitty reserved the seductive revealing of her body for Silverton. Other than Silverton—and Lord Nash, of course—no male could ever say they had seen Kitty La Bijou in any state other than decorous.

Mr. Lazarus seemed awed by his surroundings, as he strutted about with his thumbs stuck in the waistband of his trousers, the feather in his green felt hat making him look like a cockerel. Kitty didn't miss the awe in his wide-eyed gaze as took in the handsome stables, the sweeping lawns, and the fine old Queen Anne manor house.

The fine old Queen Anne manor house that would have been Kitty's home had her father not reneged on his promise to marry Kitty's mother.

So now she was here, on the inside for the very first time once they were led from the tradesmen's entrance through a catacomb of corridors to a series of anterooms near the ballroom.

Her eyes felt like they were on stalks. Of course, the back stairs and corridors were dull and utilitarian, but once they were within range of the ballroom, soft carpet covered the floors, rich draperies swathed the windows, paintings and elegant silver candle sconces adorned the walls.

And then here was the ballroom itself, richly decorated with enormous epergnes of flowers and foliage in preparation of tonight's grand ball which the play would precede.

A makeshift stage had been erected at the end of a large antechamber which directly adjoined the ballroom. Rows of chairs had been set out in front of the dais where the play was to be performed, while a long refectory table, presumably to hold the evening's supper, lined one wall.

"Lawks," Jennie whispered under her breath as she ran her hand over the fresh upholstery of one of the seats, "it's real velvet."

Kitty knew this, of course, just as she knew the layout of the reception rooms. On several occasions, she'd watched from the branches of a beech tree the arrival of the guests who'd spilled out of carriages in front of the portico before they'd been ushered into the house. Whenever she got the opportunity, she'd trespassed onto the grounds taking a detour back from one of her errands, and while she knew she'd have been horse-whipped if she'd been discovered, not all the ghosts of Hades could have frightened her away from such sights. There were ladies wearing their finest attire: opera capes over gossamer gowns, feather-bedecked head-wear, and the men handsomely garbed in the finest fitting evening wear.

These sights had stayed with her, and tonight the same would happen. She was determined to get a bird's-eye view of guests arriving for this evening's entertainment from within the precincts of The Grange. Guests arriving to see *her*—Kitty La Bijou, London's most celebrated actress—as much as to pay tribute to the evening's guest of honor, Lady Debenham. Her half-sister.

Not that anyone would know this.

The actors had been strictly instructed to keep a low profile and not to venture away from the small withdrawing room which now served as their costume and prop room just off the stage.

Most were obediently rehearsing their lines or reapplying their makeup in the designated confined space. They were too overawed by their surroundings and the officious butler to do anything but obey. But Kitty was confident she knew her way around this house. She intended to slip away and hide herself just so she could catch a glimpse of the grandeur and pomp that accompanied new arrivals.

So, as she left Mr. Lazarus intoning a monologue and Jennie prac-tising a flirtatious exchange with one of the peasants in scene two, Kitty withdrew into the darkened corridor. No one observed her go, and as she hurried down several twisting passages, her heart pounded with the thrill of her wicked truancy. Not that it should have been truancy. If her father had been a noble and honorable man who'd kept his promise to his first true love and fiancée, then Kitty would have known these corridors like the back of her hand, as the young lady of the house.

To her delight, she now found herself at the foot of a narrow, steep flight of stairs that led, she was sure, to the observatory tower. What a thrill it would be to see the sun dipping over the horizon from her secret vantage point as she watched the first guests arrive. She only wanted to see one carriage stop and disgorge its beautifully dressed occupants, and then she'd return to Mr. Lazarus.

Sure enough, it was only a minute before she saw in the far distance a small plume of dust that heralded the arrival of a carriage coming from the north. Kitty peered through the dense ivy to see the butler arrange himself in a properly respectful manner to greet the new arrivals. And then she heard the familiar tones of her half-sister, Lady Debenham, as she remarked to her companion who'd followed her out—handsome Lord Ludbridge—"Goodness, this is one little reunion I'm very desirous to witness. My lord, we must fetch Silverton." Her voice was swallowed up as she hurried inside and Kitty, who'd been on the verge of turning back to return to her fellow artistes for fear of discovery, stood rooted to the spot, clutching the railing in churning excitement, horror and fear.

Silverton was *here*? How long had that been his intention? Why had he not written and told her?

She felt ill as the view fragmented before her. Perhaps he'd not wanted to upset Kitty if he'd unexpectedly accepted an invitation to break his journey at The Grange.

And what was this about the reunion Araminta was so desirous of witnessing?

The truth roared into her head. Silverton was about to meet his intended bride *here*?

For a moment, she truly thought she was about to faint. Why had he not told her?

Of course, self-preservation urged Kitty to stick to her vantage point. Seeing the imminent encounter could only break her heart, but yet, how could she pass up the opportunity to see how Silverton greeted the woman he would soon make his wife?

The soft crunch of gravel beneath the newly arriving carriage whispered soothingly in her ears while her heart screamed in pain. Go! Of course she should go, not be caught eavesdropping like some voyeur. She dropped one hand from the railing, and half turned as the carriage door was opened by one of the footmen who'd been standing by in readiness.

Yes, she should go now!

She took a reluctant step away, ready to descend her own set of stairs and return to the catacombs of corridors that would lead her back to the antechamber by the ballroom. Mr. Lazarus would be highly distressed to find his leading lady absent at such a crucial time, though, of course, the play was not to be held for some time if visitors were still arriving. The actors had been requested to be in attendance for a start time of anywhere from seven to eight o' clock.

She heard the solicitous voices below her inquiring after the comfort of the first occupant to emerge.

Of course she could not turn away now. With equal reluctance and horrified fascination, she leaned once more over the battlement.

A large waving feather atop a purple velvet toque proclaimed the arrival of someone of great elegance in her dotage. An old woman in a travelling pelisse of brown velvet adorned with heavy roulettes at the hem straightened as she stepped onto the gravel, closing her eyes as she raised her head to the sun.

Kitty ducked at the moment recognition send shock through her. Her breath caught and her knees went weak as her hands grasped at the rough stone wall. Dear Lord, it was old tartar to whom she'd given an eccles tart earlier that day.

Self preservation spurred her to flee but then came the words she knew she ought not stay to hear. Indeed, she wished she'd been far away and so had never heard them: "My dear Miss Mandelton! I've been so eager to meet you!"

Trying to recover her breathing, Kitty recognized Araminta's crooning tones. Araminta had arranged this meeting, she realised. She must have known Miss Mandelton was making her progress from the north and, curious to see the kind of wife handsome Lord Silverton would choose, had invited them both to her birthday house party.

A great sob rose in her throat. This was too painful. She must go now. Kitty shouldn't watch this. She'd thought she'd persuaded herself that it didn't matter Silverton was succumbing to duty and taking a wife who'd bear his legitimate children. That she could bear anything as long as he reserved his heart for her. For that was what mattered. Love. Love was, above all, her sole reason for existence. It was what gave her life meaning. She'd not had a particularly loving mother or father. Nash had been her initiation into feeling someone in life appreciated her. The frenzied beating of her innocent heart had been unlike anything she'd ever experienced, and she'd assumed, would be sustained forever. She'd thought she would marry him, but by the time he'd asked her, he'd cheated on her and destroyed her trust.

Her months with Nash paled into insignificance when compared with the deep, primal need she felt for Silverton. She loved Silverton with an intensity she'd not believed possible. He made her complete. He was everything she realized had always been missing from her life.

And he respected her.

But he could not make her his wife. Yes, she *did* accept that. She'd also pledged she would never even think about that other sphere of his life that could not contain her, as long as he continued to show her the affection he did each and every day.

But just one look. One quick look to see the look in Silverton's eyes as he welcomed the woman he'd not seen for some months. The woman Silverton had chosen to spend the rest of his life with in respectable matrimony and whom Kitty imagined must therefore be beautiful and self assured, and, quite possibly, haughty and disdainful like so many of her class.

So Kitty leaned over the ivy-entwined barrier sandstone and stared down at the scene below, and found to her dismay that Miss Mandelton was none of those things.

The pair of dainty half-boots that touched the ground and the neat body dressed in a plain, dark green traveling gown with little embellishment were, Kitty saw, her best attributes. For the face that peeked out from beneath the poke bonnet was pale. Too pale for beauty. In fact, her complexion looked leeched of color. The nose was small but slightly too sharp for conventional beauty which, had her eyes been more compelling, might have been overlooked. Her brows were so pale as to be not even in evidence from this distance, and her manner was timid. She seemed to withdraw in fear as Araminta moved toward her.

No, Miss Mandelton was not a beauty.

But then, Kitty had already perceived this when she'd returned her little dog and had decided that a pleasing and kind manner were far more attractive traits than bold good looks.

She thought she would be ill.

Why had she not held fast when she'd counseled herself that it would be best if she never met the future Lady Silverton?

But they'd already met.

This was the young woman who would usurp Kitty's position. Miss Mandelton looked like she had never received a kind word in her life the way she smiled tremulously as Araminta prattled her welcome. Kitty doubted Miss Mandelton had ever said an unkind thing to anyone, either. And it was that very timidity that would tug at Silverton's heartstrings. Silverton, who couldn't abide hurting anyone's feelings.

This timid creature with her passive ways would have everything for which Kitty had longed her entire life: a loving husband—for indeed Silverton would grow fonder of his wife as she produced the children who would carry on the family line—and a family.

All her life, Kitty had longed to be part of a legitimate union with a husband who would be proud enough of wife and children that he would want to show them off. Not keep them secretly in the background, as her father had done to Kitty and Lissa and Ned and now, no doubt, the new baby.

And, as Silverton would have no choice but to do with Kitty and any children they might produce.

A great sob rose up in her throat which she choked back as she heard Silverton's voice carry over the cool, quiet air, "Octavia, my dear girl. You have come at last."

Kitty strained for any nuance that might suggest his true feelings—delight, perhaps. But there was just the warmth he might reserve for a familiar family friend.

The reflection gave Kitty no comfort. Miss Mandelton was going to marry Silverton and Kitty was not.

Her last sight of him before she turned away was as he gripped the young woman's hands in both of his, his tone bolstering, confidence boosting; while Miss Mandelton responded, stammering with overt gratitude that it was indeed good to see him, too.

For, of course, Silverton was her knight in shining armor.

He'd come to her rescue just at the right moment before she was condemned to a life of lonely obscurity, a spinster, never knowing the joys of a loving husband and adorable children.

All those creature comforts which Kitty had craved her entire life.

And which, she now realized, she would never know.

She'd managed to stop sobbing by the time she returned to the fold, as Mr. Lazarus termed the overcrowded antechamber which housed their motley array of props and costumes.

In fact, she was quite dignified as Jennie rushed forward to give her a strident serve as to how she'd abandoned them all, for Lady Debenham had just been in to inform them they'd be expected on stage in just under an hour as the last of their guests had arrived.

However, Jennie's ire had turned to enthusiasm as she'd gone on to tell her that Lady Debenham had invited the actors to participate in the dancing for an hour after the performance.

"'Er ladyship's mama didn't like 'er suggestion one bit. Said it was not respectable, but Lady Debenham would 'ave 'er way." Jennie cocked an eyebrow. "Reckon she 'ad her feelers out for our Bert. Wants to dance a gavotte with our 'andsomest feller." She giggled. "She'll be jealous when Bert kisses the leading lady on stage. Lady

Debenham's got a reputation for being fast and loose, but she don't care. What's the bet she'll be so bold as to ask Bert to partner her to make that old sourpuss Lord Debenham jealous?"

Kitty couldn't care less what Araminta did or who danced with whom. She shook her head wildly. "I'm not dancing with anyone," she muttered, aware of Jennie's surprised gaze following her before the redhead shrugged and went off to gabble her excitement to someone else.

No, if Mr. Lazarus hadn't purloined her at that moment, she might have picked up her skirts and simply bolted right out of the room and never come back.

How could she have found herself in the midst of such a nightmare?

CHAPTER 7

$\mathcal{L}$issa dubiously eyed the garment that lay upon the narrow metal-framed bed wedged beneath the tiny casement window.

She supposed she should be feeling grateful at not having to share a bed with one of the household servants. And she should, of course, be hugely appreciative of the fact that Lady Julia had, she said, seen fit for Lissa to act as Lucinda's chaperone for the night so that Lissa 'could enjoy some high society'.

Of course, that was so Lady Julia might have free rein to enjoy herself without having to keep an eye on Lucinda. A more pliant charge than Lucinda might have been trusted to behave with decorum, but Lucinda was a wild card. Lissa knew that as well as Lady Julia.

Feeling ill, Lissa donned the plain evening gown that served for any event that required a greater attention to dress than dinner *en famille* and walked, very slowly, along the corridor to knock upon Lucinda's door.

The young girl's face was flushed when she opened it, and Lissa thought how pretty she looked in a blue and cream piped gown with puffed sleeves and heavily-embroidered roses at the hem.

"Wasn't it fortunate I packed this?" Lucinda remarked, skimming her waist with her hands before offering the back of her head for Lissa's perusal. Often, Lucinda utilized any opportunity to belittle her governess, but clearly, tonight she was too excited at the prospect of shining in high society and seemed to want Lissa's approval regarding the fall of her ringlets.

After being reassured that Lucinda's ringlets, and indeed Lucinda herself, had never looked better, the young girl gripped Lissa's wrist as they began their progress toward the ballroom and begged, "Please keep as much of an eye on Lady Julia as you have to on me. You know what she's like when she's had too much Madeira."

Lissa smiled. "Well then, I promise to keep as strict an eye on her as I've promised *her* I shall keep on you." Lucinda's grin elicited the first feeling of camaraderie she'd felt for the girl. But then the girl's mouth drooped, and she was once again the pouting adolescent that bored and frustrated Lissa by turn as she asked, "And what about Lord Beecham? He showed no interest in ensuring I was properly supervised?"

"Lord Beecham leaves such matters to the mature women in his household and trusts you will not embarrass him." Lissa should not have added that piece of information in the schoolmarmish tone calculated to set up Lucinda's bristles. Immediately her charge pulled away and marched up the corridor, and Lissa wondered why she was so bad at pandering to an adolescent's precious dignity. But then, she hadn't seen Ralph in two weeks, and their enforced separation was taking its toll. He was, she knew, busy working on some business for his employer as Lord Debenham was trying to negotiate the sale of some land in Buckinghamshire, no doubt to settle some gaming debts.

Ralph was using the opportunity to pry deeper into his employer's contacts. Perhaps he'd find something conclusive that built on the letter his cousin—who was both his lover as well as being Sir Aubrey's wife—had penned intimating his criminal involvement not just in the Lord Castlereagh affair. Perhaps there was other evidence which supported his involvement in the grubby pamphleteering which had led to two members of the House of Lords taking their own lives.

There were so many instances of alleged misconduct which

pointed to Lord Debenham, yet nothing conclusive had ever been established. Maybe Lissa would be the one to supply the evidence he was involved in a plot to discredit Princess Caroline of Brunswick, the Prince Regent's wife, who evoked such violently mixed feelings among the populace and peerage.

Lissa knew this was something very much on Ralph's mind. If he could only prove that Lord Debenham had a hand in any of these matters, he would be rewarded for his services to the Home Office with a more senior role in their hallowed echelons.

He might even be rewarded with a salary or sinecure that would enable him to do as he'd declared so ardently to Lissa was his greatest dream—be in a position to marry her.

First, of course, was the nightmare that confronted her—negotiating this evening without being exposed. Would it even be possible not to attract the observation and consequent outrage of her father, not to mention any others in the area who might recognize her?

It was the reason Lissa had chosen to wear her dullest clothing and adopt a hairstyle that was as demure and unflattering as possible.

Four hours. If she could just survive four hours—one of which would be taken up watching a play that would, fortunately, enable her to fade into the background—then she could insist it was time for her young charge, who was of course not yet out, to go to bed.

Head down, she led Lucinda to several chairs at the end of a row, hoping to attract no interest. However, the audience seemed too busy gossiping with acquaintances they'd not seen since being in London, which was probably but days ago since pleasurable indulgences were all these people seemed to live for, she thought uncharitably.

She was unnerved to see Lord Ludbridge seated next to Araminta and quickly looked away, praying neither would see her, though of course that would not be possible. Lady Debenham's enthusiastic welcome had included an invitation to Lord Beecham to stay the night, but her tone had cooled when she'd seen his companion. Lissa wondered if they'd be sent on their way, poste haste, once their vehicle was repaired. Lady Julia seemed immune to shame or embarrassment, though Lissa was well aware that she courted opprobrium at every turn. Not only was there that bad business with Edgar, Lord Partington's late heir, but she was a married woman in company with a single man and his charge. She wondered how that had been explained.

But while Lady Julia had her own embarrassment to contend with, there was Lissa's own awkwardness in dealing with Araminta. She'd not seen her half-sister in some months, and of course Lissa was responsible for a number of sketches made during the fateful night at Vauxhall Gardens. This had deepened the investigation into Debenham's affairs and led, indirectly, to Araminta being pressured—so Lissa had heard—into marrying the villain.

Ought Lissa to feel some responsibility, guilt, or even sympathy for her half-sister?

Watching the self-composed beauty seated several rows away, she reassured herself that neither Araminta nor Lord Ludbridge would be likely to acknowledge her. Lissa would be an embarrassment to them on so many counts—for what she knew, what she had done, and what she was.

It was this last part that rankled.

For her entire life, Lissa had been conscious of the way others judged her on account of her parentage. Now she was sitting here in the midst of her worst nightmare, and there was nothing she could do.

Her throat felt dry, and she licked her lips as she glanced about her. Once she'd ascertained where her father was seated, she'd do her best all evening to keep her head low and out of sight.

As for Lord Debenham, he was the main reason she'd not pleaded a megrim and kept to her room. Lissa felt in her pocket for her sketchbook. Her job was to produce lightning sketches detailing the associations between people of interest to the Home Office. They wanted evidence of all the personages with whom Lord Debenham conversed in any manner that suggested clandestine matters were being discussed. Her sketches of Debenham at Vauxhall in company with Buzby and Smythe had indicated that he was in deep with men who were strongly suspected to be radicals involved in more than just grubby pamphleteering and possibly counterfeiting. If Lissa's sketches could bear that up or find evidence of, perhaps, Spencean associations, she would be lauded for a job well done.

And it had been a long time since Lissa had been lauded for anything.

KITTY WAITED IN THE WINGS, TERROR AND ANTICIPATION MAKING HER lightheaded and nauseous. Her costume would not be sufficient to disguise her from those who knew her best—namely, her father. Her name would be another shock. Silverton would not be best pleased that she was under the same roof as his future wife. In the same room. What's more, Miss Mandelton might well recognize Kitty and engage her in conversation before Kitty got the opportunity to slip away.

She dashed a tear from the corner of her eye as she angled herself behind the curtain in order to get a view of the audience. There he was. Her beloved Silverton. How commanding and dashing he looked. Yet also kind and personable. Her breath hitched in her throat as she watched him smilingly converse with Miss Mandelton, who was sitting on his right side. The fact that she was *so* plain made the reality of what Kitty faced so much bleaker. Miss Mandelton's sweetness and vulnerability would appeal to Silverton's chivalry. How could he bear to tear himself in two?

"Kitty! You're on!"

Jennie gave her a shove in the ribs and then Kitty was skipping onto the stage, a bright, jaunty smile in place; her lines perfectly memorized as her professionalism took over.

And for the next hour, she stole the show and won the hearts of all those susceptible gentlemen and whipped up the envy of the ladies.

Indeed, immediately the cast had received their applause and had been invited to stop for a bit of dancing, Miss Mandelton did hurry forward to clasp Kitty's hand and exclaim her utter delight at seeing her "old friend," while a pale and shocked-looking Silverton brought up the rear.

"My dear Silverton, can you believe it, but I met Miss Bijou only a few miles from here when she rescued Poppet for me," Miss Mandelton explained over her shoulder to Silverton, finally relinquishing Kitty's hand as she added, "And what's more, she took the naughty creature away to be cleaned so that Aunt Bertha wouldn't be in a crotchet the rest of the way here. So that makes her a very kind friend in my book. Not many people would have been so thoughtful, so I can't speak too highly of Miss Bijou."

"I'm sure your opinion is shared by many," Silverton murmured longingly as he locked gazes with Kitty over the top of Miss Mandelton's head.

A smile and brief thanks were as much as Kitty could manage, and as soon as she could in all politeness get away, she wove through the crowd of revelers—guests and actors—to seek the sanctuary of the garden.

Gulping in the cool evening air, she bent double, gripping the branch of a tree that overhung the terrace.

And then the tears came from nowhere. Great, gulping sobs that seemed to suck the life and soul from her. She thought they would never stop.

"Hetty?"

Into the soft light, there emerged a figure. A slight, motherly figure with a serene face obviously mistook Kitty for someone else, for she did not stop for clarification before she'd drawn Kitty into a comforting embrace.

"Oh, my lady, you're mistaken. I...I'm not Hetty," whispered Kitty as she waited for Lady Partingon to drop her arms and no doubt hurry away murmuring an embarrassed—or perhaps shocked—rejoinder.

Instead, she felt the momentary stiffening of the lady's arms about her. But they did not drop from her shoulders. And the voice did not harden. In fact, the very opposite happened as Kitty's father's ignorant but oh, so kind, wife, murmured, "You may not be my daughter, but you clearly are in need of comfort."

She didn't even look at Kitty, just held Kitty to her, and it was so wonderful to feel a mother's arms about her—for Kitty couldn't remember her own mother ever having offered her affection like this —that she didn't want to move away. Finally, when her sobs had subsided, and it seemed natural to speak, Lady Partington took her hand and led her farther along the terrace and into the shadows where she said, "Would it help you to tell a stranger what has made you so sad? You were truly marvelous on stage. I can't imagine someone so beautiful and accomplished could be so sad. But you are from London, are you not? Perhaps you miss your family."

Kitty couldn't meet her eye. She brushed her hand over the top of the low brick wall upon which she was resting. "I ran away from my family who disapprove of my calling, and I have a wonderful life. I'm not a bit ashamed of what I do, but I've fallen in love with a man who...cannot marry me, though his love is, I truly believe, equal to mine."

Kitty was not surprised to hear Lady Partington's slight intake of breath. Then, with the faintest trace of suspicion, she asked, "So he has just left you? And that is why you're crying?"

Kitty shook her head. What did it matter if she spoke the truth? Lady Partington was in no danger of ascertaining Kitty's true identity. And right now, it was cathartic to have the ear of one so clearly sympathetic, for, up close, Kitty was struck by just how kind and angelic a face Lady Partington possessed. In the moonlight, she looked half her age, and suddenly Kitty realized she didn't hate the woman her mother had so bitterly denigrated her entire life. She even found herself able to talk to her with a frankness she could never have managed if she'd been talking to her mother.

"He has to marry properly, and indeed there is a very worthy young lady to whom he has become affianced to please his family, but in truth, his heart belongs to me."

"And you mean to stay with this young man?"

Kitty bridled at the inherent criticism in Lady Partington's tone. What should she have expected, though? Kitty was just a lowborn actress with morals to match. Of course, Lady Partington would look down her nose at her. "He would have married me if it had been possible."

"Yet you intend to live as his...mistress...while he marries another?"

"*I* will have his heart, and that is more important to me than status or position or his money."

"My dear, you may have his heart, but it is a poor bargain for all three of you."

Kitty noticed Lady Partington sounded distressed and was surprised. After all, she didn't know Kitty. Kitty wanted to argue, but she held her tongue as Lady Partington went on, "He may think he will be happy, and that he can salvage his conscience by being all things to both of you, but if his heart belongs to you, what of his wife?"

"She will have everything she could wish for, even his affection, I believe." Kitty gulped. "But not his love, for that will always be mine and knowing that, it will be enough."

To Kitty's surprise, Lady Partington gave her a little shake. "My dear Miss Bijou, I will offer you a confidence held close to my heart. " She stared into Kitty's eyes. "Only because I would not see another innocent sacrifice her happiness out of ignorance. Do not, I beg you, go ahead with this unhappy arrangement. You say he loves you, but that duty requires him to marry another? All three of you are condemning yourselves to a lifetime of unhappiness. Think of his future wife. She knows nothing of you, is it true?"

"She is a sweet, simple soul. They are childhood friends. She doesn't expect his heart." Kitty was clutching at straws, but as she thought of Miss Mandelton, her own heart seemed to shrivel inside her. Lady Partington was only saying what Kitty, herself, knew to be true.

"Does not his future wife deserve to enter her marriage full of hope for the future? Is she not right in hoping that theirs will be a partnership that will be rewarding and fulfilling, that they will be blessed by children who will bask in the affection of adoring parents?"

"She will be given everything she could want. She will have his affection—"

"His loyalties are already divided. He will resent one or both of you. The children he has by his wife and those he has by…by you, will never know the fullest extent of a father's love as he juggles his double life, trying to fulfill his promises, but failing, not because he is inadequate or less of a man, but because it simply is not possible to give two women—a wife and a mistress—and the resulting children, what they should regard as their due. I speak from experience. I spent twenty years locked in a union without love with a man whose heart belonged to another. Yes, to a woman he would have married had his parents not prevailed at the last moment.

"I wish to God he had married her for he resented me for what I did not, could not, know. I, who had never known love, entered marriage believing we could forge a future together based on a general liking and respect, which I naively assumed would blossom into love when our children were born. Nor was it only I and his other woman who suffered. The children suffered, too. Greatly. So, I beg you, consider long and hard what you are about to enter into. It can only bring the deepest pain, recrimination, and heartache."

KITTY STUMBLED INTO THE BALLROOM. SHE'D BEEN GONE FOR SOME time, and now the actors who'd been allowed so graciously to hobnob with the grandees were being chivvied to disperse.

There was Jennie in the arms of a footman, the butler at his shoulder. Mr. Lazarus looked like he was preparing to prize the pair apart, but the lad relinquished his hold at the last moment. Kitty had little doubt Jennie would orchestrate some assignation for later.

At the far end of the room she glimpsed Silverton; head bowed as he attended to Miss Mandelton. It seemed he was attuned to Kitty's presence, however, for he immediately whispered something hastily to his future bride before making his way toward Kitty.

She turned abruptly. No, she could not speak to him and possibly give herself away in front of everyone.

And then, to her shock, her sister crossed her line of vision. Not Araminta or Hetty whose movements she'd carefully monitored but Lissa, her full-blood sister whom she suddenly realized how greatly she missed. She reached out and gripped her arm, pulling her to the edge of the room.

"Lissa!"

"Kitty, I've been looking everywhere to catch you alone!" her sister exclaimed, her voice low as she glanced about her to ensure their clandestine meeting was not observed. "Did you see Papa turn apoplectic? He's gone now, of course. Couldn't face the possibility we might acknowledge him before he had a chance to scuttle away."

Kitty nodded sadly. Once, she'd dreamed of making her father proud as she performed to wild acclaim. Well, she'd performed to such wild acclaim here under his very roof, but he'd been horrified and embarrassed.

And now he was nowhere to be seen, though that was perhaps not such a bad thing. She noticed Stephen Cranborne eyeing her with mild alarm. Kitty very much hoped he'd not divulge her true identity to Lady Partington, who had every reason to despise Kitty, just as Kitty had despised her until this evening.

Mr. Cranborne was her father's heir, but Kitty had met him only once—when she'd tumbled out of a tree and landed at his feet the year before. Kitty had sought sanctuary there when she'd been trespassing and had heard her father's voice. As she'd risen from her undignified landing, she'd declared to her father her intention to run away and become an actress. It was as if voicing the words out loud had made her dream a reality.

To Kitty's surprise, Lady Partington was suddenly at Mr. Cranborne' side, and for a moment, she could have sworn her ladyship briefly clasped his hand in hers before whispering in his ear.

Kitty turned, dragging Lissa away with her. Lady Partington mustn't learn that Kitty was the daughter of her nemesis. As much as anything else, Kitty had a very strong desire that she didn't want to cause anyone anymore hurt than had already been dealt tonight.

"Lissa, where have you been? I've searched far and wide for you, but after you disappeared from the Lamonts, I was at a loss until Mr. Lamont painted my portrait and I saw your name on the back of his sketchbook."

"We cannot speak here, Kitty," said her sister as she sought refuge in the shadows with Kitty. "It's wonderful to see you, and I can't wait to hear more about Mr. Lamont and about you, but nor can we reveal who we are to each other. You understand that?"

"Just as Lady Debenham is going to great lengths not to reveal what we are to her. Not that she knows who I am—other than the actress who helped her the night her baby was in danger of being delivered too early."

"Oh, Kitty, I *must* talk to you, only not here. Where are you staying?"

When Kitty mentioned the name of the inn where the theater troupe had bespoken rooms, Lissa nodded after a quick glance over her shoulder. "I must get back to my charge now. Tonight was Miss Martindale's first evening out in broader company, but it's her music teacher, Lady Julia, whom I must ensure doesn't create a scandal. I can see Lady Partington's bristles are already set up. Oh, Lissa, it's so good to see you again. I'll visit you if I can before I leave, but at least I know where to find you."

CHAPTER 8

*B*ut it wasn't Lissa whom Kitty expectantly admitted following a soft rapping on her door later that night.

"Silverton," she murmured, stepping aside reluctantly though her heart was at war with itself. She opened her mouth to tell him what she'd determined earlier that night, but immediately the door closed behind him, he swept her into his embrace, bringing his lips down to hers in a passionate, all-consuming kiss that brought her spirits soaring to the surface once more.

Kitty went limp in his arms as he carried her to the bed, his passion for her greater than ever, it seemed, and she responded with equal ardor, though she knew what they had could not be sustained. Not after what she'd seen and heard tonight.

He barely spoke but to murmur endearments and words of passion as he quickly divested her first of the simple night shift which was all she wore, before attending to his boots and coat.

Kitty's heart was in danger of tearing in two. Not one word of the parting speech she'd rehearsed could she say in the face of her rising need for the one man who gave richness and meaning to her life.

But at what cost? How could she bear to share him?

"I love you, too, Silverton," she whispered against his lips, though not so loud he could hear her. She simply had to say what was in her heart. And to show him that she was his. For tonight.

When her body was laid open to his loving, she closed her eyes and allowed her mind this last time to take her where this wonderful man took her every time. With his mouth on her breast, his right hand gently stroking her cheek, his left stroking up her inner thigh and then to that magic spot at the very core of her where her heart, body, and soul seemed to meet, Kitty clung to him, trying to muffle her whimpers of desire when he moved over her. She was ready for him. She was always ready for him for she loved him so dearly.

Silverton claimed her, bringing her to an earth-shattering climax. For a long time afterward, she lay silent in his arms, every fiber attuned to his rhythmic, labored breathing.

She must remember every nuance, the exquisite sensation of his heated skin, lightly sheened with sweat, his chest hair tickling her cheek, the wonderful essence of him wafting through her senses.

He *felt* rock solid, and he was in so many other ways, too. But he would not be there in the way she needed him to be; not if she were to escape the miserable cycle into which she'd been born. She wanted children. Children born within wedlock. Granted, Lord Silverton would be a more constant and loving parent than her own father, Lord Partington, had been. However, while her children by Silverton would enjoy their father's protection and affection, they'd not have his name and, in this world, one's name was everything.

And so she must leave him but dear Lord, making that break would be the most painful thing she would ever do.

Kitty reached across to stroke his face and murmured, "Your conscience must smite you," then gave a gentle, ironic laugh as she felt him stiffen, the only indication that her words had found a mark.

"It's not as I would wish." He spoke with difficulty as he stared at the ceiling, one hand resting behind his head, the other tightening over her fingers as he turned to face her. "I love you, Kitty, but I am duty bound to Miss Mandelton."

"And to the rest of your family. I understand." A searing pain ripped through her, but she showed no emotion as she stared into his eyes, mirroring the flickering candle that sat on a low table beside the bed. "I thought I could accept it, too. Your arrangement, I mean. I thought I only wanted your heart...that I didn't need more than that." She swallowed, trying to keep at bay the rising tide of emotion. "But I know, now, that it's not enough. If I were to sacrifice my hopes of children, it would be different, but that's too much of a risk and too much for me to accept."

He rose onto his elbows and turned to clasp her shoulders. "What are you saying, Kitty?" There was a hint of panic in his voice.

"That I will never risk having a child who would be branded a bastard. I have endured that burden my whole life. And if I cannot be your wife, I cannot risk such a possibility as your mistress."

"You would leave me?"

Her sigh felt as if it were dragged from her very depths. "I *am* leaving you, Silverton." She felt like weeping but knew she must be strong. This was the only future for her. Gently she stroked his beloved features, both to comfort him and to commit them to memory as she tried to strengthen her argument.

"It's not just the children we might have together...out of wedlock. It's what I'd be doing to Miss Mandelton, too. After my performance at The Grange, I chanced upon a woman who confided to me the pain she'd endured as an unloved, *legally wedded* wife. I would not do that to anyone, and I would not repeat the situation my mother has endured for the past twenty years."

"We can make it work, Kitty," he whispered as he pulled her into his arms, but Kitty shook her head as she stared over his shoulder at the wall.

She repeated dully, "I want marriage, Silverton. I told you from the start, when we were simply friends, only it was such a strange and dramatic set of circumstances by which I became your mistress with you on the way to meeting the wife your family had chosen for you. I always felt confident of your love, but when you marry, your first obligation would be toward your wife and—when they start arriving —your children. You would soon be out of my reach. I can't do it."

"I would always be within your reach. You have my heart, Kitty. You will *always* have my heart."

"But at what cost, Silverton? I've met Miss Mandelton. She deserves better than what she'd have to make do with if you remained true to me." She brushed away a tear, adding, "What we have together *is* pure and true. I know you don't love her, and I understand the duty that compels you to follow through on an obligation made a long time ago, but that's not compensation enough for me."

Gently but firmly she pulled out of his arms, finishing her speech from the safety of the carpet as she draped her discarded shawl over her nakedness. "Miss Mandelton's life would be barren and miserable if she learned your heart belonged to another. Believe me, I know what that feels like from experience, and I could not live with myself for thrusting it upon someone else. Certainly not someone as good and deserving as Miss Mandelton."

LADY JULIA WAS MAGNIFICENT IN POMONA GREEN. DEBENHAM followed her with his eyes as she danced the minuet which, he was amused to see, included a clearly reluctant Stephen Cranborne in the set. The woman appeared to have no shame after the terrible drowning that had occurred two years earlier. Terrible tragedy, of course, but Stephen Cranborne could thank Lady Julia for the fact that he was now Lord Partington's heir. Her drunken revelry two years ago had led Partington's bacon-brained nephew Edgar to a premature death, and everyone knew Cranborne would be a much steadier man in charge.

That didn't make Debenham like him any more. In fact, it enraged him to think that the fertile valleys of Cranborne's lands yielded so much more than Debenham's sparse and rocky dominions further to the north. No wonder Araminta had chosen to stage her celebration here when they were so comfortably accommodated a little more than two hours from London. She detested his country seat as much as he did, though there were times when he would've liked to have banished her there for a few months at a time.

That said, since she'd done her duty and given birth to young William of whom he was ridiculously fond—far fonder, it would appear, than his wife was—and she had regained the luscious curves which, with her pride and beauty had most attracted him, there were compensations to having her near.

His reverie was disturbed by the intrusion of an old acquaintance of whom he was not terribly fond. Debenham raised his laconic gaze to the Earl of Barston's heir whose gaze was fixed upon Lady Julia.

"She could be mistaken for any one of the debutantes about, eh? Experience to burn, though. Three children in the nursery and a roving eye."

It occurred to him that Barston could have been referring to Araminta in a couple of years. The young man went on, "Lord knows how she can get away with this fanciful charade of chaperoning Miss Martindale hither and thither when everyone knows she's Beecham's fancy piece."

Barston was well known for his petulance when he didn't get what he wanted. Perhaps he'd had his eye on Lady Julia once. Or perhaps he still did. Debenham had often gambled with him when he'd been in his cups complaining over this or that. He didn't particularly like the fellow whom he thought a puling namby-pamby boy, so he wasn't much inclined to continue the conversation until Barston said something that made his ears prick up.

"A good thing Sir Archie ain't here to see his wife in the arms of Cranborne of all people." For the pair were now in a waltz hold and galloping to the corners of their square, and Cranborne was smiling for the first time. "I'd be more than dashed grieved with matters in such a pretty pickle on the home front if I were Sir Archie." Barston's hangdog mouth was, as usual, turned down at the corners, his expression more than unusually sour.

Debenham looked at him inquiringly. The fellow looked like he didn't need much encouragement to unburden himself. He sent Debenham a sly look and said, "Common knowledge that Lady Julia tricked him into marriage, though she did the right thing and produced twin boys. Seemed she could then do what she liked after that. And she did." He chuckled. "I was there on the occasion that produced the third son."

"Good Lord!"

Barston shook his head. "No, not with me." He jerked his head in the direction of Cranborne who, once again, had taken Lady Julia into a waltz hold to gallop into the other corner of their set. "Reckon fate'll play into his hands, and he'll be the one to have fathered Sir Archie's future heir after that awful business with the twins."

"What awful business?"

"Didn't you hear? They got rheumatic fever not long after the new baby—Cranborne's, I'd wager a dozen monkeys—was born, for you only have to look at it to see Cranbourne's nose and forehead. One twin died; the other is unlikely to live past his teens. And if that's the case, it's the third son who'll inherit. Cranborne's spawn."

Debenham frowned, trying to dredge up the little he knew about Sir Archie, whom he detested almost as much as he detested Cranborne though he pretended otherwise. "I did hear murmurs. It was shortly afterward that Lady Julia took on her self-appointed role of music maestro to young Miss Martindale, wasn't it?" He racked his brains. Yes, there was a buzz of scandal at the time. Not regarding the dubious parentage of Lady Julia's third son, but the fact that Sir Archie's wife had left within several months of the birth to go gallivanting across the country, claiming kinship with either Lord Beecham or Miss Martindale who'd recently lost her family to scarlet fever. He couldn't quite remember.

But the upstanding, seemingly celibate Cranborne and Lady Julia? He pretended skepticism though it didn't take much imagination to wholly believe Barston's insinuations with regard to Lady Julia whose roving eye was well known.

"Speculating is one thing, but if you're so sure, why not confront Sir Archie and make mileage out of it?"

Barston looked surprised. "Blackmail?" He shook his head. "Sir

Archie's too powerful in government circles for me to want to get my own head lopped off. Nevertheless, I stand by what I say."

"On what basis? You sound as if you have proof. How could you if you had nothing to do with the business?"

Barston looked affronted. "I was a guest of Sir Archie and Lady Julia the night Cranborne stopped by on his way to answer Lord Partington's summons to size up his new heir." When he could see he had Debenham's interest, he dropped his voice as he warmed to his theme. "That was before that knucklehead cousin Edgar or whatever his name pitched up." He chuckled. "Lord, but that did set the cat among the pigeons. He was a deserter, did you know? The biggest coward who walked the earth, and now Lord Partington was landed with him as his heir. Thanks to Lady Julia, of course, he didn't last long."

He put his head on one side. "Anyway, going back a bit, this happened the night Cranborne was Ledger's guest and hadn't yet met Lord Partington. Well, Sir Archie and his good wife had hatched a wager whereby they planned to fleece young Cranborne of a tidy sum, knowing he was off to meet his rich and influential benefactor, Lord Partington, the next day. I should say it was Lady Julia's plan, for Sir Archie was swimming in the River Tick. Sir Archie was easily led, too, and he set everything up, just as she instructed."

"And what was the wager?" Debenham was becoming increasingly interested.

"It was over a pair of mating spiders. Sir Archie bet that the female wouldn't devour the male, but Cranborne, being a keen zoologist or whatever you'd call 'em, pooh-poohed the idea and bet a fortune on it. Course, he had to take a piss at some stage while the rest of us were waiting. That's when he was detained by the lovely Lady Julia, coming back down the passage. Her role was to distract Cranborne so Sir Archie and I could swap the spiders and declare Cranborne's theory had failed. Well, Lady Julia detained Cranborne for a very long time, I can tell you. Sir Archie sent me to find them, but I never reported back the true story."

Debenham licked his lips. "And what was that?"

"They were in a storeroom. I could hear the panting and the full climactic glory, though I told Sir Archie they were having a conversation about his grandmother's portrait." He shrugged. "Anyway, Lady Julia's next son was born nine months later."

"The son you predict will become Sir Archie's heir?"

"Did I hear you mention Sir Archie?"

Debenham glanced up at the new voice to discover it was Lord Beecham. He shrugged. "Ah Beecham, as you know, I have little liking for the fellow." His gaze encompassed the room and alighted upon his wife's cousin. "And, like you, even less liking for our esteemed do-gooder, Cranborne." He threw a speculative look at Barston but then shook his head upon a sigh. "Alas, if only it were possible to prove paternity."

CHAPTER 9

*D*ebenham leaned back against the windowsill and eyed his wife appraisingly after he'd shooed Jane from the room. It was a habit of his to lounge about in her dressing room while Araminta put the final touches to her toilette prior to an evening out. It also happened to be a habit she loathed. Now he brushed his hair back and muttered admiringly, "I've always admired you in red, darling."

Araminta put her hands to her now slender waist and touched the expensive silk of the gown, for which she still needed funds to pay the dressmaker if she were to continue to enjoy her services. The woman was extremely deft and creative, and Araminta didn't want the embarrassment of being dunned if Debenham balked at the bills she was going to have to ask him to pay, having exceeded her previous quarter's pin money.

"No doubt that is why you gifted me such an exquisite pearl choker when William was born. It would have gone very well with this gown, don't you think?" She raised an eyebrow to reinforce her meaningful look. "You told me you needed it only temporarily to settle a few accounts, and that it would soon be returned to me. But weeks have passed. When do you suppose you might follow through on your promise?"

Debenham chuckled. "So impatient, my love. And a scenario frighteningly similar to the strange disappearance of your ruby and diamond choker which has never been adequately explained. You'll get your choker back, but I do have other priorities. Namely, protecting my good name. Some of those gentlemen with whom we conversed so amicably tonight would see me at the end of a noose, including your charming cousin, Stephen Cranborne, don't you know?"

Araminta turned her head away. She knew her Cousin Stephen wanted to discredit her husband, and if the consequences weren't likely to be so dire for her, she'd happily have helped him.

The unfortunate fact was that Cranborne's mission to discover the letter she'd thought she'd burned was making life extremely difficult for Debenham and, in turn, for Araminta.

Well, if Ralph Tunley really knew where it was he should give it to her brother. Her darling Teddy would be only too pleased to hand it over. Many times, Araminta had toyed with the idea of telling Debenham that his secretary, Ralph Tunley, possessed the letter that had the power to severely handicap Debenham in public life. But it was too dangerous to put it so plainly. Debenham would punish Ralph; not that Araminta cared particularly for Ralph. In fact, it was highly distressing, if not horrifying that Teddy's own brother should have allied himself with a governess, an illegitimate governess— Araminta's own half-sister, Lissa. She really was going to have to do something to nip that little romance in the bud. Perhaps she could reveal Ralph's suspected duplicity—though not if it threatened Teddy's love for her.

"Cousin Stephen would never see harm come to his own brother-in-law. No, he'd never be so duplicitous," she murmured.

"Ready to drive the knife in the moment I make a wrong move." Debenham chuckled. "Ah, but that is the way of survival. Stephen Cranborne truly believes he will best me, but I assure you tonight was very profitable in ensuring that if anyone is bested, it won't be me."

Araminta made her voice light as she affected more interest in the fit of her gloves. "And how do you plan to effect that, my love?" It was important to discover her husband's plans if she were to be successful in doing her part in the background. Poor Debenham truly thought he was clever, but the truth was that in addition to being a gambler and a womanizer with an overinflated sense of his gifts, Araminta was going to have to work hard to ensure he didn't fall victim to hubris. Of the two of them, Araminta was the one who really knew how to manage people to best effect.

He stroked his whiskers. "How do I plan to effect that? In fact, this very evening the most extraordinary information has just come into my possession."

"Information? You intend to blackmail someone?"

He looked mildly shocked before his facial features assumed their habitual sneer. "Blackmail is such a distasteful word, but as it's unkind to speak in riddles, let me just say that the dangling before a personage of the strong suspicion of their past demeanors in order to extract something of value could be termed blackmail."

"Debenham, speak plainly. What is this information you've discovered?" Lord, but her husband could be exasperating.

"So you can inadvertently reveal it to the world? No, dearest Araminta. I'm happy to speak in generalities but not specifics. Suffice to say that I have heard of a great scandal that could rock the entire foundations of society. Curious, eh?"

That was putting it mildly. "You're teasing me, Debenham. Who does this scandal involve?"

"I shan't tell you. In fact, I'll be honest and say that my informant hasn't given me sufficient information to act upon beyond saying that it involves a child. A child who is to become heir to a great estate to which he is not entitled."

Araminta dropped the pearl earring she was about to hook through her lobe. Robbed of air, she could only raise her eyebrows. All the strength seemed to have seeped from her limbs, and she had to sit down at her dressing table once again.

"Why?" He asked the question for her, seemingly unaware of her horror. "Because, of course, the child was sired by the faithless wife's lover. Now there is just the matter of proof."

Araminta's world swam before her eyes. She couldn't look at Debenham. He was playing with her. Waiting for her to ask the question before he launched into a fierce and bitter diatribe as he threw her past behavior into her face. So he knew, then, that William was not his? Dear God, what would happen now? If he didn't kill her, he'd make her life a living misery. He'd cast her out, and she'd be shunned. Ridiculed.

"So...you know then?" she whispered between dry lips. He was stringing her along, enjoying watching her squirm. Soon he would confront her with her crime. Araminta couldn't bear it. She tried to hold back the tears. Debenham would make the most of her agony. He was cruel at the best of times.

He sent a thoughtful look through the window. "To tell you the truth, I'm not entirely certain of the specifics," he murmured as he chewed his lip. "The seed was sown tonight after someone intimated that such a scenario had occurred within our ranks. My plan, my dear Araminta, is to discover all the sordid details beyond all reasonable doubt, and then reveal it to the world—or else claim a great sum for my silence."

THERE HAD BEEN NO PLEASURE IN DANCING THIS EVENING AMIDST lavish surroundings. In fact, Lissa considered the night she'd been forced to spend under her father's roof the most painful of her life.

Everything had been contrived to rub salt into the wound, reminding her of what might have been hers had justice prevailed.

If Lucinda had been difficult, Lady Julia had been a nightmare. A hideously embarrassing nightmare as she'd tried to flirt with Stephen Cranborne, of all people.

Thank the Lord Lissa had finally escaped after having to spend just the one night in that poky little attic room. She wouldn't have been surprised if Lord Beecham had insisted they were the first to leave. Perhaps there'd been a scene, for Lady Julia had sulked the entire journey home while Lord Beecham had glowered out of the window.

And now, at last, Lissa was here in Ralph's lodgings Mrs. Nipkins having obligingly left to visit her sister for the evening, enabling two clandestine hours for her to be with the most wonderful, clever, enterprising young man in the entire world.

The moment she'd walked into the kitchen, he'd seated her on his lap. Now he was brushing out her braids while he told her about a play he'd seen the previous week, and for the first time in weeks, Lissa was laughing.

Of course, it was dreadfully tempting to be a good deal more sinful, and indulge in kisses that might get out of control with Mrs. Nipkins out of the way, but both of them had discussed the dangers and come to the conclusion that if they were to marry with their reputations intact, they must make very sure that no scandal attached to their names. It was one thing to be alone when that was courting disaster by its very nature.

Lissa closed her eyes as she raised her face to the low ceiling and the enjoyment of the moment rolled through her. Ralph was the only person who could make Lissa laugh. He made her forget her troubles and her dissatisfaction with life. She'd hoped her new posting with Lord Beecham would provide her with excitement to make up for her lack of marital prospects in the meantime, but everything had been so dull, peppered by horrible interludes like spending the night at The Grange.

In the midst of laughing at Ralph's account of two barristers who'd nearly come to blows outside his office, they both jerked upright at an urgent series of knocks at the door. Cautiously Ralph rose, and barely had he turned the knob than the flimsy barricade was thrust open, and Kitty burst into the room and quite literally into Lissa's arms.

"What's happened? Is it Mama?" For that was the only calamity Lissa could imagine causing such angst in her little sister.

Kitty was sobbing so loudly it was some time before they were able to get anything coherent from her. Lissa pushed her down into a chair while Ralph rustled up a cup of tea from the kettle boiling over the hob, with a detour to fetch his brandy.

"It's not Mama," she finally said when she could talk. She raised her head and sent Lissa a baleful stare.

Immediately, Lissa understood. Her lover. "Oh, then he's tired of you already," she remarked as sympathy drained from her. This was the first time Kitty had visited her. For her sister to have tracked her down, she'd have imagined the reason to have been of the utmost calamity. Though she supposed it was when one's main means of support was suddenly taken away.

"No need to use that tone. I know you disapprove, but the fact is, *I* ended it!" Kitty faced her sister furiously. "Yes, I ended it after I met Miss Mandelton and realized I'd have to share Silverton. Like Mama. Even though I love him more than life itself."

"Don't be dramatic, Kitty." Lissa couldn't help sounding short. "Besides, loving someone more than life itself is not possible."

Ralph returned to the room with glasses for them all and eyed his beloved askance. "You would not lay down your life for me, dearest?" he asked, looking hurt, then pouring them each a tot as he went on, "I'd lay down my life for *you*. Actually, climbing that drainpole outside the Lamonts was rather risky business. I'm just disappointed it wasn't appreciated more—"

"Ralph!" Lissa stamped her foot, torn between rushing around the table and hugging sense into him, and maintaining a more sober attitude for Kitty's benefit. Kitty had to learn, someday, that she couldn't act like the baby of the family forever, chasing impossible dreams. "You're playing semantics! You know that I would risk my life for you, but I'd not lay it down passively because my love for you was greater than my own appreciation of my life."

"But passively loving someone with passion and to distraction is surely as noble as violently loving someone and recklessly throwing themselves into danger in order to save them. My point is that my love for you, Lissa, and I would hope, yours for me, is as valid and noble as your sister's is for the man she loves. Therefore, she is in as great a need of comfort at this moment as you would be had I *not* survived a fall from the second floor of the Lamont House when I rescued you all those months ago."

"Yes, but Ralph—"

"Will you both stop!" Kitty's shriek had them turn their attention from their minor disagreement to Kitty, who was now sitting up, her eyes flashing as she said, "As I said, he did not 'cast me off' as you so derisively put it, Lissa. Our love is purer than that. That is why I made this sacrifice. Yes, sacrifice! I've never done anything noble before. I know you think of me as the spoiled little sister who chose her own happiness before that of anyone else's, but you, Lissa, were not condemned to living for the rest of your days with Mama who has never been grateful to us for anything we've done, having to shop every day in the village, never escaping from the horrible whispers. I know that becoming a governess was something you'd rather not have done, but that you did it for the good of the family. But what if you'd been given no choice but to slave away for Mama? Do you not think you'd have found a way to leave? Just because I followed my calling when I got the opportunity and became an actress rather than a governess, doesn't make me less dutiful than you. Perhaps more scandalous, but not less dutiful, Lissa."

"She does have a point, dearest."

Lissa glared at Ralph. "Am I to have no support from you?" she began.

But he put his hand on Kitty's shoulder and reminded her, "Kitty came here to find you, in the dead of night, after she gave up the greatest love of her life, for the sake of his happiness and that of his bride-to-be. I think we should applaud her, pour another tot of brandy, and discuss how she might best go on from here."

Generously, he refilled all their glasses, except Lissa's whose was untouched and sat down.

Lissa reached out for Kitty's arm and gave it a squeeze. "Ralph is right and I'm being righteous. I'm sorry." She smiled a little tearily at her lovely young man and was grateful for his kind and reasonable approach. Lissa hadn't had much love growing up and knew that her responses, especially toward Kitty, could be interpreted as unfeeling, though it was because there was little leeway for sentiment when life was harsh and difficult. Lord knew how long she and Ralph would remain in their unsatisfactory nether world, unable to marry because of the impecunious situation which had seemed on the cusp of change a few months ago but which had stagnated. Tonight was the first opportunity she'd had to spend a few hours away from her duties toward Miss Martindale, and she'd hoped to spend it in Ralph's arms. But Kitty deserved sympathy.

"It was a brave thing you did, Kitty, if you truly loved him. For, of course, you'll not have his support and that places you in a precarious position. What will you do?"

"I still have my job. My wages have gone up at the theater, so I won't be on the street. Silverton would not accept the ruby necklace I tried to return to him."

"Lord, the one that Debenham gave his wife, and which caused all that trouble when she sold it and he went hunting it down so he could use it to pay a gambling debt?"

Kitty nodded. "You know the story, then? Nash gave it to me when he asked me to marry him."

Lissa shuddered again at the thought that her own once-innocent little sister had been the mistress of the rakish Lord Nash before moving on to his friend, Silverton.

"But when I rushed off from the church, thinking it was a sham marriage, my necklace was recognized by the friend of a woman of dubious repute whom I shall not mention in your hearing, Lissa."

"You mean, the woman who runs the brothel in Soho, Maggie Montgomery?" Lissa forced herself to utter the shameful words as she stared defiantly from Kitty to Ralph. "I'm not so protected or precious I can't utter truths when they're required."

"It was actually Mrs. Mobbs who recognized me and who is Maggie Montgomery's friend. She was my landlady when I first came to London, and she also finds homes for motherless babies, so she's not a bad woman, but Maggie Montgomery is, and she knew Lord Debenham was searching for the necklace that Nash had procured from a visit to...Maggie Montgomery's."

Kitty's bit her lip as she recounted the story which Lissa hadn't

BEVERLEY OAKLEY

heard in such detail. Indeed, its very sordid nature made her blanch though she kept her thoughts to herself.

"Lord Silverton was doing the noble thing, looking after me following my mad flight from the church—"

"Looking after you?" Lissa put her head on one shoulder. "So you ran straight from the church where you were to marry Nash, and into Silverton's....arms? And thereupon became his mistress. What? A month ago? Six weeks? And now it's all over?"

"Silverton and I had been friends far longer than that!" Kitty ground out. "You make it sound grubby and coarse, and it was anything but that. Anyway, Silverton paid twice over for that necklace to ensure I was safe from Debenham and Maggie Montgomery and anyone else who had evil intentions. And now he's insisted I keep it."

"Was your parting amicable, Kitty? He wasn't...violent when you wanted your freedom?" Ralph's concern made Lissa feel guilty. Of course, she should have been equally concerned about this part.

"Oh, he begged and was torn, but he knew he had his duty toward his family first, and that Miss Mandelton was relying on him. He didn't want me to go and begged me to reconsider, and I nearly lost my resolve, but all the time, at the back of my mind, was the image of my life turning out like Mama's." Kitty put her head in her hands and hunched over the table. "I want a loving family with children who can grow up proud of who they are. As much as I love Silverton—and I do, *passionately*—I couldn't condemn my children to the life you and I have lived, Lissa."

Lissa swallowed. Awkwardly, she put her hand on her sister's soft, golden hair and stroked it, realizing she'd never done such a thing since Kitty had been a little girl.

And as she thought about her sister's words and considered her sacrifice, she realized that what Ralph had said was true. Kitty *was* to be commended for her brave and noble sacrifice.

CHAPTER 10

*K*itty hunched over the table with Lissa and Ralph on either side of her in Mrs Nipkins tiny dwelling.

She had always felt her sister's disapproval keenly, but there was nothing she could do. She wasn't going to become a governess like Lissa. She hadn't the patience. And didn't it make far more sense to trade on the talents she did have?

She wiped her streaming eyes with the back of her hand and thought of what she must do now. She'd only just parted from Silverton, but it felt like a lifetime. He'd insisted there was no urgency for her to leave the lodgings he'd leased for her, no doubt hoping she'd change her mind.

But Kitty was so terrified of losing her resolve to do the right thing that she knew she couldn't stay there while Silverton was in town. All it would take was another distressing visit like the last when he'd arrived unexpectedly, pleading with her to stay with him, and she'd weaken.

So tomorrow she must start looking for a new abode. In the meantime, her loyal maid Dorcas was packing Kitty's things and making her own inquiries as to a suitable place for them through the friends and contacts the poor thing had made when she'd been indentured to Mollie Montgomery.

Kitty and Dorcas's friendship had been cemented when both had just arrived in London from the country and found lodging with Mrs. Mobbs, but while Kitty's star had risen, and she'd become the most celebrated actress in the country, Dorcas had been tricked into signing a contract that forced her to serve in Mrs. Montgomery's wicked house of ill repute. Kitty and Silverton had tried to rescue her, before she'd been given her freedom on condition she perform some villainy for Mollie. Kitty still worried that somehow Mollie and her henchmen would find Dorcas and threaten her into some dubious business that would serve their ends if she didn't return to her previous hated life.

She was about to thank Lissa and Ralph for their kindness, when to everyone's obvious shock, there came another rap upon the door followed by a breathless voice.

"Mr. Tunley? Are you there?"

Kitty gripped the tabletop and glanced at Lissa. The voice belonged to a woman; a young woman by the sound of her cultured tones. Kitty's mind whirled. Perhaps Silverton had enlisted the help of a female friend to beg Kitty to return. But no respectable young lady would venture into these alleyways after dark. No, this couldn't be about her.

"Mr. Tunley. I know you're in there."

Kitty saw Ralph and her sister exchange concerned looks before Ralph went to open the door.

By the time a tall, slender young woman dressed entirely in black had swept in, Kitty had found a hiding place behind the curtain which separated the scullery from the bedchamber on that level. She'd recognized the voice and had no wish to be observed in discussion with Lissa and Ralph. The unexpected newcomer was Araminta, and Araminta was devious. And vengeful. She'd need to know the connection. She also, no doubt, knew Kitty had been in possession of the ruby and diamond necklace that had once belonged to her and had caused so much trouble.

"Mr. Tunley, you must help me!" Araminta now cried, and through a chink in the curtain, Kitty watched her push back her veil.

"Araminta?" Lissa gasped, and her sister swung around, her eyes dark with panic. And then surprise.

"Lissa?" She nodded to Ralph as she clearly tried to compose herself. "I'm sorry to burst in unannounced. I did not expect to see you here at such a late hour."

Kitty was still getting over her astonishment, when Ralph calmly put his hand beneath Araminta's elbow and led her to a chair by the dwindling fire which he bent to attend to, tossing on a couple of pieces of kindling before settling himself against the mantelpiece since there were not enough chairs for all of them.

"Something has happened, Lady Debenham? To my employer? Yet surely you would not have ventured out alone, at this hour, to tell me? How can I help?"

"Indeed, I *wouldn't* have ventured here alone if you were not my last hope, Mr. Tunley."

"Your last hope, Araminta?"

Kitty was taken aback by the scorn in Lissa's voice and the fact she used their sister's Christian name.

"You think I'm being dramatic?" Araminta drew herself up, offended. "Is it dramatic to seek out the only person who may be able to help, when the alternative is for my husband to exercise his talent for cruelty and cast me onto the streets or worse?"

Kitty wondered at the nature of Araminta's misdemeanor, though she imagined she'd learn it soon enough through Lissa's expert line of questioning.

Lissa was not one to beat about the bush. "Cruelty? You surely knew what you were doing when I accompanied you to Vauxhall Gardens that fateful night a year ago. You threw your lot in with his Lordship and left your sister Miss Henrietta somewhat vulnerable to the drunken rage of Lord Debenham. I think she got the better deal when she married Sir Aubrey and you, Debenham. But are we to sympathize with you when you made your choice? It was not so long ago that I saw the two of you together at your birthday at The Grange.

I'm surprised your sister was prepared to have him under the same roof, but Lord Debenham appeared mightily pleased with you for producing a son and heir a timely nine months after your nuptials." Kitty was swamped by memories of the role she'd played the night Araminta had nearly lost her baby. "Isn't that what every man wishes?"

"Oh yes, I gave him what he wanted because I knew that to do otherwise would put me in the gravest danger." Araminta closed her eyes upon these enigmatic words and twisted the fabric of her skirts nervously before looking up. "Obviously, I take a grave chance in coming here and even telling you anything of what I'm about to reveal, but…it's my only chance of salvation. You, Mr. Tunley, are of course my husband's trusted secretary. I do not know if *I* can trust you, but I don't know what else to do." She glanced at Lissa and said, "You helped me all those months ago to secure the letter that incriminated my husband, but it wasn't the real letter. Oh, but if it hadn't been for that terrible, terrible night, none of this would be happening now."

Kitty had never seen Araminta cry, but her sobs were so wrenching Ralph obviously thought it incumbent to reach for his now dwindling supply of medicinal brandy, while Lissa found one of Mrs. Nipkins's discarded squares of fabric to use as a handkerchief.

"I'm confused, Lady Debenham, but I gather you have come to demand that I hand over the real letter to you? That poses a number of questions. First, that you believe I am holding it for reasons of my own. But also, why now? Why the urgency that sends you alone into the night, this of all nights?"

Lissa interrupted, saying bluntly, "Unless you've strayed and your husband has found out. It *is* Lord Ludbridge, Ralph's brother? I don't know what Ralph can do to help. Yes, he's your husband's secretary, but he's in no position to intervene on your behalf if your husband—"

"No, nothing like that!" Araminta snapped. "Since my marriage, I have been the truest of wives, and no evidence to the contrary could be found to tarnish my good name." She took a heaving breath, closed her eyes and clenched her fists. "It's just…what happened *before* I was married. During that night at Vauxhall."

"Rather a great deal," Lissa remarked drily. "And since we're speaking bluntly, as you've just conceded, the reason you were coerced into marriage with Debenham was because of what you did that night."

"What I *attested* to have done. There's a great deal of difference. What Debenham blackmailed me into *attesting*." Araminta spoke crisply, and Kitty was surprised at the antagonism between the sisters that suggested a great deal of familiarity of which she'd been unaware. She hoped the truth of her own relationship with Araminta would never be made public. Araminta would not like it one bit.

Araminta fiddled with her veil. "Debenham forced me to say that I'd visited him in his supper box because apparently, there was other evidence to suggest he had spent it in company with the two criminals suspected of involvement in the Castlereagh Affair. But Debenham has many other enemies. If that letter got into the wrong hands, he would be ruined."

Lissa and Ralph exchanged looks, just as Araminta added, "And if that happened, so would I."

"You want me to get you the letter? I'm afraid I can't do that, though it might come as some consolation to know that, on its own, it provides insufficient proof of anything." He looked truly regretful. "Surely my brother has told you it's impossible to hand it over to you. I do not have it. A very serious investigation involving your husband is underway."

"Teddy did not tell me it had gone so far!" Araminta went pale, and her mouth dropped open. "You are his trusted secretary, Mr. Tunley, yet you are plotting against him? Surely you understand that if he's ruined, so will I be! And if I tell Debenham that *you're* a traitor—just like you're accusing him of being—*you* will be ruined," she threatened. "You'll have no job, Mr. Tunley. Perhaps something even worse will happen to you."

Kitty stared through a chink in the curtain at the three of them sitting in the cramped parlor—Lissa and Ralph and, between them her beautiful half-sister, Araminta, whose showy presence in this run-down hovel was so utterly unexpected.

She was horrified and fascinated in equal measure. Why had Ralph been so blunt about plotting against Araminta's husband?

Ralph poured Araminta another brandy and pushed the glass across the table. "Debenham is not known for his kindness toward his minions. Look at his valet, who suffered an unfortunate accident when Debenham suspected he had this particular letter. Nothing could be proved, of course, and his valet continues his uneasy employment. I believe Debenham holds to the adage to keep one's friends close and one's enemies—or suspected enemies—closer. He's certainly never professed to like me." He leaned back and studied Araminta's tense, mutinous face. "I sometimes wonder why he keeps employing me other than that he's too lazy to find someone else to keep his affairs in order. I assure you, though, that with regard to his financial matters, I am entirely honest. But, by all means, tell him about the investigation, if you wish, Lady Debenham." He raised his hands, palm upward. "My belief, however, is that an outcome more conducive to your future security and happiness can be achieved through you joining your efforts with ours."

Araminta looked aghast, just as Lissa did, and Kitty felt.

Ralph put his head on one side. "Am I to infer that you want that letter so urgently now because you plan to use it as insurance against what you fear your husband might find out about you, Lady Debenham?"

Araminta did not react with the outrage Kitty had expected. After taking a deep breath, knocking back the brandy in one mouthful, she clasped her hands together and began calmly, "Debenham told me in idle conversation of a little matter he'd heard about...that he is, in fact, investigating something which, he believes, could be of financial benefit to him since he knows that to reveal the truth would ruin... someone's reputation."

Kitty could see the sheen of sweat on her brow from her hiding place just a few feet away as Araminta went on, "Every hint he dropped suggested the person in question could be me. You're in a position to discover what I need to know, Mr. Tunley. You shall be well rewarded if you can tell me exactly who my husband is investigating and what he knows."

Ralph betrayed no surprise, though Kitty was astonished that Araminta would be so forthcoming. Still, if she wanted Ralph's help, Kitty supposed she'd need to tell him this, and more.

Rising, Ralph began to pace. "You've given me very little go to on, Lady Debenham, other than that you believe your reputation is in danger. You've also said nothing to my earlier suggestion."

"What?! That I betray my husband on the promise of safeguards to ensure that I am not ruined in consequence?" Araminta looked perplexed. "Are you more than just my husband's lowly secretary? This investigation...are you involved, *personally*? You've intimated as much, yet you live *here*? Why should I believe your grandiose claims?" She was gaining confidence as she spoke, as if a plan was slowly forming in her mind. Kitty could read the signs. Araminta had always been devious. Suddenly, she was afraid for Ralph.

Yet Ralph just lounged by the fireplace, watching her with interest as she went on, "I could tell Debenham you're plotting against him and he would do his worst." She smiled. "But if you help me, I won't."

"So you're blackmailing *me* now, are you, Lady Debenham?"

"Of course not! I'm just suggesting to you what you suggested to me earlier, but using different words."

"Don't be puerile, Araminta," Lissa bristled. "You *are* threatening Ralph if I ever heard it, yet Ralph is the only one who can help you, which is why you came here tonight."

Araminta looked outraged, then burst into tears. "Don't be angry. I'm not blackmailing anyone. I'm just terrified of what Debenham will do to me—"

"Do you mean, if he uncovers the truth about you, Araminta?" Lissa supplied. Her nose twitched as if she'd suddenly come in contact with something very unpleasant. "And what, exactly, might the truth be? Don't be so disingenuous. If you want Ralph to help you, then he needs an assurance you won't reveal him to Debenham."

"And yet, I don't know how I *can* help you since you've given me no information whatsoever, Lady Debenham," said Ralph.

"Well, you are his trusted secretary. I hoped you could trick him into revealing his sources. He's being so evasive saying only that 'someone' had said something. Perhaps you could find out who that someone is and what that something was?"

"Ralph can only do that if he is still Debenham's trusted secretary."

Araminta nodded at Lissa. "Of course, you have my word that I'll say nothing to Debenham about any of this, including the fact Mr. Tunley could get that letter I want and that Debenham wants it even more, no doubt. If Mr. Tunley is prepared to act in my interests, I'm more than happy to act in his. And what I ask is quite simple. I just want him to quiz Debenham, find out what it is Debenham thinks he knows, and then report back to me."

Kitty wondered what terrible deed Araminta could be guilty of that she would go to such lengths. An affair, no doubt. The idea appalled her. Imagine making one's sacred vows and entering marriage full of hope for the future only to indulge in a grubby and clandestine union with someone else.

Then she remembered that's why she'd rushed over to seek comfort from her elder sister—because she couldn't bring herself to force Silverton into behaving so dishonorably toward Miss Mandelton that she'd given him up.

Lissa leaned across the table. "How can Ralph know where to begin questioning Debenham if he has nothing to go on?"

"So you will help me?" Araminta's eyes widened as if she'd received the first piece of good news all night, ignoring Lissa's question. "If I say nothing about Mr. Tunley to Debenham, then Mr. Tunley *will* help and protect me? He'll get to the bottom of whatever scandal it is that Debenham's investigating and then will report back to me immediately?" Nervously. Araminta nibbled at the tip of her glove and looked at each in turn. "You'll say nothing of this to anyone else?"

They all shook their heads.

"So, Lady Debenham, what, exactly, did your husband say that has you so concerned?" Ralph spoke in such a comforting tone, and Kitty saw the way Araminta melted. Goodness, even Lissa's expression softened when he spoke as if she were as besotted with Ralph as...well, Kitty was with Silverton.

Araminta drew herself up, liking the attention, no doubt, now that it was directed with more sympathy toward her. "All right. Debenham likes to crow about his triumphs, and on the night of my birthday, he was obviously delighted at coming into some information which he believed he could use to his advantage. That's the only time Debenham is really happy. Well, he told me that in casual conversation he'd been told of a case where, unless certain monies were paid, a man of great consequence would be informed that..."

She'd started off with such assurance, but now she could not go on. Helpfully Kitty supplied, "His wife was unfaithful?"

Araminta nodded. In a soft voice, she added, "It's worse than that, though."

Kitty wondered what could be worse while they all waited in silence for her to go on.

"And that the child he believed was his, was...not his own."

Kitty's surprise was so profound she was glad she didn't tumble out from behind the curtain.

"But...how could this be of concern to you, Araminta?" Lissa asked. "I thought you were here because you were, well, terrified for yourself?"

"Rumors are as damaging as the truth." She raised herself proudly. "I just need to know the people involved that Debenham is so occupied with ruining. I've heard rumors that...that he could be trying to manufacture evidence against me."

This was said in such an odd manner, Kitty wondered whether Araminta had come upon the notion as she spoke. "And you, Mr. Tunley, are in as good a position as anyone to solicit that information in a manner that would be discreet enough as to not raise his suspicions. You see," she added quickly, "I'm...very much afraid that the woman in question is a dear friend of mine. I fear Debenham has got it into his head to ruin my friend's husband by insinuating that his wife has cuckolded him, or at least provided him with an heir who is not his."

"A *friend* of yours, Araminta?" Lissa asked.

"So, I'm to ask your husband the name of the woman whose husband he's blackmailing?" Ralph looked bemused. "And you came here in the dead of night to ask this of me?"

"Because you were so concerned for your *friend*?" Lissa interjected. "It's you, isn't it, Araminta? You'd not be this concerned unless you were in Debenham's firing line, and unless you had something to hide." She sighed. "But then, you knew you'd have to divulge that to us before any investigation could actually begin, didn't you?"

Araminta shook her head. "It's not me," she declared. "I have nothing to hide. I gave Debenham a son nine months after we were married. Nine months after the night he tricked me into agreeing to his marriage offer by arranging that my reputation was besmirched at Miss Hoskings's betrothal ball." She gave them a challenging look. "Debenham blackened my name, forced me to marry him, and I've paid for it every day. If someone else is trying to blacken my name by suggesting to Debenham that his child is anyone else's, then I need to know what I'm dealing with in order to defend myself. Given that you all know my husband's character, and the vulnerable position I'm in, I'd assume you'd consider my concerns, and my request to you, perfectly reasonable."

She rose, Ralph poised to see her out as she pulled down her heavy veil.

"My, my," he murmured as he closed the door and Kitty emerged from behind her curtain. "Your sister has a heavy burden to bear if she's so afraid of Debenham."

"Araminta doesn't deserve pity," Lissa bristled. "She's grown up in indolence, cosseted and spoiled by our father—"

"Hush, my love." Gently Ralph put his finger to her lips. "Araminta did not, I think, enjoy all the benefits I think you assume. Regardless, since her marriage—a marriage, it appears she'd not have chosen willingly—she has been forever under the strain of trying to please an exacting master. I believe I am in a very good position to sympathize with poor Araminta. We both know exactly how exacting Lord Debenham can be."

Lissa sighed. "I think I'm in a particularly uncharitable mood tonight because we so rarely get an opportunity to be together, and Mrs. Nipkins will be here soon." She put a restraining hand out toward Kitty, who rose at her words. "See, I have no tact. I'm so glad to see you, Kitty, and I want to comfort you, yet I've rebuffed and all but dismissed you. Forgive me."

She ran a weary hand across her forehead. "My charge, Lucinda, has been taxing my patience, but it's Lady Julia who has me at my wits' end. She detained me, all but in hysterics, as I was trying to leave to see Ralph, and poured out her woes over her children whom she says her husband has forbidden her to see. I can't believe it of Sir Archie. He's such a mild-mannered gentleman. I think it's her excuse for remaining under Lord Beecham's roof. She says she sees herself as a proxy mother-figure to Lucinda, and she *is* Lucinda's godmother, but I know Lucinda despises her. Enough of that." She waved her hand in the air. "Sit down, Kitty, and continue where you left off before Araminta so rudely interrupted you. It has been a strange night."

Kitty sat slowly, the thought that had been churning in her head from Araminta's words taking shape.

"Yes. Lady Debenham must also be at her wits' end if she sought Ralph out...here."

"The least likely place she'd be recognized, I suppose," said Ralph. "I doubt she's ever ventured into any of these rookeries alone in her life before."

Lissa gave a humorless laugh. "She was happy enough to venture into a disreputable inn to try and elicit that letter from Lord Debenham's valet, Jem, if you recall."

"And she nearly delivered her child early at Mrs. Mobbs's lodgings after I took her there," added Kitty. "Not that she'd want *that* to be made public."

"Good Lord!" Lissa, who was busying herself with the fire, looked over her shoulder. "What tall tale is this?"

Ralph's mouth dropped open.

"Araminta was alone in her carriage on her way to visit her sister when the coachman stopped at her cries, just as I was issuing out of the theater. We took her to Mrs. Mobbs's which was not far."

"Not to Debenham's townhouse?"

"She refused to be taken there."

Lissa looked scandalized. "She'd rather give birth to her husband's heir in a rat and flea-infested hovel—"

"You are referring to my choice of lodgings for the first little while I was in London," Kitty reminded her with mild indignation. "Mrs. Mobbs mightn't be the most fastidious of housekeepers, but she was good to me, and she was good to Araminta."

Lissa spoke again. "So all progressed well. Or rather, didn't, since the babe was persuaded to wait."

Kitty frowned, recalling the infant's mewling she was certain she'd heard. But then, the walls that separated Mrs. Mobbs's dwelling from the one next door were paper thin, so it could have been any newborn. "I...suppose so. After all, Araminta didn't give birth for another six weeks."

Lissa stood. "Well, the fact is that our half-sister is apparently in grave fear of being exposed for some terrible misdemeanor her husband believes she committed." She put her hand on Ralph's shoulder and smiled sweetly. "Ralph, I think you have no choice but to quiz Lord Debenham—and others—as far as you are able to, without incurring suspicion, to find out what the gossip is and which scion of the nobility is in danger of being exposed for cuckoldry."

CHAPTER 11

"You look troubled, Stephen. Come, my love, and tell me while I rub your shoulders."

The sound of Sybil's voice was enough to clear Stephen's furrowed brow. Smiling, he turned to greet his beloved as she entered the potting shed. With his keen interest in horticulture—and insect life—the small dim room at the bottom of the kitchen garden offered a welcome refuge during the day for the couple to discuss the more intimate matters pertaining to daily life.

Not that Stephen meant to concern Sybil with the troubling epistle he'd picked up from the silver salver the footman had offered him a little more than an hour before.

"Ah, just what I need," he murmured, sinking onto a footstool and resting his cheek against her hand as she gently eased the tension from his shoulders.

"You have something on your mind, Stephen. Is it Humphrey?"

He was glad she'd asked the question in such direct terms, enabling him to dispute this—in fact, dispute that there was a problem at all. Darling Sybil, so pure and trusting, had endured so much unhappiness at the hands of her cold and unloving husband, Stephen was not about to weigh her down with problems that would terrify her, but about which she could do nothing.

Nor had Stephen any idea yet as to how he would go about responding to the demand for payment if he didn't want to see the reputation besmirched of a certain lady with whom he'd been on intimate terms.

The certain lady must refer to Sybil, of course, and the letter hinted at revealing the scandal of her apparent faithlessness with Stephen. Little matter that Lord Partington had sanctioned their union. Little matter that Lord Partington had been the first to stray, literally the day after their wedding night, abandoning his hapless betrothed, Miss Hazlett, at the altar to wed Sybil, only to return to his apparent true love, Miss Hazlett, before the ink had dried on his wedding vows.

No, Humphrey, Lord Partington, would be unaffected by the scandal, as would Stephen, for as men, they were permitted to stray. The only person whose reputation would suffer was Sybil. Though perhaps that would be the impetus needed for her to run away with Stephen to the Continent, where they would be free to love each other as they were only permitted to do, here, in secret. Of course, she'd never do that to her children. Hetty and Araminta were safely married, but Celia was only a baby.

A terrible thought struck him as Sybil gently nuzzled his ear. What if the blackmailer went further than to reveal Stephen's affair with Sybil.

As matters stood, Humphrey acknowledged their daughter, Celia, as his. But what if the writer of this extortion demand—for that was what it was—had knowledge of Celia's true parentage? What if the scandal revealed the fact that Stephen, not Humphrey, was Celia's real father?

Celia was the principal reason Sybil refused to run away with him. She knew that to do so would be ruinous to the infant's future. At least with Hetty and Araminta respectably married, there could be no harm to them.

As much as Stephen adored Sybil, he knew she was right. He

couldn't succumb to his feelings if it made baby Celia ineligible for a portion of her father's estate and, with her illegitimacy recognized, unable to contract any decent marriage.

"Why, Stephen dearest, your cheek is awfully cold. How long have you been alone in this draughty room? Let me warm you."

Feeling her softly rounded body enfolding him in her loving embrace was cathartic. Sybil had been the first and only woman who'd shown him true love. His beautiful, feckless mother had gambled away the fortune she'd inherited from her father, and then that of her husband, leaving virtually nothing for Stephen.

He gazed up at the mud-spattered window, half-covered with tentacles of ivy. The horrors of the Peninsula Campaign were like a long-distant memory of hunger, pain, cold, and privation. They had, however, fostered in Stephen a self-reliance which had stood him in good stead when he'd returned to England with little more than the clothes on his back.

He'd hardly been able to believe his luck when Lord Partington had solicited him as his heir. Now he was a young man with expectations. He would inherit a grand estate, and for nearly two years had spent a great deal of time at The Grange. To all appearances, he and his benefactor enjoyed a convivial relationship, but the truth was that while they rubbed along well enough, Lord Partington was happy enough to leave Stephen to his own devices—or rather, his wife—while he indulged himself with his mistress of more than twenty years, Miss Hazlett.

Far in the distance came the sound of thunder.

"Is it Celia? You know her grizzling mood is brought on only by the fact she's cutting teeth." He heard the smile in Sybil's voice. "You mustn't worry that it's an indication of her temperament."

"Lord preserve us that she should inherit Araminta's temperament," Stephen murmured, smiling as he held Sybil closer. "To think that I might have been leg-shackled to *her*."

"No, instead of my lovely young daughter, you chose her aging mother. Oh Stephen, and you still haven't rued the day?"

Stephen wished Sybil wouldn't speak like this, even in jest. For him, it was Sybil's warmth and loving heart that mattered most. He also thought her the most serene looking of any woman he'd ever come across. Indeed, in the two years since they'd been lovers, he believed time and age had only imbued her with greater loveliness. It was as if a light glowed from within her.

"I'll never rue the day, my love. Even when you are ninety years old, and I'm a spring chicken of seventy-five, my heart will forever be yours. But talking of Araminta, she seemed agitated when I last saw her. No longer smelling of April and May, it would seem?"

"When was Araminta ever smelling of April and May? Certainly not with Debenham." Sybil sighed. "Araminta brings her own problems upon her shoulders, but I'm sorry that this marriage is such a difficult one for her. The only blessing I can see is that she's provided Debenham with an heir in such a timely fashion. If he finds fault with her in other ways, at least she's done him proud in this one respect."

"Indeed, she has," Stephen agreed.

BACK IN LONDON, THERE WAS NO SYBIL TO RUB HIS WEARY SHOULDERS to soothe away his troubles. The Home Office was not a place to put his cares aside, but he could not remain at The Grange. He and Sybil had been discreet about their affair for two years and to the best of Stephen's knowledge, no one, not even the servants—suspected.

His fears multiplied, of course, as he went about his work. A suspected move to blacken Princess Caroline's name was afoot. Personally, Stephen thought she was doing a fine enough job on her own, though he had found her surprisingly fetching when he'd met her briefly the year before. Certainly, she was blunt, if not at times coarse in her language—as he'd been warned—and untidy about her person, but he'd found her frankness and directness refreshing. The great surprise was that she should ever have become consort to the fastidious Prince Regent, though, of course, the inducement of 160,000 pounds by his father to cover his debts could explain anything, he supposed.

And there was the matter of how to explain Debenham's involvement in the Spencean uprising several years before, and the attempt on Lord Castlereagh's life. So far, there was no evidence beyond the damaging letter. Damaging, simply not incriminating enough on its own though it hinted at much broader involvement on Debenham's part. Perhaps Debenham had tucked his head in since then, and if that were the case, did Stephen really want to push ahead to uncover more dirt on his Cousin Araminta's husband? No one had been killed or maimed in the conspiracy. Perhaps the time had come to simply leave Debenham out of their investigations and concentrate on another line of inquiry.

Like who was behind the blackmail letter Stephen had received. He'd said nothing to anyone while he gathered his resources to make the necessary payment by Thursday next. What else could he do? Allow the Pandora's Box to be split open and the world to know that he and Sybil were lovers, thus casting doubt on Celia's paternity?

Stephen could not bear such shame to taint either Sybil or Celia. He was a man, and his lack of dependency made him far better placed to withstand the opprobrium to follow.

But Sybil? And Celia? No, he simply could not risk irreparable damage to the two females in his life he loved more than his own.

"Distracted?" Stephen hadn't realized he'd been standing, staring at a tray of jewelry for he didn't know how long in *Phillips*, Regent Street's most high-class jewelers. He'd thought to buy a token for Sybil. Something to match her green eyes. He wanted to see them light up because they'd been clouded with worry when they'd farewelled one another three days before, and Stephen couldn't bear Sybil to be worried.

Of course, Sybil knew something was in the wind. She could read him like a book. Just another of the little things he loved about her. Sybil also knew the nature of Stephen's work and one of the things he loved about her—yes, another! —was that she never pushed him to divulge anything merely to satisfy her curiosity.

He looked up to find Ralph Tunley gazing at him from across the dim space, for the evening shadows were closing in though the trade being done by the *Phillips* store was brisk.

Stephen had met Tunley a few times, though the young man didn't frequent the social haunts favored by his brother, Lord Ludbridge. He supposed that a sixth son forced to remain in the employ of a villain like Debenham would have little in the way of funds for entertainment.

He nodded. Although it had not been stated to him directly, he understood that Tunley was among a band of shadowy informers placed in positions of importance to monitor the activities of suspected traitors, and those with undesirable intentions toward the Government and the Crown. Like Stephen.

"Good day to you, Tunley. About to dip a toe in Parson's mousetrap?" He indicated the tray of betrothal rings in front of Tunley.

"Lord, if only I could afford it!"

"At least you're not swimming in the River Tick to support what can't be sustained like I was at your age until fortune favored me. Take heart; anything can happen."

"I'm of an optimistic turn of mind, but I'd rather it be through my own enterprise that I make, if not my fortune, then at least a respectable living that would enable me to make a certain young lady a marriage offer."

"The West Indies Company, perhaps?"

Stephen didn't miss the brief flare of excitement before Tunley resumed the impassive look he'd obviously needed to perfect for his line of work. In a resigned tone, he said, "That is just the kind of adventure I'd have leaped at had I not been bound by sentiment." He tapped his heart. "You can laugh, but no inducement could tear me from within walking distance of a certain young lady who is very dear to me."

"You must feel the pressure more days than others in your present position," Stephen remarked, and Tunley laughed at the oblique reference to Debenham.

"Lord, yes." He dropped his voice as he glanced about to ensure they were not being overheard. "Care to join me for a pot of porter?

We can go just around the corner, for it's occurred to me that you might be very well placed to aid me in a little inquiry I am bound to investigate."

Stephen happily accepted his offer and was expecting more in this vein as he slid into a nook. Instead, he discovered a much more serious underlay to Ralph Tunley. Clearly, that was why Tunley had succeeded so long in Debenham's employ, for it was easy to disregard him as a fixture—a bland and unassuming one.

Now, Tunley said, wiping the froth from his mouth, as he put down his drink. "Cranborne, we both answer to the same master; I know that. So I won't beat about the bush. Someone has been making blackmail attempts which have already claimed the lives of several of those unwilling to pay up."

"Murdered?" A frisson of dismay ran through Stephen as he recalled the looping handwriting of the letter he'd received dancing in front of him like a macabre reminder of how precarious his position was.

"No, no, they've taken their own lives. Lord Calder's death came shortly after he received a letter threatening to reveal certain secrets. A blackmailer is in our midst, and will continue his work with impunity unless more people are willing to step forward and admit they've been targeted. The reason I'm saying this is because you move in more exalted circles than I; in fact, among the very people most likely to have the secrets and the money to keep them that way."

Another wave of discomfort swept through Stephen. Tunley may well be right, but Stephen was not about to divulge either his blackmail demand *or* secret to him right now. He stared into his half-finished porter. "How do you go about persuading people who are prepared to pay money to a blackmailer to safeguard their secrets that they should instead tell *you*."

Tunley sent him a sudden, disarming smile. "Trust. I invite trust, which is perhaps why the other night I was visited by a distressed young woman who suspected she might be the next target. She asked for my help as she'd become aware of the activities of a blackmailer targeting high-profile society individuals. Fearing that her own secret may be divulged—though she did not tell me the nature of that secret —she exhorted me to discover and apprehend the blackmailer."

"She came to *you*? Why?"

"She knows of my connections. Our connections. She hoped I'd be in a position to help, just as I would hope to be in a position to help you, if you went so far as to trust me."

Stephen's arm jerked in surprise as he brought his tankard up to his mouth. Surely Tunley knew nothing of—

Tunley cut off his train of thought. "Of course, if one has no dark secrets, one is not at risk of exposure, and you, Mr. Cranborne, are renowned for your exemplary life—that is, after your untidy youth."

"Untidy!" Stephen laughed, partly out of relief. "I was no different from any other soldier of war wanting what scant comfort was available." There was no point in regretting the wantonness of his early days. From the moment he'd learned he was to be a man of consequence and left his grandmother's cottage with little more than a couple of trunks, he'd taken his duties seriously. In fact, he'd made a vow in front of his grandmother that he'd make something of himself given this unlooked-for opportunity. And indeed he had, traveling by horseback across the country to The Grange.

Unbidden, the image of the top of a golden head of shiny hair came to mind, and he nearly reeled with…. horror, yes, horror! The golden ringlets he'd gazed down upon in youthful rapture as their owner had pleasured him in a small storeroom, in the most unexpected encounter of his life, did not belong to his golden-haired Sybil, whom he'd encountered for the very first time the following day when he'd finally arrived at his destination.

He ought to feel shame, perhaps, for his ongoing affair with Lord Partington's wife. Yes, the wife of his very own benefactor and the man to whom he owed so much. The truth was, that while he might be her knight in shining armor, she was so much more to him. He'd rescued her from…how had she put it? 'A barren, emotional wasteland.' How could that be sinful? No, Stephen didn't regret his ongoing actions one bit, and he intended to continue loving Sybil for as long as they both had breath.

What he did regret was his naivety the day previous to his auspicious meeting with his benefactor's wife; yes, he bitterly regretted not understanding in time that Lady Julia was a conniving minx, who'd flattered him in order to entice him into that conveniently located storeroom just down the passage from where her husband had staged, and then altered, the outcome in a bet over a pair of mating spiders to ensure he fleeced Stephen out of one thousand pounds. Lady Julia was complicit in this plan to cheat Stephen, only she'd taken perhaps more pleasure along the way than her husband knew about.

He squirmed at the memory. She'd pushed him into the semi-darkness, fondled his groin, murmured words of passion and then taken him in her mouth. Stephen had not known what it felt like to have a woman of class—as he'd thought her at the time—show interest in him like this, or show such lack of restraint. Of course, he was wiser now. Of course, he should have understood there was more to her motives than met the eye. But he'd spent six years fighting on the Peninsular before, injured, he'd lived in quiet solitude with his grandmother; his mother having drunk herself into her grave long after his father had died a similarly ignoble death.

He knew he could not excuse his actions, which made him feel grubby and disloyal to Sybil, even though he'd not met Sybil until later.

Lady Julia, clearly, had not felt the same remorse. Fortunately, Stephen didn't often encounter Sir Archie. Whenever he did, though, he wondered if Sir Archie knew to what lengths his wife had gone when, no doubt together, they'd hatched the plan for her to divert Stephen on his way back from pissing in the chamber pot farther up the passage. Yes, Sir Archie was indeed complicit in the plan whereby he and his friend Barston would swap the tiny male spider Stephen had confidently predicted would be vanquished by the female, with another. The reversal of what Stephen knew to be a natural act of nature had been engineered into a false outcome, seeing Stephen lose every last farthing he possessed in the world, and more.

True, Lord Partington had engineered matters so Stephen could have his revenge, but the fact was that Sir Archie had acted with thorough ignobleness, though Stephen knew he now held some position which required that he had dealings with the Home Office. Fortunately, their paths did not cross.

Yet, did Sir Archie suspect how far his fair wife had gone in their shared quest to distract Stephen? Did he know—Stephen shuddered at this—that when she'd almost pleasured Stephen to the pinnacle of his endurance, she'd unexpectedly hiked up her skirts and straddled him, climaxing at the very same moment Stephen had? As if she'd truly found their lovemaking as incendiary as he had? No wonder Stephen had—for about ten minutes—entertained thoughts of jumping astride his charger the very next day and taking Lady Julia into the sunset with him. What had he been thinking? She had twin boys in the nursery. He hadn't given a thought to that little fact. He'd thought she was choosing love with Stephen above all else.

And then, the next day, Stephen had met Sybil. Simple reflection of her calm sweetness made his insides stop their churning. She was everything he needed. Everything and more.

"Wild days," said Tunley. "It seems you left your past behind when you arrived back on English soil a little less than three years ago. You can't pretend you don't know you're in the sights of every designing mama who has a debutante to launch. You are in London on Government business, and you dutifully attend many social events, yet you show no discernment, and as soon as possible, you return to the country."

Stephen licked dry lips and managed a weak smile. "I had no idea my movements were so minutely scrutinized. What interest might you—or others— have in my conduct if it has so little impact on anyone else?" He was deeply worried now. All this time he'd thought he'd been so clever, avoiding interest, gossip and, ultimately detection. The thought that Tunley, so self-effacing, should have taken such a keen interest, bordered on terrifying.

He dismissed the irrational notion Tunley's question might be prompted by suspicion that Stephen had something to hide; that Stephen had joined the ranks of the blackmailed, almost before it had even lodged in his mind. Of course, Tunley knew nothing of Stephen's secret life. What Tunley was demonstrating, however, was that he took account of minor matters in an almost scientific way; that he played a key role in the move to nail down the increasingly active blackmailer who was wreaking havoc among the ton.

He wanted to prize from Stephen anything that might be of minor interest, something that might be potentially useful.

Tunley shrugged. "I'm suggesting that while I can conduct my observation from afar, you might be able to tell me more of interest, given that you move in more exalted circles than I do."

The comparison flashed through his mind that Tunley's impecunious situation was not dissimilar to Stephen's if one turned the clock back three years. Both had been born into wealthy families and brought up as gentlemen, but shackled in their expectations since a fat pocketbook wasn't part of the deal.

Stephen had found luck, of course, by being invited early to The Grange as Lord Partington's acknowledged heir. Tunley was hoping honest toil would see him rewarded. Presumably, that was the intention when he took on the role of secretary to Lord Debenham—or rather, continued in it.

"You're an asset to King and Crown, and we serve the same master," said Stephen, "but I don't know that it makes me ready to divulge my secrets to you."

"*Your* secrets? Why, that's a confession if ever I heard one." He peered more closely at Stephen. "And if perchance you ever received a poison pen letter, you're insinuating that you'd rather hold onto your secret than tell me?" He shook his head. "You'd choose to trust that your blackmailer will be satisfied with the filthy lucre he mines from you, rather than divulge your secret to a man who might be able to help you?"

Stephen nodded, decided. "I trust you enough to concede that I have a secret, but I'm afraid I would go to any lengths to keep it hidden," he said.

"Even if that means satisfying the ever greater demands of a ruthless blackmailer?"

Stephen nodded.

CHAPTER 12

*O*ctavia's hand felt small and insubstantial in Silverton's grip as he led her onto the dance floor. He could tell she was nervous, so his smile was bolstering for her benefit.

The light was kind to her sallow complexion. He'd thought she looked tired and somehow diminished from the last time he'd observed her back in the country. But then, she'd been comfortable in the domain over which she reigned; assisting his mother with her jam-making, he recalled, being the last time he'd seen her. He'd not expected then to make her an offer.

He'd *never* expected to make her an offer. He'd acted rashly, of course, penning her the letter inquiring after her thoughts on matrimony with him after he'd learned Kitty was to be marrying Lord Nash.

The whole Nash affair had been a debacle. And if Silverton felt he'd been shackled to a marriage he did not desire, it was through his own lustful impetuosity.

Kitty had been in the church saying her vows to Nash, for God's sake, when Nash's father had objected, seeming to bear up the fact that Nash was planning a sham marriage. When Kitty had rushed out of the church, Silverton had felt only the most enormous relief. Now he could have her at last.

She'd all but admitted she loved Silverton, but would marry Nash because she was fond enough of him to accept what she wanted above all else—honest matrimony.

How ironic that Silverton's hasty seduction had put paid to Kitty's chances. Yes, she had the man she loved, but she'd never get the marriage Nash offered. And that was because of Silverton. His lovely, good-natured Kitty had not appeared to harbor a grudge. Besides, that was not Kitty's way. Her sweet purity was what he loved about her.

He forced himself to remember that Octavia had a similar sweet purity. What did it matter that Octavia was plain and shy and disliked the social whirl? That, other than her good and pure heart, she couldn't be more different from Kitty?

Another pang.

"Are you all right, Silverton?"

He glanced with surprise at Octavia as he positioned himself opposite her for the cotillion.

She looked concerned. "I wondered if a sudden pain had beset you."

"Lord, I'm as fit as a fiddle." Then, as they had a moment to fill before the dance began, "Don't worry that I'll turn into a gouty old codger or leave you a widow too early, dearest." Silverton had thought long and hard about how he must train his heart to do what it ought. If he could trot out the terms of affections and similar endearing sentiments, then he might find that the processing of turning his sympathy for Miss Mandelton into love, would yield results.

That is, as long as he steered well clear of Kitty. So when Octavia suddenly giggled and said, "Oh, I don't worry about that a moment. I hear that's what happens in *The Happy Wildflower*. Miss Neville said it was very good, and I'd love to see Miss Bijou on stage again. Do let's see it, Silverton."

He hoped the horror that swept through him was not palpable. No, he would not, *could* not see the play in which Kitty was performing to packed houses every night.

"Not possible. Not a seat to be had," he murmured and was relieved when she accepted this, though with a little sigh of disappointment. Yet even a vague and innocent reference like Octavia's, which brought Kitty to mind, revealed how susceptible he still was to her charms, and made it clear how much harder he must try to extirpate her from his mind. That was what he *must* do. The dozens of letters he'd written Kitty had all been returned with a sweet but short message each time, telling him that their love for each other had nothing to do with the underlying issue of honor and duty, and what they owed Miss Mandelton and their families.

Silverton shook his head to clear it of these rogue thoughts of Kitty, and racked his brains for something to say that would thoroughly deflect her, in case she returned to the subject. "You dance beautifully, has anyone ever told you that?"

Her pale eyelashes fluttered in surprise, making it clear that no one ever had, and nor would they, in all likelihood, for Octavia was not gifted with grace and rhythm. Her shyness was exacerbated by her awkwardness, which became more pronounced in social situations.

"Lord Silverton, you are either completely without perception, or completely in thrall to me if you are able to utter those words without obvious gall." Her self-deprecating giggle was suddenly rather endearing, and he laughed with her, glad that for the first time he could acknowledge feeling comfortable with shared humor, even if it was over a deficiency of hers.

"If, however, I looked like that dark-haired young woman in the blue silk over there, whom I perceive, now that we're closer, is Lady Debenham, I might believe you."

"Lady Debenham?" Silverton raised an eyebrow and lowered his voice. "I would far rather my intended bride had your temperament, looks aside."

Octavia's eyes flashed as if she couldn't believe he'd say such a thing, and she bit her lip. "Scandalous," she murmured as Silverton clasped her in a waltz hold to dance her to the other side of their square, twisting her head to look over her shoulder at the former Miss Partington. "Lady Debenham looks like an angel," she sighed. "An exquisite, dark-haired angel."

"An angel she is not." He was about to change the subject, but on impulse added, "And if she perchance invites you into her orbit, I would encourage you to politely decline."

Octavia looked at him sharply. "Would you choose my friends for me when we are married, Silverton?"

"No, no, you mistake my meaning," he said hurriedly. "I'm simply warning you that Lady Debenham has a way of drawing the unsuspecting into her net. It is easy to be dazzled by such beauty, but her interest is usually dependent on how one can serve her. My caution stands. Beware."

MEANWHILE, HETTY WAS TRAVERSING THE DANCE FLOOR IN THE ARMS of her own handsome husband, uncaring of the looks her graceful sister was, as ever, courting.

The previous season, she and Araminta had been rivals for the same delicious gentleman, Sir Aubrey. If the rumors were true that White's Betting Book had listed Miss Henrietta's chances as so marginal compared with her sister's, there were more than a few young men who'd lost sizeable sums.

No, Hetty had been the out-and-out winner, and all this time later she still felt as though she were floating on air.

The music finished on a dramatic chord, and Sir Aubrey released her. "Dazzled as ever, Lady Banks," he said with a bow and a fond smile as he rose.

"And to think that last season you didn't even notice me." She sent him a sly look. "It was Araminta who caught your eye on the dance floor."

"And you who snared my attention in every other way," he said with a sly reference to Hetty's decidedly un-debutante-like nocturnal pursuits.

Yet she did not blush. "Still waters run deep, and beauty is in the eye of the beholder. I'm sure there are a few more clichés I've neglected to mention, all of which could probably be applied to Miss Mandelton over there."

"Now there's an unlikely match." Sir Aubrey released Hetty's hand. "Perhaps you should go and talk to her now that she's been abandoned by her betrothed. She looks a little lost."

Hetty loved her husband's unexpected many kindnesses. Poor Miss Mandelton was standing near the window embrasure looking decidedly uncertain of herself, she noticed, so with a smile and a nod at Sir Aubrey, she crossed the room to her side.

Following the direction of her gaze, she saw that she was staring at Araminta, whose gown of blue sarcenet clung to her curves with all the allure of the risqué French beauties in the fashion books Hetty used to pore over longingly.

But she was no longer jealous. She had Sir Aubrey's love and loyalty, and a beautiful son in the nursery. There was nothing else she wanted.

"My sister is very lovely, but she is not always known for her kindness. Are you enjoying yourself, Miss Mandelton?" she asked.

Miss Mandelton jumped, as if she'd been caught out in a terrible crime. "I'm very transparent, aren't I? But when one looks like me, you can imagine why I'd be a little envious." She sent a self-deprecating look at her bony body, angular and flat-chested, then touched her hair. The heat from the ballroom had caused it to go frizzy about her face. "Lady Debenham *is* beautiful. She must have many…friends."

It struck Hetty that Miss Mandelton must be lonely. "Not many at all, because she's not very nice most of the time. But the gentlemen like her well enough, it appears." She smiled. "Do you have a friend here tonight?"

"Only Silverton. He's always been my friend. I don't have brothers or sisters, you see." She paused. "His mother is my dearest friend. I help Lady Silverton with her charity work on the estate."

Hetty forced a smile. *Hardly an auspicious reason for marriage*, she thought, *wondering if Silverton were marrying for love or expediency.*

Regardless of how pleasant Miss Mandelton was, it did not augur well for him to be marrying for the latter.

She was about to make some appropriate response, when she saw Miss Mandeton's gaze focus on a young man with curling dark hair and a pallid complexion staring pointedly at the exquisite Araminta. He was in a darkened corner, and Araminta was passing within a couple of feet of him, yet although he stepped out in front of her, she made a point of not acknowledging him as she detoured past him.

Envy and despair marred his features. Hetty, of course, had once known these emotions well; she hoped she'd managed to control them more effectively than poor Mr. Woking, whom she'd never liked but for whom she now felt rather sorry. "The cut direct," Hetty muttered. "Araminta is famous for it. Ah! But he persists. A devil for punishment."

They watched as for some seconds the young man spoke earnestly to Araminta, his gestures suggesting he was upset. Araminta tossed her head and began to walk away, but he followed, taking her arm and drawing her into the darkened corner where he continued to gesticulate as if he had a torrent of passion to express.

Octavia was clearly fascinated as she watched the young man stalk across the ballroom following his obvious dismissal, weaving his way in and out of the crowd, his brow thick with distress.

"My sister was once betrothed to young Mr. Woking," Hetty told her, then laughed at Miss Mandelton's shock. "Yes, I think Araminta rather desperately felt she needed a marriage offer, and when he proposed, the timing was right. She quickly regretted it though, and reneged on the poor gentleman who has never recovered, it would appear. My feeling is that he made rather a lucky escape."

"A lucky escape? Why, your sister is the loveliest woman I've ever seen."

"Hardly reason enough to marry her, though."

Miss Mandelton's lips parted. "You made a good match. I've seen the two of you," she blurted. "You and Sir Aubrey seem so suited. His eyes follow you everywhere." She blushed furiously, and Hetty felt ridiculously gratified.

"It nearly went horribly wrong. My sister wanted to marry Sir Aubrey. It's hard to imagine he actually chose me." She touched Miss Mandelton's sleeve. "There's no telling what dictates a gentleman's heart, is there? And you and Lord Silverton are obviously very well-matched."

She'd thought to bring a smile to Miss Mandelton's face, but the young woman looked even more downcast. "I hardly know him," she confessed. "He was the best friend of my brother, Tom. But then Tom died and Silverton sort of...inherited me."

Hetty floundered. "The greatest love flourishes from friendship, I'm told."

Miss Mandelton gave a rather helpless shrug. "I feel out of my depth here in London. I wish I could go home, but I can't. If I don't take this chance to marry, I will never get another." Her mouth trembled. "And I keep telling myself how lucky I am. Silverton is such a nice man."

Hetty's drew in her breath sharply. She glanced about her, afraid they might be overheard. "But you don't love him?" she whispered.

Miss Mandelton shook her head, staring at Hetty with an expression close to panic. "I like him very much. But that's not the same thing, is it?"

CHAPTER 13

The days seemed endless to Lissa. After the horrors of the night spent at The Grange, followed by the equally horrendous journey home during which Lady Julia and Lord Beecham had literally bristled with hostility, she'd thought she'd relish days of uninterrupted dullness.

But now Ralph was just like the old Ralph she'd fallen in love with —brimming with enthusiasm for the task at hand. He didn't seem to notice that Lissa was becoming increasingly lackluster. When she asked him if there was any special task she ought to be performing— after all, she'd been placed into Beecham's household for a reason— he'd just chucked her under the chin and told her that the greatest good she could do was to stay safe. Stay safe because Ralph was gathering evidence that he was sure would implicate Debenham in a range of unsavory dealings, and once Debenham was dealt with, then he and Lissa could be married.

The last time he'd said that, Lissa hadn't responded with the same enthusiasm she'd mustered on the first few occasions, and Ralph had asked, concerned, "Dear heart, you do still want to marry me, don't you?" To which, of course, Lissa had replied in the affirmative, since that's what she wanted more than anything.

What she wanted only slightly less was for some kind of excitement in her life. Lucinda was surly and clearly unhappy. She showed Lissa the minimum of respect. She showed Lady Julia even less respect, so that was something she supposed. Lord Beecham was forever berating his ward, demanding that she address her piano teacher with civility; to try that curtsey as she took her leave 'one more time.' Yet even he seemed out of sorts these days with Lady Julia, who was now a regular overnight guest. As for Lady Julia, her forced brightness was most definitely at odds with the general gloom of the household.

On yet another evening, while Lucinda played a few desultory tunes at the piano, and Lady Julia and Lord Beecham appeared to be engaged in yet another of their quiet but heated discussions, Lissa picked up the pencil and sketching pad that lie upon the table in front of her, and idly began to draw. She hadn't drawn in months, though she instructed Lucinda in pen and ink sketches, which were not very good, but which Lucinda proudly brandished in front of Lord Beecham from time to time in the hopes of some praise, no doubt.

Lissa wondered why the girl tortured herself. Granted, Lord Beecham had a certain autocratic bearing which might be appealing to a naïve and inexperienced girl. But at nearly forty, he was far too old for her, and his nature was not overly sympathetic. A hopeful spirit like Lucinda's would shrivel up in no time. Lissa was charitable enough to acknowledge that Lucinda was not a bad girl. They simply did not rub along well together, though perhaps the environment had more than a little to do with the general malaise Lissa was sure they both—all—suffered from.

At a jarring chord, they all looked at Lucinda, who blushed fiercely but kept her head down.

Lissa wondered how she'd fare when she was presented. She could be pretty when she was animated, but that rarely happened these days. Her corn-colored hair was dressed simply, and her gown was plain as befitting a girl not yet out. Really, Lucinda wouldn't turn heads, Lissa decided, quickly sketching the forlorn expression on her face before turning her attention to Lord Beecham.

Certainly, his face was handsome enough though the vertical lines in his cheeks, and his bristling eyebrows, would see him age into a venerable, if not rather frightening, gentleman.

Lady Julia was the beauty of the gathering, though Lissa wondered where the attraction was beyond that. Or if it did. Lord Beecham seemed increasingly irritated by her these days. Now the pair was muttering something together in rather vexed tones about a child. She caught the name of Lady Julia's son whom Lissa had heard was not well. There's been no mention of Princess Caroline lately. No mention of anything worth passing on to Ralph. She felt superfluous. At least in her detested position at the Lamonts there was some tension and excitement, even though Cosmo Lamont had tried to imprison her, if not worse, which was why she'd been so careful to ensure her talent for drawing was not discovered by her current employer who might seek to exploit it, just as the odious Mr. Lamont had done.

"Goodness!"

Lady Julia's exclamation coincided with Lissa's realization that she had been entirely unaware of the fact that her picture was exposed for all to see who might rise at that moment and pass by. Which was exactly what Lady Julia had done.

"Beechy, look at this!"

"Please, I really would prefer not to—" Lissa soon realized it was useless to try to exert her will when it opposed Lady Julia's. The page nearly tore clean out as Lady Julia tugged the sketchbook from Lissa's hands and brandished it in front of her paramour. "Do you see the way you looked at me? There it is! Plain to see. As if I were— No, I shan't even say it!" She spoke rapidly, under her breath, as if unaware that both Lucinda and Lissa were staring at her.

Lord Beecham took Lady Julia's arm and tried to draw her back, clearly aware of their audience in a way Lady Julia was not.

"After all I've done for you!" Lady Julia cried, her voice rising. "I came to your aid when you were at your wits' end over what to do with your ward. You wanted to dispose of her in some school for ladies, but it was her mother's dying wish that she become your ward, and that you should find some suitable female to help ensure the girl didn't entirely disgrace the family name when she was presented."

"Julia, stop—!"

But there was no stopping Lady Julia now she'd started.

Lissa saw that Lucinda had gone pale and was gripping the back of the sofa as she stared from Lord Beecham to Lady Julia.

"Oh, you were only too happy to find an excuse to have me here when it suited you. I've done more than my share of dirty work for you. And I've tried, believe me. I've tried to instill some feminine graces into that girl, but she is obstinate and obdurate. She offers me no respect. Not that she offers her governess any either. Eyes only for you, Beechy."

Lissa heard her young charge's gasp, before the pale-faced girl pushed past her and ran from the room.

"That's enough, Julia!" Lord Beecham thundered. "Where is the respect you owe *me*? And the thanks for taking you in when your husband was no longer to your liking? Or did he cast you out? That the truth, really, isn't it? Well, you can leave now! Miss Hazlett!"

Lissa took a step back, her heart hammering. She should have heard nothing of all this, of course, and now could only be at fault for being in the wrong place when tempers were at snapping point. There were just the two of them now, and Lord Beecham was pointing his finger at Lissa as if he were about to give her a piece of his mind.

"Miss Hazlett!" he repeated, his face apoplectic. Lady Julia seemed to have upset him more than was warranted, although something like this had been brewing since the day they'd returned from Araminta's party. Suddenly, it seemed he didn't know what to say. "Go upstairs and do what you have to in order to placate that wretched child!" he finished lamely. "And don't let me hear another word about tonight." His shoulders slumped as he turned to the sideboard where she heard him draw the stopper from the whiskey decanter. Lissa didn't wait to hear the liquid splash into the glass.

She hurried from the room as fast as she could and up the stairs, pausing outside Lucinda's room. Muffled sobs could be heard. Lissa knew what it felt like to be unwanted. Of course, she should go in and offer what comfort she could though the girl would push her away and make it even clearer how much she despised Lissa.

With a sigh, Lissa carried on up the passageway to her own room.

WITH A FINAL FEATHER IN HER HEADDRESS, KITTY WAS RESPLENDENT and ready. The giggles of the chorus girls on the other side of the curtain had risen to a crescendo. They were nearly onstage while Kitty had another five minutes before her debut.

Taking a deep breath, she glanced about her dressing room. The multiple bouquets of hothouse and garden blooms ought to have eased her pained heart, but only exacerbated its torment. A moment ago, when she'd been fully in her character, she'd been able to put aside the pain of being Kitty La Bijou, celebrated London actress. Or just Kitty Hazlett, unacknowledged daughter of Lord Partington. A hard and unyielding man, who believed his illegitimate daughter had none of the rights of his nobly-born offspring, and therefore no right to marry into the strata of society from which he'd effectively barred her through his own selfishness.

Not that that mattered when she only wanted Silverton. Oh Lord, how she wanted him.

Four minutes.

She heard the call as if through a curtain of despair. In a moment, she'd have to plaster a smile on her face and dazzle the crowds like she did every night. The only times she felt respite from the perpetual ache in her heart was when she was performing.

"Come!" she called out in response to a rap on her door, expecting to see Mr. Lazarus.

To her horror, it was Nash. Nash, the man she'd nearly married only a few months ago. She didn't have time to order her thoughts before he was standing before her, clutching her hands having deposited a dozen long-stemmed red roses on her dressing table.

"Now that Silverton is to be married, and you are no longer his mistress, will you come back to me?" He looked grim, rather than loving. "I am prepared to take you back, even after everything you've done."

"As your mistress?" she clarified.

He looked surprised. Then he gripped her hands even tighter. "I could hardly make you my wife after you declared before the world you'd rather be mistress to my adversary than wife to me. Even if I wanted it."

"And would you?"

"What?"

"Want me for your wife?"

"I want *you*, Kitty!" He dropped her hands to put them to his face; his tone anguished as he muttered, "It's irrelevant if I want you for my wife, because that can never be after your appalling behavior. But I'm prepared to forgive. I hear you'll be giving up the lease on your house now that Silverton has given you his congé. Well, I'll set you up in finer lodgings than that, and we can be as we were before."

"As we were before, Nash?" She felt dead inside. "How could that ever be? When I fell in love with you, it was like a thunderclap. I came to London expecting to meet the man of my dreams, and you materialized in front of me like the dashing prince I'd been searching for my whole life."

Clearly, he did not see where she was going with this. His voice became fond. "Was I not good to you, Kitty?" He drew her into his embrace, resting his chin on her head. "Did I not get you everything your heart desired? A fine house, beautiful clothes, your own carriage. Jewelry to cement our union. I even asked you to marry me, for God's sake, despite knowing how opposed the pater and rest of my family would be. Silverton wasn't prepared to do that, was he?"

"But he didn't cheat on me," Kitty whispered. "He didn't go from my bed to find his pleasure at Mrs. Montgomery's, or take the woman I called my friend into his bed the moment I was unavailable."

Nash drew himself up. "Am I never to be forgiven? One lapse—"

"Two...that I know of."

"Every fellow has the occasional lapse! Will you not forgive me, even when you know that you alone are the woman I yearn to love and cherish?"

Kitty closed her eyes and clenched her hands at her sides as the sounds of the theatre pulsed around the two of them, alone in her dressing room. She ought to think about her future. In a few years, her looks would have faded and with it, her fame and acclaim. A clever woman would amass now what she'd need in retirement, not look a gift horse in the mouth, as the saying went. And Lord Nash was any woman's dream with his brooding dark looks and his fine, athletic physique. He was an exciting and considerate lover. Generous, too. And he was offering her everything he'd given so freely before.

Except marriage.

"I can't go back to you when I'm still in love with Silverton," she said softly. "It wouldn't be fair."

"I'd make you forget Silverton. Kitty, please." His tone was beseeching. As if he truly didn't care that she'd not be wholly his? How could he? Kitty would rather die than be with someone whose heart she knew belonged to another. It was the knowledge that Silverton would inevitably drift closer to the worthy Miss Mandelton as their babies were born that fueled her need to withdraw from him while she still had the strength.

There was a rap on the door. "Miss Bijou. Thirty seconds."

Kitty glanced back to Nash and shook her head. "I'm sorry, Nash. Your offer is very generous, and you're a good man. But I just can't turn back the clock."

Rejecting him didn't make her feel any better or any more powerful. She performed her role with all the usual finesse, judging by the rapturous applause. And then she wondered how she did it as she stepped forward for a final encore, her arms full of bouquets.

"You were marvelous, as usual," Mr. Lazarus congratulated her afterward. Actors and chorus girls milled around her, excitedly chattering about how first rate the night had been. Kitty felt in a daze. Had she really been so rash as to sacrifice what might be her only chance at finding at least some kind of mutual love? She had loved Nash, hadn't she? Why, only two months ago she'd been prepared to be his wife.

And then, as she returned to her dressing room where she could thankfully be alone, another rap sounded on the door and she turned, her heart thundering more painfully than it ever had in her life when Silverton walked into the room.

He was alone. But he would not be for long. She knew that, just as she knew in the intense, pained look they exchanged that she could never feel the kind of love for anyone that she felt for Silverton.

"Oh God, Kitty, I've missed you!" he murmured, closing his eyes and not advancing farther after he'd closed the door behind him.

The frenzied buzzing of actors nearby, the strong smell of lead paint and powder and dust made her head swim. Or was it that her senses were so overloaded she wasn't sure how much more she could take?

It was too much. Kitty dropped the flowers she was holding and ran across the room and into his embrace. His arms went around her tightly, and as his lips came down upon hers, she felt the most incredible rush of euphoric joy. This was what she was made for. Love.

But only Silverton could do this to her.

The urgency of knowing how short their time was together only escalated their passion. As his tongue breached the seam of her lips, and his hands skimmed her breasts, half exposed by her low bodice, the ache between her legs was like a cruel reminder of what she could never have. Never again could she run her hands up his toned chest, or twine her fingers in the light hair that dusted his muscled torso. Nor would she feel his hot mouth closing about her nipple or pleasuring her most intimate parts, before he took her in a final climax of urgent want and need, thrusting into her and filling her with joyful satisfaction.

For he belonged to another now.

With a soft moan, she pulled out of his arms. He didn't try to reclaim her. His hands were at his sides now and his expression one of the greatest sorrow.

"You will not come back to me, will you, Kitty?" He said it like he understood the terrible dilemma that had torn them apart.

"It's not only me. You couldn't do that to Miss Mandelton, I know, Silverton," she whispered. "Even if I said yes, you know you couldn't live with yourself."

"Kitty, I wish to God I—"

She turned, pressing the palm of her hands to her eyes. "Don't say it," she rasped. It hurt just to breathe. "You can't marry me. An actress, another man's acknowledged mistress. I am forever out of your reach because of who you are and what you owe your family. And for the path I've chosen."

The truth echoed around her head. *And for the path her* father *chose. A bastard could never amount to anything.* She'd heard it so many times.

She managed a teary smile as she put out her hands. "Forever friends, Silverton?"

Gravely, he took them.

"Forever friends, Kitty. And if you should ever need my help in any way, you have only to ask."

Kitty blinked back her tears. "You're a kind man. That's why I loved you." She had to put it in the past tense. "And have you brought Miss Mandelton to the theater? I think you would not have come otherwise, perhaps?"

He nodded. "It was her great desire to bring me along, even though she's seen the play before. We are the guests of...Lady Partington. I was there when she invited Octavia."

Kitty had to grip the edge of the dressing table as her knees buckled. She swallowed. "Lord Partington did not come?"

Silverton looked pained. "He did not."

"But of course not," Kitty whispered. "He's made it very clear I am not a daughter who has made him proud. Something of an irony that Lady Partington, who has been so very kind to me, is here. I doubt she would have been had she known who I was."

Silverton shrugged. "You might be surprised."

Kitty gave a small laugh. "I think I'd prefer not to put it to the test. Now, give me a moment to gather myself, and then I shall greet Miss

Mandelton with all the aplomb you could desire. And with not a single pained or reproachful glance in your direction." Like the true actress she was, she plastered on her most carefree smile and shooed him to the door. "Begone, dear, kindest of men. I shall rejoin you downstairs as soon as I've changed."

CHAPTER 14

$\mathcal{H}$etty had never believed it was possible to be so happy. She'd been married more than a year, and yet frequently she awoke to find her darling Aubrey gazing at her as if he'd married her only yesterday.

Another wonderful thing was that Aubrey was only too happy to indulge her with her desire to visit her darling mama so frequently. He and her parents got along famously these days, so trips to The Grange were always happy affairs with much fussing over the babies. How lovely there were only a few months between baby Celia and her little Lysander so that they could grow up the best of friends.

Right now, the adults were in the drawing room discussing their plans for the day. Aubrey and Lord Partington were of a mind to go shooting on the neighboring estate, while Hetty and her mother wanted to attend the market in town.

"Can't we take the babies?" Hetty asked, but her mother shook her head. "It's too chilly today, and Celia is only just getting over a cough. Let's leave them snug and warm and in Mabel's good care, and then you and I can stop for a bun and tea at Sally Forrester's afterward."

By the time they'd put on walking dresses and pelisses the weather had worsened, but Hetty was feeling ebullient. She and Aubrey had enjoyed the most delicious lovemaking, and just before they'd parted ways as they'd meandered along the path at the back of the house, he'd snatched her hand and pulled her into the bushes for a deeply passionate kiss that only underscored the fact she was the luckiest girl in the whole country, if not the world.

John Coachman drove them the short distance to the village and helped them out. The usually quiet square was crammed with people from all over the district here to sell their wares, and Hetty was keen to buy some ribbons for a new bonnet she was making for Lysander.

She wished she had her baby with her to show him off, but her mother had been right; the chill was too much if one had the choice, though there were plenty of infants accompanying their parents who were selling everything from gilt gingerbread to oysters. Despite the gray skies it was a festive atmosphere, and Hetty was enjoying the contrast with her usual quiet days at The Grange or the London revelry Aubrey often cajoled her into enjoying with him. Yes, she'd finally agreed, there was a time for babies and a time for her husband, and if her husband wanted her company to Lady This's ball or to the opera or ballet, she was only too happy to be seen with the dashing and gallant Sir Aubrey. It wasn't just the unusual streak of white that cut through her husband's inky black locks that turned people's heads, but the magnetism of his hazel eyes and his feline grace. Hetty was sure every woman under thirty was madly jealous of her.

Of course, Araminta was jealous, and the thought was both disquieting but also gratifying. Who would ever have thought Hetty would have won Sir Aubrey when Araminta had gone to such lengths to have him?

But Sir Aubrey had chosen Hetty. And what a happy, loving marriage it was. Of course, Hetty shouldn't give Araminta a second thought, but knowing that Araminta was so unhappy with Lord Debenham was worrying. Who knew what her sister might get up to if she were dissatisfied with her lot?

Several rods containing a variety of brightly-colored ribbons blew in the breeze, attracting Hetty's attention, though really it was the cherubic child in the crib in the corner that most engaged her. Hetty loved comparing babies, especially when they were around the same age as her own. It was an endless fascination to learn whether they were crawling or taking their first steps or at what age they'd first smiled.

"What a darling little boy," she remarked to the woman who came to assist her. "What's his name?"

The woman beamed. She looked like a well-satisfied farmer's wife with her ample bosom and rosy cheeks as she laid out the ribbons, beckoning to a girl she referred to as Rosie, who looked about twenty, to come and help.

"My little one is not quite as old as yours," Hetty said to Rosie. "What's his name?"

"Hamish," replied the girl with an embarrassed glance at the older woman. "'N I ain't 'is mam."

The portly, pleasant-faced older woman bustled around the back of a collection of boxes and scooped the baby out of its crib, obviously eager to show off her pride and joy. Hetty was delighted, and even more so when the child gripped the finger she offered it, gurgling with delight.

"I'm sure one never gets tired of cuddling them, no matter how many there are," said Hetty. "I have a little boy called Lysander. He's my first, so I'm still getting used to it all."

"Hamish is my first, too," the farmer's wife told her, putting her cheek to the child's. "Blessed, we were, my Jacob and me, to be granted a babe this late in life."

Hetty could see by the rapturous look in the woman's eyes how much this child meant to her, for surely the woman must have been over forty. Suddenly, she felt a pang for her own child back in the nursery at home. It was rare for more than a couple of hours to go by without Hetty sidling off to give her son a cuddle.

"May I hold him?" she asked, stretching out her arms. The little boy was well rugged up in swaddling clothes with a white knitted bonnet tied beneath his chin, so she wasn't concerned that the cold would harm him.

"'Twould be an honor, ma'am." Smiling broadly, the woman held out the baby who immediately began to squirm and protest.

'Hush now, Hamish," she crooned, trying to settle him and attempting to retie the ribbons that held his cap on. But the baby was not about to cooperate. With an impatient sweep of its hand against its head, it dislodged the cap which went sailing through the air to land on the counter.

"Now, now, Hamish, the lady just wants to get you a cuddle," said the farmer's wife in mild remonstrance as she took back the child, glancing at Hetty. "Isn't that right, ma'am?"

But Hetty couldn't answer. She was too occupied with the sight of the child's hair—a healthy crown of inky black locks throwing into sharp relief the swathe of white hair at its left temple.

Hamish's mother seemed not to notice Hetty's shock as she replaced the boy's cap then turned to put him back into the cradle.

"Now, ma'am, any of these ribbons take your fancy? We have every color in the rainbow, plus more, and if you've a mind for some fancy lacework, there'll be some of that to show you next market day after me Jacob has done his rounds."

Distracted, Hetty pointed to a midnight-blue ribbon. "I'll take two yards, please." What else could she say? The child was back sleeping in the corner, yet Hetty's mind was crammed with questions, all of them far too probing and impertinent to ask.

She paid, put her purchase into her reticule, and then went to the tea shop to meet her mother who also remarked upon her distraction.

"I'm…missing Lysander because I saw a baby that reminded me so much of him," she said, frowning. No, she wasn't going to mention the hair. She just couldn't.

"Oh darling, you're just like I was with my first." Her mother smiled and reached across the table to pat her hand. "It's so hard to be without them, and I will admit that it is a darling age. Celia's a little more of a handful now that she's walking, but every age is delightful. Now wipe that worried frown off your face. I'll be finished my tea soon, and then we can meet John Coachman."

Hetty rose. "I think I'll dash back and get another length of ribbon," she blurted. "No need to hurry on my account. I'll be back shortly."

She tried to keep her pace measured and sedate as she returned to the stall, deciding that, yes, she would ask at least some of the probing questions that might help her ascertain the lineage of the ribbon seller's child.

But as she rounded the corner and started walking toward the stall she was surprised to see, from a distance, the young woman Rosie sitting upon a stool in a dim corner holding the child, and astonished when she got closer to see that the child was suckling at her breast.

The young woman rose and reordered her clothing just as Hetty reached the counter, and her shock must have been apparent for Rosie immediately explained, "Mrs. 'Ancock got the babe when I still 'ad me milk from me second." She glanced over her shoulder, perhaps to ensure her mistress was out of earshot, before adding, "She can't abide goin' nowhere wivout the little 'un, even though it ain't 'er own. That's why she takes me along fer when it needs feedin'."

"The child's adopted?"

Rosie nodded. "Everyone knows it, so I ain't tellin' secrets. Mr. 'n Mrs. 'Ancock bin married twenty-two years 'n 'spected ter go ter their graves childless, 'cept it seems their wishes fer a babe was granted when Mrs. 'Ancock were gived one by a respectable young lady wot weren't in a position ter keep it."

Hetty stared at the baby. "He's…a very nice-looking child," she said lamely, but the questions were swirling around her head. "How old is he?"

"'E were a newborn when 'e came ter Mr. 'n Mrs. 'Ancock 'bout three months ago."

That made him about six weeks older than Lysander. Hetty smiled weakly. No, she couldn't ask them, for what would this young woman know of the child's parentage?

So she asked for a red ribbon, only realizing she had no use for such a color as she traipsed back to rejoin her mama, hoping not to be quizzed on her disordered wits.

All she could think was that if Sir Aubrey had no brothers in the country who might have sired a child with such distinctive white and black hair, then who else other than Sir Aubrey could be the child's father?

Her husband had certainly made no secret of his rakish reputation when he first got together with Hetty, and though he might be a reformed man now, there was no telling what he might have got up to in the weeks preceding his unexpected and impulsive marriage to Hetty.

She felt ill. In all the fourteen months they'd been married, there'd been no secrets between her and Sir Aubrey. Or so she thought.

And then another thought occurred. Perhaps Sir Aubrey had no idea he'd fathered a child on a respectable young lady, who'd had no choice but to give it away. Indeed, Hetty had been in the very position where that might have happened to her had fate not dealt so kindly with her.

The thought was too distressing. Imagine having to give up one's own child because of the shame? Hetty thought she'd die if that had been thrust upon her.

No, there was only one solution. She could not confront Aubrey, but she must also put out of her mind any angst or recrimination toward him. No doubt he was oblivious to the fact he had a son growing up on a farm to the north in far more straightened circumstances than their own beloved Lysander. But if Hetty were to keep enjoying her loving family unit, she would have to do what she could to ease her conscience.

She had no idea exactly what she would do; but she had to do something.

CHAPTER 15

Stephen was glad to be back at The Grange and to note that Sybil was her usual serene self. Clearly, she had not been rattled as he had by suggestions that someone knew something about their affair.

This evening, Lord Partington was dining with them as Hetty was still in residence. Even when he was with his mistress, and it was just the two of them— Sybil and Stephen—they took infinite care in front of the servants never to disclose the nature of their relationship. In fact, Stephen was almost certain, and proud of the fact, that none of them could have discovered their secret. Dinner was conducted with the usual decorum. Hetty chattered the most. She seemed happy these days, he was pleased to note. Sir Aubrey was clearly a better match than he'd have believed. In fact, the couple appeared as smitten a year after their nuptials than they'd been when they'd wed so hastily.

He wished he could have married Sybil.

The syllabub was delicious, Sybil declared, smiling down the table as Stephen gazed at her. She was so easy to please. He smiled back, quickly transferring his look to Hetty, though not before he caught the flare in Sybil's eye. She wanted him to come to her tonight, even though she sat at her husband's right hand. He could tell. Much as

Stephen wished he could legally sleep with her every night, there was something enormously erotic about the veiled glances they shared, her sudden flush of consciousness as he fixed her with a smoldering look.

Suddenly, he was in a fever of impatience to get dinner finished. His Lordship might request his company for coffee and port though Stephen doubted it. The old man looked out of sorts tonight. Perhaps he might go straight to his own apartments. Stephen doubted he'd head off to the little house by the bridge to see Miss Hazlett with Hetty visiting. He thought of Lord Partington's daughters by his mistress—Lissa and Kitty. They were both beauties—clever and enter-prising, too—who could have married well under different circum-stances. *Lord Partington was a harsh father to his bastard offspring*, he thought. Just as he was a harsh husband to Sybil. Stephen knew if the slightest whisper got about regarding his affair with Sybil, they could consider it finished.

It was why he was prepared to pay any amount to keep it secret.

At last. The ladies were rising. Stephen and Lord Partington rose too, nodded to each other and with relief, Stephen saw that his Lord-ship had no desire for anyone's company tonight. In fact, his leg seemed to be troubling him, particularly as he limped from the room with the aid of Puddles the butler on one side and Sybil on the other.

"I'm ready for my bed, too," Hetty said on a weary sigh. "Lysander was up three times in the night. He's cutting another tooth, and I fear tonight won't be any better."

Stephen murmured the required sympathy and prepared to follow her when one of the footmen handed him a note. Discreetly.

He made sure he was alone when he opened it.

Meet me at the boathouse after dinner if you can manage it. The writing appeared to have been scrawled in haste. It certainly wasn't Sybil's usual hand, but perhaps she'd tried to disguise it. After all, it wouldn't do to fall into the wrong clutches. It was obviously also the reason she hadn't signed it.

He crumpled it, then tossed it on the fire on his way from the room, his groin suddenly aching with need.

The night was dark, and he had to take a lantern to light his way. He took the back route through the kitchen garden—and a rug for them to lie on—and hurried to make it there though he knew he'd be first. Sybil had left the dining room only seconds before him, but she'd probably see Lord Partington to his apartments since her husband was so obviously in pain. He hoped she'd not offer to rub his legs, but then, of course, she wouldn't otherwise she'd not have written the note to Stephen. It had been a week since Lord Partington had been under the same roof as them, due perhaps to the fact Hetty and Sir Aubrey were staying so he wanted to keep up appearances. No wonder Sybil was on fire to be with Stephen for it was rare they were apart so long.

The note filled him with ridiculous excitement. He'd not expected this of Sybil, but she was always one to surprise him. It was just one of the many things he loved about her.

The quickest route was across the lawn, but as he might have been observed from a window with his lantern, he took the meandering path that skirted the great expanse of lawn, dipped into the forest, and arrived via the northern side of the lake. Perhaps Sybil would suggest they take a boat and row across to the island. It was a mild night, and there'd be even greater privacy for them in the little rotunda there.

It didn't matter. His mind was too busy conjuring up delicious scenarios just to give it something with which to occupy itself, for the main object was that soon he'd hold Sybil in his arms, and feel her soft golden hair beneath his chin as he embraced her and breathed in all that was good about her...then took his fill of her wondrous sexual allure with as much eagerness as she.

He stopped at the threshold of the boathouse and glanced back at The Grange. The light was on in Sybil's bedchamber where Mabel her dresser would be preparing for her mistress's return, just as Sybil would be preparing for Stephen's arrival.

He was hard with anticipation as he trod lightly over the threshold and into the darkened boathouse. A candle guttered in the base of one of the rowing boats at the far end, and he could make out the shadowed form of his dear heart. She appeared to be staring in the opposite direction but turned as she heard him, rising and putting out her arms.

"Stephen."

Her voice arrested his progress. Shocked, he halted. "Who is that?"

"You do not know me?" She sounded disappointed. She rasped in a breath, and her voice broke. "I know it's been a while and that you weren't expecting me, but I thought you might have known my voice. Might even have been a little...pleased?"

There was a hopeful note to her voice.

There was only horror in his. "Lady Julia! What are you doing here?" What could she want at this time of night? Certainly not something he was prepared to give. She'd been flirtatious at Araminta's ball the previous week, and he'd been polite but distant. It was not possible she could have misinterpreted any of his responses for encouragement.

"I need your help, Stephen." Her voice caught. "You do not sound pleased to see me, and perhaps that's only to be expected, but I do need your help since it's because of you that I'm in such dreadful difficulties."

"Me?!" Incredulity, even more horror, and just a little shard of terrified guilt sliced through him. "I don't understand you." She couldn't be alluding to what—dear God—he never wanted to think about if he could help it. Besides, too long had passed.

"You are the father of my son, Stephen, and Sir Archie knows it, and now Lord Debenham is threatening to reveal the truth to the world." She heaved in a sob, and her face looked haggard in the candlelight. "You must help me for I don't know what to do."

"I am the father of your son?" He leaned against the prow of the boat and stared at her. "You cannot know that." Shock made his voice faint. "Nor could Sir Archie could ever prove that."

Lady Julia ran a hand across her brow. "Indeed he could." She straightened, then stepped over the center bench seat and sat down, smoothing the skirts of her cobalt-blue traveling dress over her knees. Her figure was as neat as he remembered it, and her bright golden hair as carefully coiffed, but she'd obviously dressed for a journey rather than an attempt at seduction. He hoped so anyway.

"Lady Julia, there's nothing I can do for you. You come here claiming I'm responsible." A sudden thought occurred to him. "Edgar?"

"Lord, we never went *so* far and no one has ever suggested impropriety to that extent. There is no doubt that you are the father of my third son. The son that will in all likelihood inherit from Archie."

"How can that be?" He said it more to himself but she replied, "That night I detained you in the storeroom, and you took your pleasure—"

"No! *You* took your pleasure." He was starting to shake now. This was his worst nightmare. She couldn't prove this. Nor could Sir Archie and, good God, nor could Lord Debenham.

Her voice hardened. "You certainly didn't object when I went down on my knees and took you in my mouth."

The words sounded so coarse, but she spoke the truth. He had thrown his head back, astonished that after so many years living a rough soldier's life a woman found him attractive. A woman wanted to pleasure him. One he hadn't even had to pay.

And what happened afterward? He shook his head to clear it of what he simply could not think of just then.

But that a child had resulted from such a grubby two-minute encounter seemed inconceivable.

She sniffed. "You were handsome and amenable, and after Sir Archie's little troubles, I was needing release in the same way as you, Stephen. Do not imagine it's only men who take pleasure from the act."

Oh, he knew that. He thought of Sybil and the many and varied times they'd found ways of pleasuring one another. After a week of abstinence due to Sir Partington's continued presence at The Grange, Stephen knew how much both he and Sybil were looking forward to finding release in one another's arms and bodies.

"Sir Archie was...?" He had to clarify what she seemed to be implying.

"Not was. *Is*. Sir Archie has been impotent since a terrible fever that plagued him about six months after our twins were born. Of course, that causes its own problems. Anger. Frustration. Well, you can imagine what he was like when I fell pregnant. I didn't know what to do. I tried to pretend it wasn't happening, but then the doctor was called after I'd fainted, and he confirmed the happy news." She said this in tones of mild sarcasm.

"What did Sir Archie do?" Stephen felt sick.

"What *could* he do? Was it more manly to admit to being cuck-olded, or to have another child in the nursery that proclaimed his manly prowess when we both knew he would never be the man he once was?"

He was at an impasse. "Why are you here? To force me to tell the world what could never otherwise be proved?"

"God, no! I want you to prevent Lord Debenham from telling the world. He's got to be stopped. He wants money for his silence, but it won't end there."

Stephen frowned. "You came here with Lord Beecham last week, did you not? He and Debenham know one another. Can't Lord Beecham ensure his silence? After all, I presume you and Lord Beecham are on more than passing friendly terms." He spoke wryly, but she responded with acidic dignity.

"Lord Beecham has nothing to do with this, nor does he know about you and me. I am Lucinda Martindale's godmother, and it is only right and proper that I help launch her since she's become Lord Beecham's ward. It's true he accommodates me on occasion, but with my husband's consent."

"So you have fallen out of favor with both your husband and Lord Beecham, and so you've come to me. Are you saying you have nowhere to go? Are you blackmailing me into giving you the refuge both your husband and paramour have withdrawn?" He couldn't help but speak so slightingly when he was so enraged at what had occurred. Yet, he had to accept culpability. He realized that, though acceptance would not come quite yet.

She raised her head and sent him an icy glare. "Since you are clearly so opposed to such an idea, I shall relieve you of that possibility on one condition—that you find a means of silencing Lord Debenham."

"Silencing him."

"That's right. After all, it's in your interests as much as mine."

"And how do you propose I do that? Invite him to my club for a cozy heart to heart and tell him that I'd appreciate it if he didn't proclaim to the world—" He stopped suddenly as the reality hit him like a force. He had fathered a son. A boy just a couple of months older than his precious Celia. A boy who, from what he'd heard, was likely to inherit Sir Archie's name and estate.

A red haze hung behind his eyes. "I wonder that your husband hasn't threatened to silence me forever, knowing what I've done."

She shrugged. "He isn't happy with you, but he doesn't have the courage to kill you, if that's what you're afraid of. He'd rather Debenham said nothing, and has made it clear that it's in my interests —as regards the comforts I've enjoyed as his wife—that Debenham is silenced. I've assured him that I will do whatever I can to see to that."

"So he sent you here tonight to speak to me?"

"Of course not. I've been staying with Lord Beecham, who has been angry with me ever since I danced with you at Lady Debenham's ball. He accuses me of trying to make him jealous. He's obsessed with me. I don't know what he'd do if he discovered you'd fathered Horatio."

Dully, he said, "So that's his name."

"Of your son? Yes. He looks a great deal like you, too. So will you agree? To silence Lord Debenham, so Archie and I can rest in peace knowing that Horatio will grow up with no slur attached to his name?"

"I have no idea how I might manage that." Stephen felt the energy drain from his shoulders. Now he realized the blackmail note he'd received from Debenham did not refer to his affair with Sybil, as he'd assumed. Well, it was some consolation, but he didn't think Sybil would think too highly of what had occurred between Stephen and Lady Julia the night before he'd met Sybil.

He wondered if Barston had whispered in Debenham's ear. Of course, nothing could be proved, but that didn't seem to be enough for Lady Julia. "I will endeavor to ensure his silence as it is in my interests as much as yours." He felt stiff and much older than his years as he stepped backward. "I presume you have a carriage waiting for you nearby. Do you wish me to escort you to the road?"

"I would appreciate that, Mr. Cranborne," she said, holding out her hand so he could help her step out of the boat. "You always were the gentleman."

CHAPTER 16

*K*itty returned from the theater to her little house feeling a great deal less magnanimous than she'd left. She'd farewelled Silverton for the last time. She was proud of the manner in which she'd conducted herself, but it didn't make her feel happier. In fact, she'd never felt more forlorn in her life.

The hackney put her down in front of the sweet little house that she'd vacate in a few days, as soon as she found suitable alternate lodgings. It would have to be far less luxurious, but she was no man's paid plaything now. She had gifts from Silverton that would ensure she got by in comfort for the next few months. He'd insisted upon that, and of course, an actress's wage was barely enough to feed and house her though Kitty was luckier than most.

A light was on her room she saw as she crossed the road though the rest of the house was in darkness. The servants must have gone to bed. She hoped Dorcas might have waited up for her. She could do with someone to talk to. Someone who understood her heart.

"Miss Kitty?"

Kitty startled as she let herself in and heard the voice from her drawing room, for it was not like Dorcas to sit in semi-darkness and wait for her. She entered the room and saw that the Argand lamp was low and placed on a table beneath the window illuminating two figures. Only when she strained her eyes did she see that they sat close together. For a moment, she thought they'd been holding hands, except that it wouldn't have been like Dorcas, for her companion was a young man and Dorcas had sworn off men since her terrible experience at Mrs. Montgomery's.

"Miss Kitty, this is Mr. Prism," Dorcas said as she stood up this time. The young man beside her was already standing, and in the gloom, Kitty could see he was tall and reed-thin, with an earnest look enhanced by wire-framed spectacles. Anything else was impossible to make out.

" My apologies for calling so late, Miss Bijou," the young man said. "I came by earlier on account of something important to tell Miss Dorcas, only she insisted I stay until you returned."

"I certainly don't mind Dorcas having a visitor, if that's what you're concerned about," Kitty assured them, while her mind roamed over Dorcas's various past associations. She was certain Mr. Prism was the only young man Dorcas had ever spoken of with any fondness, having finally escaped from her indenture at Mrs. Montgomery's house of ill repute.

"Dorcas, why don't you turn the lamp up and organize a drink for everyone?" she suggested as she went to her favorite chair in the corner. Yes, she remembered now. Mr. Prism was the young man whose father had sent him to Mrs. Montgomery's for his twenty-first birthday initiation. He and Dorcas had spent the night talking. Mostly about his father's disreputable activities, she recalled, though perhaps about Dorcas too, though Dorcas was likely too bashful to have mentioned that part.

Kitty slid another look toward them as she lowered herself into the lovely comfortable leather chair that would be hers no longer after tomorrow. Her interest in Dorcas and Mr. Prism was swept away momentarily by a pang for everything else she was about to lose. For two months, she'd never known such pure pleasure and delight.

"Miss Bijou, I came here to tell Miss Dorcas something that I thought would be of interest and, possibly, importance to both herself and to you. First, might I preface this information with a few words on the enormous esteem in which I hold you, both as London's most beautiful and accomplished actress, and as a most honorably intentioned employer who has helped Miss Dorcas so immeasurably in extricating herself from the appalling situation in which she found herself. And finally, on that note—but of no less importance—is the fact that I would like to say in front of you and Miss Dorcas that in no way am I prejudiced by Miss Dorcas's past life which forced her into actions against her moral inclination. I, too, have spent most of my life forced into actions against my moral inclination, but I know that what is important is what one believes is right and true, and what is in one's heart, for we are all too often indentured to masters who care nothing for right and wrong, and only for how to line their pockets with gold. And that is why I am here."

After the long pause that followed this incredible speech, Kitty finally said, feeling rather taken aback by such candor, "I am enormously gratified that you should make such an effort to reassure Dorcas of your esteem. I am flattered by your kind words, too."

"Miss Bijou, I came here neither to flatter nor to impress, but to impart important information." He glanced at Dorcas, and the look they shared was so telling, Kitty's previous gentle amusement was swept away by the realization that there was something more at play.

Dorcas swayed closer, brushing against his arm and taking his hand in hers to give it a quick squeeze before she released it, saying in a hurried whisper, "Tell Miss Kitty 'bout Lord Debenham...'n Lord Silverton."

Shocked, Kitty sat back in her chair, indicating for the others to do the same.

Lord Debenham? The last time she'd heard his name was in the company of Lissa, Araminta, and Mr. Tunley as Araminta had poured out her fears that Lord Debenham was searching for material to use for blackmail purposes. Material that might somehow implicate Araminta.

But the idea that Silverton was somehow linked to Lord Debenham made no sense. Silverton deplored the man's morals and behavior. He'd been doing his best to uncover information that would add to evidence of wrongdoing on Debenham's part; evidence that would implicate him in the plot to assassinate Castlereagh.

Her shock must have shown, for quickly Dorcas reassured her, "Mr. Prism don't mean Lord Silverton's bin linked ter anyfink bad. Yer remember them letters Mrs. Montgomery wanted me ter plant in 'is study?" The girl blushed for, of course, it had been part of the terms of her release but had come to nothing after Dorcas had confessed virtually the moment she'd done the deed. "Lord Debenham were part o' that only now 'e's tryin' sumfink else."

"Oh," Kitty said faintly. It was all she could manage right now as she took in the horrifying ramifications. If the ruthless viscount was continuing a vendetta against her darling Silverton, where might it end? Swallowing, she added, "I have no liking for Lord Debenham, but surely if Silverton has nothing to hide he has nothing to fear?" It was a foolish hope, she knew. It also bolstered her determination following her recent discussion in Ralph Tunley's lodgings to do all she could to assist in bringing the villainous viscount to justice.

That, she now knew, was what Lissa and Mr. Tunley were intent on doing, but if Kitty could help achieve an aim which in turn helped Lissa and Mr. Tunley to finally wed, so much the better.

Grief lodged in Kitty's throat. Lord Silverton could never be hers, she knew, but if Kitty couldn't be happy with the man she loved, nothing would give her greater pleasure than seeing Lissa finally able to marry Mr. Tunley. Finding a way to apprehend Lord Debenham would go a long way toward achieving that.

"Brandy, Mr. Prism? Thank you, Dorcas." She settled back with the drink Dorcas handed her, taking a sip of the fiery liquid which she decided she'd need. "Now, please tell me what this is all about."

With a long, earnest look at Dorcas, Mr. Prism seated himself once more on the sofa beside her and proceeded to speak.

"Miss Bijou, I am a clerk. My father's desire has been to see us rise in the world, and I am the beneficiary of his noble aims. But his aims are all that are noble. I am the respectable front of his nefarious operations. He will go to any lengths to further add to the family coffers, and I have always—"

"Yes, yes, thank you, Mr. Prism, but what exactly can you tell me about Lord Silverton?" Kitty's heart thundered in her chest, and she barely dared hear the answer.

Dorcas cleared her throat. "Miss Kitty, I fink I'd better begin by tellin' yer 'ow it come 'bout that yer fine gennelmun were mentioned. Yer see, I were in the market buyin' fish when I 'eard me name bein' called from a carriage wot 'ad stopped nearby. When I went over, it were Mrs. Montgomery who said she 'ad sumfink ter tell me 'n would I come ter 'er establishment."

Kitty sent her a look of horror.

"You surely didn't, did you, Dorcas?' Kitty asked, and Dorcas shook her head vehemently.

"I said she could tell me wot it were there, 'n so Mrs. Mongtomery told me that she could give me a lot o' money if I told 'er a few things that would be 'elpful fer doin' good."

"Mrs. Montgomery...doing good? I hope you didn't believe her, Dorcas."

"'Course not. But then she said that as I 'adn't carried out properly 'er instructions 'bout them letters wot were s'posed to show up Lord Silverton fer the villain 'e is, then she were goin' ter 'ave to get 'er lawyer on ter me if I didn't come back willing-like 'n work fer 'er." Dorcas looked thoroughly frightened at this and rubbed an eye with one fist. Mr. Prism slid his eyes across to her and patted her hand while a furious blush spread across his cheeks.

Kitty was about to speak up in defense of Lord Silverton's good character when Mr. Prism cleared his throat, and bringing back his straying hands to clasp them demurely in his lap said, "It so happened that in the greatest of coincidences, I was passing by, and I happened to see Miss Dorcas talking to Mrs. Montgomery. As I drew nearer, I heard Mrs. Montgomery telling Dorcas that Lord Silverton had come into possession of a necklace through illegal means which he'd given to his—"

"Mistress? No, I'm not upset by the term, but by the falseness of the charge. Lord Silverton paid twice over for that necklace. It had belonged to Lady Debenham, but she'd given it to Mrs. Montgomery to pawn for her, I believe." She clenched her fists and added fiercely, "Certainly, it was never stolen! Neither by me nor by Lord Silverton."

"We assuredly know that you and Lord Silverton are in no way blameworthy in this, being such pillars of respectability—"

He reddened at this, and looked relieved when Dorcas interrupted. "It were eva so good to see Mr. Prism again, but I were fearful ashamed that 'e'd think badly o' me assumin' I were still workin' fer 'er establishment."

"Nor would it have changed my opinion of you, Miss Dorcas," he assured her vehemently. "I have been ill-used by my father. I know what it is to be forced to perform immoral acts against one's good conscience, and so you and I are alike. Dorcas was forced against her will to do what made her soul shrivel inside her." His eyes grew bright in his pallid face and he leaned forward. "But when I overheard what Mrs. Montgomery was saying to Dorcas, I realized that Dorcas and I could redress the balance because of what we know, and because we both want to work for what is right, and we both understand something of the evil network that operates at Mrs. Montgomery's."

He paused to draw breath and Dorcas burst out, "I were talkin' te me friend, Sal, wot's one of Mrs. Montgomery's girls—yer met 'er once, Miss Kitty—'n she told me that Lord Debenham pays 'is favorites ter give 'im information wot 'e can use ter blackmail people fer money. She reckons it were Lord Debenham wot blackmailed Lord Calder, causin' him ter take 'is life."

Kitty remembered Silverton's dismay at losing his friend, and his suspicions regarding the blackmailer.

But while the insidious fear surrounding Mrs. Montgomery's power seeped through her, so did the thought that she could help bring justice to Lord Debenham with the aid of these two before her. Each of them had some insight into Mrs. Montgomery's evil empire or knew—more than most people—about Lord Debenham's nefarious activities.

She leaned forward excitedly. "Dorcas, Mr. Prism, I'm so glad you're here. The three of us *can* make a change for good. We can work together to redress some of the wickedness we've seen but been unable to change."

Excitement began to churn inside her. Imagine if she, Kitty, could be known for something other than for her lack of respectability as an actress, or the unacknowledged illegitimate daughter, or the mistress of two of society's most eligible bachelors. Imagine if, in her own right, Kitty could be known for bringing to justice a nemesis to society.

"Are you telling me you're here because you know something important? Something that really could go toward convicting Lord Debenham?"

Mr. Prism and Dorcas nodded in unison, then Dorcas said, "There's an engraved pewter box, yer see, that 'e 'as unda lock 'n key. No one knows 'bout it, but it contains all 'is secrets." She lowered her voice. "*All* o' 'em. And Sal, she reckons she knows 'xactly where 'e keeps it."

CHAPTER 17

*A*raminta stared at the scrap of paper lying on the elegant round table in her private dressing room, and feared she was about to be sick. She'd been doing that a lot lately. Being sick, but the occasion now was nothing to do with the nausea that had plagued her each morning with regular monotony, and which she dreaded might be her worst nightmare—another child. Lord Debenham's child. She contoured her slender waist and closed her eyes, reflecting on how recently her body was hers again. The body that drove men wild. She hadn't intended ever to become pregnant again.

Then she did another turn about the room, her hands clenched into fists, before returning to stare once more at the note. Perhaps she'd been mistaken in the way she'd read it the first time.

Lady D. Your husband wants to know why you gave away your ruby and diamond necklace. Shall I tell him, or would you like to make a donation for my silence? Meet me at 5 o'clock inside the Western gate, Highgate Cemetery, with five hundred pounds.

Araminta gripped the table, afraid she was going to faint. Who knew the story of the necklace?

Kitty La Bijou, of course.

A gust of wind down the chimney stirred the letter at the same time as a thought speared Araminta's mind. Who *else* knew about the necklace? Well, the awful woman to whom Miss La Bijou had taken Araminta when she was giving birth.

One of them must have sent the blackmail note. Araminta had been sure she'd pulled the wool over credulous Miss Bijou's eyes, but that greasy creature—what was her name? Mrs. Mobbs—she must have told Miss Bijou. Could Miss Bijou be responsible for this? Swiftly she seized the letter and crumpled it in her hand and threw it at the fireplace.

Jane appeared in the room at the very moment she let out her cry of frustration.

"Can't fit inter yer fav'rite gown fer this evenin', m'lady?" Jane asked, unfazed by her mistress's distress as she calmly picked up the piece of paper that had missed the blaze. She raised her eyebrows. "Or did someone write yer sumfink yer didn't like?"

"Go on, read it then! I know you're dying to, and perhaps you can then tell me what I should do!" Hissing out a breath, Araminta began to stalk from one end of the room to the other while Jane held the paper up to the light.

Fragmented multicolors made her vision swim. "I was so sure Debenham believed I'd pawned the necklace and there'd be no more questions. But someone wants to tell him the truth, don't they?"

"Are yer goin' ter give 'em the money?" Jane sat on a stool and began to roll up a pair of discarded stockings.

"With what? I have no more pin money for this quarter." Araminta ran her fingers through her hair before turning an imploring face toward her maid. "What should I do, Jane? Do you think the letter comes from Kitty La Bijou? Should I confront her? Tell her what ill will come to her if—"

"Yer might consider 'oney a better bet than vinegar, m'lady. Not that I reckon Miss Bijou 'as anyfink to do wiv it. Nah…but she might know, though. Have yer thought about that, then? Why not go to 'er sweet, like, 'n ask her ter 'elp yer? That's wot I'd do. She 'elped yer afore."

"You really don't think she's taking advantage of the situation? Of what she knows through helping me before?"

Jane rolled her eyes. "Trouble is—if yer don't mind me sayin' m'lady—is that yer believe others fink the same as yer. Miss Bijou, it seems ter me, is a good sort 'n would more likely 'elp yer."

"Oh, Jane, what have I got to lose? Only everything if Debenham finds out." Another wave of nausea threatened to swamp Araminta, only this time it wasn't on account of her fear over the letter. No, it was purely physical, and as soon as Araminta had delivered up the contents of her stomach into the chamber pot, she threw herself onto the bed and burst into noisy tears.

"Debenham has his revenge, truly he has, without slicing my throat!" she wailed as she clutched her stomach and hung her head over the edge of the bed.

She opened her eyes at the cool dampness of a flannel dabbing at her temples and stared dolefully into her maid's face.

"You're not looking at all sympathetic, like you ought, Jane," she sniffed, "but truly, I don't know what I'd do without you. You won't leave me, will you? I know I'm perfectly horrid to you sometimes, but you will promise you'll stay, regardless—won't you?"

"Well, no' *regardless*, m'lady, fer that would give yer quite some license," Jane acknowledged with a brief, wry grin. "But I ain't goin' nowhere in a 'urry. Not while Jem's still got a place wiv 'is Lordship."

"Yes, I did have to pull some strings about that considering Debenham was all for having Jem deported for stealing that letter, so you owe me a promise you'll stay."

"Well, it weren't proved beyond doubt that it were 'im, were it, since it were neva found in 'is possession 'n yer tried ter take it from 'im."

"No! *You* took it, Jane, and you gave it to Hetty." Araminta suddenly remembered how aggrieved she was on this score. "*You* should have been deported, Jane, and maybe I'd have seen that you were, if I hadn't intervened because I needed you more. Oh, but what am I going to do?"

"About anuvver bairn? Well, reckon there ain't nuffink yer can do.

It'll be like last time, only easier. Second babes are always easier 'n yer first; well, it did come mighty quick so I reckon yer one of the lucky ones."

"Well, at least Debenham's more likely to leave me alone for a while." Araminta seized on this hopefully while a raft of ideas crowded her mind. She could go to the country, and she and Teddy could...

"Wot is it, m'lady?" Jane asked as Araminta let forth another wail, for she'd just thought of how soon her body would become bloated and hideous. Teddy would be disgusted. She had to act quickly and entrance him before that happened. Besides, he might be able to help her. Ralph Tunley had said the letter he had was insufficient to convict Debenham of anything, and that was some small relief. Maybe Araminta might find in Teddy an ally who would keep an ear out for whispers. Whispers that might implicate her husband in anything more underhand than his misdemeanors all those years ago now regarding the Castlereagh affair, and the nonsense over his suppos-edly radical leanings. Debenham didn't have the energy to involve himself in political affairs. All he wanted was to gamble— and have enough money to get him out of financial difficulties.

"I want you to send this note around to Lord Ludbridge, Jane," Araminta said decisively, feeling a lot better as she scribbled a hasty missive which she handed to her maid.

"And then I want you to lay out my new gold net evening gown. I'm going to the theater tonight."

"To see that Wildflower play?"

"No, to see Miss La Bijou."

THE LATE-AFTERNOON SUN SLANTED THROUGH THE PLANE TREES IN THE small park opposite the Beecham household, as Kitty said vehemently, "So you see, Lissa, I can help you, if you'll only let me."

Lissa couldn't get over the hope and enthusiasm on her sister's face. Back home, Kitty had always been the wayward, frivolous younger sister whom Lissa had brushed off as simply not pulling her weight.

Even just a couple of weeks ago, she'd bemoaned to Ralph about Kitty's latest appalling transgression. First actress, then mistress to not just one gentleman of the ton, but two!

Now Kitty was here in the garden opposite Lord Beecham's townhouse, wearing a fashionable and becoming gown of Pomona green, telling Lissa how she should go about ensuring justice was done so that Ralph would get the promotion he so desired, which would enable him to marry Lissa. It was beyond anything!

The afternoon sun that filtered from the thick band of low cloud was making Kitty's ringlets look like spun gold, and her skin look golden with health.

Lissa dropped her head, though she didn't stop walking, and looked at her scuffed half-boots. "You have no idea what you're talking about," she muttered. "Do you think if there'd been any way to have helped Ralph do what he had to do, I wouldn't have been leading the charge?" It hurt her to the quick that Kitty insinuated Lissa had just sat idly by, drilling Miss Lucinda in deportment and mending Lady Julia's torn undergarments.

Kitty's mouth dropped open. She looked about to sally forth, but Lissa went on, "You've done exactly what you wanted, Kitty, but how has that benefited anyone? All right, I'll speak plainly, though you won't like to hear it. Have you given a thought to Mama since you ran away from home and dragged our name through the mud?"

Lissa turned her head away from the hurt look on her sister's face. She thought she'd seen a tear glisten, but Kitty was the most accomplished of actresses.

"What good name?" Kitty asked. "That's why I ran away. I had no name. Except "bastard." So what did I have to lose? As to not having contact with Mama, I send money home to her every fortnight, and I know I'm more generous than Papa. I bought her that shawl she'd so coveted, but which Papa said was too expensive. I *have* thought of Mama! What have *you* sent home to Mama?"

Lissa didn't like the combative tone. Even less did she like the direct question, for the truth was that her wages were so pitiful Lissa hadn't been in a position to send *anything* home.

Lissa strove for the high ground. "Look at the clothes you're wearing!"

"What about them? They are in the first stare. There's nothing tawdry or showy about them. Araminta or Hetty would wear just the same if they had such good taste. You're jealous, Lissa. You weren't beyond borrowing clothes from Araminta whom you profess to despise. I'll wager you felt mighty grand attending a ball and looking like you were venturing forth for your grand debut. I know you pretend you don't care, but you do! And now that I'm able to enjoy freedom and nice clothes you're jealous."

Lissa clenched her teeth. "I'm not jealous if it meant I had to...do the things you've lowered yourself to do to get them."

Kitty gasped. "Are you casting aspersions on my reputation? Do you think I'd give myself to a man I did not love? I've done nothing that our Mama hasn't done. She's lived in sin for twenty years, and what joy has it brought her? What joy has it brought any of us?" She looked on the verge of angry tears. "I simply came to see you because I thought you'd want to help Ralph do what he's been charged to do—uncover the nefarious dealings in which Lord Debenham is involved, and by so doing, uncover the other villains in his circle who are causing such unhappiness."

Stirred into action, Lissa stopped in her tracks and swung around. "A year ago, I was lauded for the role I played in this very conspiracy. My drawings brought the Foreign Office hot on the heels of Lord Debenham."

Kitty frowned. "I knew nothing of this. How *did* you meet Araminta?"

"She recognized me, and when she needed someone to accompany her to a coffee house to purloin an important letter his Lordship's valet had supposedly hidden away, she sent a message around. Well, the letter was proved a fake, and besides, it wasn't sufficient evidence on its own. Nevertheless, I was commended by a high-ranking figure in Parliament, a diplomat who placed me in my current governessing position with the express idea of keeping an eye out for anything I could pass on. I shouldn't be telling you this because I compromise everything, and because you can't keep a secret, Kitty, but I will not have you saying I've done nothing. Lord, the inaction is torture. Barely seeing Ralph is torture. Having to pander to Lady Julia and Miss Lucinda is pure torture. Don't you preach to me about what's right!"

"Well, don't you suggest I'm not in a better position than you are to discover gossip and other important information. I have a much wider network than you do. And greater access to important people who can yield the right information. I can be more persuasive. I have friends who know how to be very persuasive. And here I am, suggesting to you that we join forces and share information, yet all you do is make me feel small. Like when we were children. Small and unimportant."

Lissa drew a breath for forbearance, but also because there was truth in what Kitty was saying. She'd always felt protective of her younger sister, but also slightly exasperated by Kitty's lack of insight on occasion.

"I'm not insinuating you're not open to the idea of doing whatever you can, Lissa. I just think you're too busy trying to make me ashamed of myself that you've lost sight of what's more important. And you know what that is? It's bringing justice to Lord Debenham and his cronies so you and Ralph can be married, and so I can at least prove to Lord Silverton that I *would* have made a brave and worthy wife." Impatiently, she dabbed at the moisture in the corner of her eye.

"Come, it's probably time to turn back," she muttered, breaking off a leaf from an overhanging branch. "You'll have Miss Lucinda to attend to, and you're both going to Lady Richmond's ball tonight, I know. But you will marry Ralph someday, and you will be happy. I will watch Lord Silverton being married in four weeks' time and know that I will never be happy."

Lissa put out her hand and squeezed her sister's briefly. "You will find someone else," she said. "You're young and beautiful, and you are feted by the whole of London it would seem. I am proud of you, even if you think I'm not. Already, in less than a year, there's been Lord Nash and then Lord Silverton, and while I don't approve of your... liaisons, it proves there'll be others."

There was a curious look in Kitty's eye as she whispered, "I can't believe you're insinuating what I think you are, Lissa! That I can so easily transfer my affections. I knew Lord Silverton for months as a good and loyal friend. I would do anything for him except ruin his future and relations with his family. No, there will never be another of his caliber. He and I were good together. We love each other. There's no changing that! Just like there's no changing the way you feel for Ralph."

"Now!" Her trembling mouth turned up into a smile. "If you're going to be out on the town tonight, you can't possibly disgrace the family name with the poor ensemble that is all you have at your disposal, so I shall send Dorcas around with several suitable possibilities."

Lissa was glad the conversation had ended on a better note, but she shook her head. "I can't possibly, Kitty."

"No, I insist!"

"It's not your generosity I'm turning down. I truly thank you. But I couldn't possibly turn up somewhere in what would be a gross putting forward of myself, suggesting I had ideas beyond my station. It would look like I wanted to cast Miss Lucinda into the shade."

"Ideas beyond your station?" Kitty's look was sad. "Lissa, you are the daughter of Lord Partington. Is it 'above your station' to wear a beautiful gown to an event that...that Araminta and Henrietta will be attending in lavish ball gowns? Don't you want to show them up? Prove you're just as good?"

"But I'm not."

"Not as good as *Araminta*?! Please!"

They both grinned at that, and then Lissa ended the camaraderie with a worried look at the fading light. "I'll have to go in now and see to Miss Lucinda." She put out her hand feeling much more charitable toward Kitty now, despite the fact that Kitty was as impulsively misguided as ever. Kitty had always wanted to be better than Lissa knew that they could be. They'd been born in sin. Their brother Thomas could ride above the stain to his birthright through industry and the backing of influential sponsors.

Kitty had sunk to the lowest depths of degradation possible, but Lissa could still cling to tenuous respectability as a governess.

"Oh Lissa, you'd look just lovely in the pale green silk and roses. I do wish you'd consider it!"

"If it'll make you happy to say I'll consider it, then all right." Lissa tried not to show her sadness as she gazed at Kitty's animated face. Already her sister had put the unfortunate aspects of their conversation and situation behind her, and was gaily contemplating future happy pursuits. But what would happen to poor Kitty when her looks were faded? She'd have nothing.

No, it would be up to Lissa to maintain her impecunious little sister, when Kitty had run through all her funds, and there was no gentleman to support her.

"I wish you well for tonight's performance, Kitty," she said, turning.

"And I wish you well for finding out something important at Lady Richmond's tonight." Kitty put her hand on Lissa's arm. "You are very clever at keeping things close to your chest. I don't wonder you were chosen for a position of such discretion, and I'm sure you'll find out exactly what we need to find out if we're to help Ralph. I want to see the pair of you happily married, truly I do!"

"That's very sweet," said Lissa, thinking how far distant any such a possibility seemed right now. "And I'm sure you'll do whatever you can to find out who else might have an axe to grind with Lord Debenham though, of course, Araminta only wants such information so she can protect him in order to protect herself." She sighed. "I'm sure it's all far too complicated for you to have to worry about. Goodnight Kitty."

CHAPTER 18

*K*itty plastered on a cheerful smile as she farewelled her sister, but it was hard to keep her shoulders back and walk without showing the real depths of her sadness. Lissa and Ralph were deeply in love and all that held them apart was a lack of money.

Kitty and Silverton were madly in love, but the factors that held *them* apart were insurmountable.

Still, she was an actress, a *celebrated* actress, she had to remind herself. In a few hours, she'd be performing on stage and presenting herself to an adoring public as if she hadn't a care in the world. Lissa clearly had little admiration for the choices she'd made, nor for her ability to make any difference in solving a mystery that had such important ramifications for her sisters—Lissa and Araminta—but Kitty would show her.

She just wasn't sure how.

Therefore, it was an enormous surprise when directly after the performance, she was given notice by her dresser that a lady wished to see her in private and was there somewhere they could repair to.

"A lady? Did she say who she was?" Kitty wondered fearfully if it could be Miss Mandelton come to accost her having heard rumors about her past liaison with her future husband. Not that she believed

Miss Mandelton would have the courage to do such a thing. Carefully nurtured females such as she were trained to keep their heads demurely down, preferably over stitching their husband's shirts or infants' nightcaps, and to pretend they had no knowledge of the deviant underworld to which Kitty belonged.

"She didn't say miss, but I knew it were Lady Debenham."

"Lady Debenham!" Kitty sat down abruptly at her dressing table. She glanced at the door. "Tell her she can speak to me here and we'll be private. Make sure no one else interrupts us, Betsy."

What on earth did Araminta have to say to her that it required such cloak and dagger? Araminta would have recognized Kitty at her birthday celebration at The Grange, and was no doubt horribly uncomfortable at the memory of what she and Kitty had shared when Kitty had taken her to Mrs. Mobbs's.

"The audience seemed to like you well enough." Araminta swept in, ostrich feathers waving, her beautiful gown molding her form. "You certainly played a passable nymph. I daresay you can be whomever you choose, and that's quite a gift."

Did Lady Debenham know that Kitty was also Lord Partington's daughter? She knew Lissa was, but judging by the airy way she tossed her fur tippet over one shoulder and seated herself upon the spindly chair Kitty had pulled across from the window, Kitty doubted that she knew Kitty was also her father's daughter.

"Now," said Araminta, "you are no doubt wondering why I'm here, and since my husband is waiting at home to take me to Lady Richmond's ball, I shall be brief. The fact is, Miss Bijou, that I have a problem, and I need you to help me get to the bottom of it. You were in possession—and no doubt still are—of my ruby and diamond necklace."

So that was it. She wanted it back. Anger bubbled through Kitty's veins as she said, "I was given that necklace by Lord Nash who paid for it, honestly. When your husband demanded it back, nevertheless, my...friend, Lord Silverton, paid him its value so I could keep it." Crisply she added, "Therefore, the necklace has been paid for twice over, and I refuse to relinquish it."

"I'd heard there was quite a story to that necklace. However, I'm more interested in how it came into Lord Nash's hands than anything else."

Kitty looked at Araminta askance. "I'm not sure a lady like you would want to know."

Araminta glanced at the door and then thrust her chin out at Kitty. "I need to know the truth. Where did Lord Nash acquire the necklace?"

Kitty sighed. "He bought it from an unsavory woman called Maggie Montgomery. It was one of the objections I had to marrying Lord Nash. That, and the fact that the necklace had belonged to you first, though I didn't know that at the time." When she saw the confusion on Araminta's face, she explained, "Maggie Montgomery is the madam of a house of ill repute...if you know what that is."

"A brothel!" Araminta jerked as if stung. She began fanning herself furiously but waved away the drink Kitty offered her. "I need your help, Miss Bijou. You helped me once before, and maybe you think I wasn't grateful enough, but let me assure you I was." Stopping abruptly, she bit her lips. "That is, assuming you were discreet."

"I vouchsafed nothing about assisting you when it looked likely your babe might come early, if that's what you mean."

"Just as well for you..." However, Araminta said the words distantly. She seemed more concerned with other thoughts until she refocused her gaze upon Kitty and said suddenly, "I need you to come with me this evening and meet someone. Or rather, someone intends to meet me at midnight, and they want five hundred pounds—which I don't have."

"A ransom demand?" She remembered Araminta's evasiveness during the conversation she'd overheard between Araminta and Ralph. "Over what?"

"I'm not telling you. But I want you to meet this person in my stead, and I'll be watching to see who it is. It's twenty minutes before the clock strikes so we'll need to hurry."

"You're asking me to do this dangerous thing out of the goodness of my heart?"

"Of course not. I'll pay you well, naturally."

"What if I have other plans? I'm sorry, Lady Debenham." No, Kitty wasn't sorry, but furious that Araminta thought she could toss out directions in such a manner.

Araminta looked outraged before she forced a smile. "Do you?"

"Do I what?"

"Have other plans?"

"Well…"

"Your liaison with Lord Silverton has ended, has it not? Very charming man. I remember I met you the first time in his company. But perhaps you have already allied yourself with someone else."

"No, I have not! But all right, I'll go with you." Kitty would have anyway if Araminta had not been so selfishly beastly about assuming she would. A blackmail attempt? Kitty imagined Araminta would be ripe for all manner of blackmail attempts the way she conducted herself; however, since Kitty and Lissa were hoping to discover the identity of an extortionist who was operating amidst the ranks of the ton, this was a good start.

Araminta was quiet as they climbed into a hackney and made the short journey to the cemetery where they were to meet the black-mailer. She was more nervous, perhaps, than she'd first appeared, for when Kitty asked, "Are we here?" she made a strangled noise and indicated for Kitty to lead the way as they left their conveyance and trod a twisting path through a small pine forest.

A quiet section near the eastern entrance had been chosen as the meeting place. The moon gave good light, but there were plenty of opportunities to find concealment. Ancient yew trees lent an eerie atmosphere, and Kitty yelped at the sound of an owl hooting in a tree branch just above her head. Araminta hung back near the gate while Kitty took the lead, showing more confidence than she'd expected to feel. Like Araminta, she was now heavily veiled.

Shortly after arriving at the designated meeting place, Kitty heard the soft tread of footsteps upon the gravel. Suddenly, she was terrified. Perhaps Lord Debenham had planned to take his wife to task, and it was, in fact, himself who was going to confront Kitty. He'd be completely unimpressed if he discovered the woman who supposedly had stolen his wife's necklace was here in Araminta's place. Oh Lord, she hadn't considered that. Lord Debenham? Indeed, it was quite possible though she'd discounted him because he'd already received payment from Lord Silverton. Of all London's gentlemen, he was the one who terrified her most.

But it was a woman, large-busted with ostrich feathers in her brassy hair, and a terrifyingly familiar voice who stepped into a pool of moonlight as if she'd stepped in front of the stage lights. She was veiled, but the gaudy scarlet and black high-waisted gown with its overdone embellishments that accentuated her ample proportions, proclaimed exactly who she was. Kitty had seen Mrs. Montgomery wear this gown on numerous occasions.

"So Lady Debenham, have you the money?"

Kitty could only gasp as she shook her head.

"Then what have you instead, dearie? That little one takes a fair bit of feeding. Reckon he's chewed up more than a diamond and ruby necklace is worth.

Kitty could not stay here and look that awful woman in the face. Equally, she wasn't at all sure she could stomach what she was hearing. A baby? What did she mean? Had this anything to do with Araminta's first season which had ended under a cloud?

She needed to answer, but the words caught in her throat. She shook her head, distressed, and suddenly Mrs. Montgomery whisked her veil away from her face.

"Kitty La Bijou!"

"Mrs. Montgomery!" Kitty didn't know what else to say, which didn't matter as Mrs. Montgomery let out a tirade. "What are you doing here? Do *you* have the money I'm after to keep my silence?"

Kitty cast around for Araminta, and suddenly she was there, breathless, and obviously more courageous for having Kitty's presence.

"So *you're* the woman who's been trying to blackmail me!" she shrieked. "And you know Miss Bijou? Well, let me tell you, Mrs.... Montgomery, I have friends in high places, and you will not succeed in your evil schemes. I've heard whispers about you, and I could ensure your entire business is ruined with a few words from me. So desist from your claims now, and all will be well. But if I hear a whisper that you've broken your silence, I will see you destroyed."

Araminta, whose icy, controlled anger had been whipped up like that of a fiery, avenging Valkyrie, was most impressive, Kitty thought. Though perhaps if Araminta had been subjected to Mrs. Montgomery's merciless wardenship like Dorcas had, she wouldn't have ventured so much. Still, the effect on Mrs. Montgomery was most surprising. Kitty had thought she'd be about to witness a battle of momentous proportions as Mrs. Montgomery gave as good as she got. But instead, the woman drew herself up, her body rigid, her face immobile, giving nothing away.

Araminta took a menacing step forward. "If my reputation is besmirched, Mrs. Montgomery—thank you, Kitty, for the name—I will know you're responsible, and I promise you that I will see you destroyed, in turn. Now, is that the last of your threats?"

Kitty couldn't believe it. She left the scene with Araminta clearly in the ascendant, a vanquished Mrs. Montgomery pledging to keep her silence. As they hurried through the trees, Kitty dwelt on the unanswered questions that needed satisfying, but as soon as they reached the hired equipage, Araminta turned and said, "I suppose I can't leave you here. I'll take you where you need to go, but if I hear that a word of what's transpired tonight has been made public, I'll know it was you."

"Or Mrs. Montgomery," Kitty added, climbing into the carriage.

"Well, she told you why she was blackmailing me so now you know, and if you tell a soul I'll—"

Kitty wasn't often spurred to anger, but indignation flared, and she ground out as the carriage lurched forward, "Don't threaten me, Lady Debenham. There's more I know about you than you think, but because we are also closer than you think, I've held my tongue, and I've been your ally tonight when it could have gone so badly."

Araminata's mouth dropped open. "Well, I thank you for coming along. But it's very strange that you know that woman, don't you think? Considering…well, what she is."

"What are you insinuating?" Kitty had never been closer to striking anyone. "What kind of person do you think I am? I'm in love with a man who can never be my husband because I am not respectable, but I gave him up so he could be with the bride his mother would have him wed, whereas *you*…" She shook her head. "You gave away your baby, didn't you?"

Araminta was clearly rattled and not nearly as robust in spirit as Kitty had assumed, for she immediately burst into tears. "

"So you guessed? Or did that awful woman you took me to that night—your landlady—tell you?"

At first, Kitty had no idea what she was talking about. Then the terrible realization struck her. She *had* heard a baby mewling that night. And it had been her half-sister's. Kitty had helped Araminta. Aided and abetted her in this terrible deed. The carriage was rattling along at a sedate pace through a disreputable part of town, and she could hear the sounds of street brawling and fighting cats. But nothing so sordid or terrible as what she was hearing now. "No! Surely it can't be possible. Your baby was born *that* night? While I was there?"

Araminta dropped her hands. Her eyes were luminous and glistening with tears. A mortal terror crept into them. "I thought I heard Mrs. Montgomery tell you so."

"She mentioned a baby. I assumed…perhaps it was the reason your first season had been cut short. I'd heard rumors…"

"Rumors about *that*?" Araminta's cry was strangled.

Kitty shook her head, incredulous. "You…gave away Lord Debenham's heir? But…why?"

"Oh Lord, are you so stupid! Why did I assume you knew everything? I chose you to be my proxy tonight because I thought you harbored suspicions, and I decided it was better to keep you close and find out what you know while I was at it. Well, I'm not going to say another word." She hunkered down with her hands covering her face, but Kitty persisted.

"You've told me too much now not to tell me the rest. You are clearly in great danger if Mrs. Montgomery knows that you gave away Lord Debenham's heir…for a diamond necklace."

Araminta dropped her hands and, in the first physical gesture ever between the two sisters, gripped Kitty's wrists. Her fingers were surprisingly strong, and Kitty wondered if she'd been in the habit of pinching her younger sister. She'd not seen much of Hetty but remembered when she'd spied at The Grange that the younger sister often looked sad, or as if she'd recently been in tears, however at Araminta's birthday she'd looked radiant. Now, when she chanced to see Lady Banks as she was now out in public, she looked the picture of newlywed bliss, and Kitty had heard remarks whispered about the uncommon fondness of Sir Aubrey for his unlikely wife.

Clearly, Araminta did not enjoy such marital felicity. Giving Kitty a final vengeful squeeze, she dropped her wrists and leaned back into the squabs. "You have no idea about it! The child was early and clearly not Lord Debenham's. Can you imagine what would have happened to it, or to me, if he'd learned the truth? His pride would not have borne being publicly cuckolded, yet as the child was born within wedlock, he'd have legally had to accept it. But he'd have had his revenge. Both on me and the child. What option did I have other than to ensure it went to a good home? One that your landlady found, and for which I paid handsomely. I can't tell you what trouble that diamond and ruby necklace has caused."

"Indeed," Kitty remarked, wryly, her thoughts nevertheless mostly consumed by the shock at learning this news. "But…but you *have* a child. One that Lord Debenham is happy to consider his heir."

"Yes, and I shall answer no questions about that. Suffice to say that Lord Debenham is satisfied."

"He's not kind to you?"

Araminta rolled her eyes. "No, he's not kind. In fact, I wish he were dead."

Not knowing what to say to such a terrible desire, Kitty peered a little closer and saw that she was biting her lip, clearly trying not to cry. Then Araminta burst out, "Promise me you'll not blackmail me! I truly thought you knew...had discovered the truth that night...and that it was you who'd sent the blackmail note."

"But you asked me to come with you."

"I'd thought to expose you. I expected no one would come at midnight, and then suddenly you'd announce that you knew everything."

"And then what were you going to do? Hit me over the head?"

Araminta let out an amused snort. "I hadn't thought that far. Actually I was going to propose that if I saw to you achieving your heart's desire, or something within my means to grant you, that you'd withdraw your threats to expose the truth about...you know."

"Well, it's beyond your power to grant me my heart's desire, since all I really want to do is marry Lord Silverton who is due to wed Miss Mandelton in a few weeks. And I want to see Lissa happy and able to marry Ralph. Those are the two things I want more than anything, but even though you're not in a position to grant those, I'm certainly not about to unmask you. I should warn you about Mrs. Montgomery, though. She seemed quite cowed when she left, but she's pure evil. I wouldn't trust her at all."

Kitty was still thinking about the child and that she should question Araminta more, but then the carriage came to an abrupt halt, and the jarvey called out that they were at their destination.

"Good night, Miss Bijou. You shall have to walk from here, I'm afraid. I do acknowledge that I owe you a debt of service, though." Araminta appeared distracted as she glanced up at the window of her townhouse. A light shone in a window of the second floor.

"Are you afraid?" Kitty had always been impulsive and knew she had no right to ask such a question.

Araminta looked at her for a long time, and a play of emotions crossed her face in the gaslit gloom. Then she laughed as she gripped the door frame. "I'm married to Lord Debenham. What could I possibly be afraid of? And now he's taking me to Lady Richmond's ball, where I shall dance the night away with not a care in the world, and people will whisper and wonder if I really am happy with a man who has such a sinister reputation, but then they will say, 'Well, lucky for Lady Debenham she produced an heir for her husband in a timely nine months. At least, she has done her duty.'" She leaned forward, gathering her cloak around her and preparing to quit the carriage as the jarvey stood with the door open, adding in a whisper, "And the fact I've done my duty is the *only* thing that keeps me safe from my husband's erratic temper."

CHAPTER 19

*A*nother London entertainment. It was strange how weary *not* dancing made Lissa feel. No one ever danced with the governess, and although Lissa would strenuously deny wanting to, the truth was that each time she accompanied Lucinda and Lady Julia to such events, she was ever more consumed by the idea that this was a world from which she was forever barred, and yet it was...Ralph's world.

"The girl is looking in fine form. Let us hope she behaves herself." Lissa glanced up at Lady Julia, who muttered this as she wafted past in crimson chiffon leaving the lingering scent of bergamot behind her; a musky, sultry scent that matched the look in her eye which she directed toward Lord Beecham whose side she now joined.

Lissa wondered what had happened that the pair had mended relations, since Lady Julia had returned recently from a few days visiting her husband at their country house. Certainly, she appeared to be in high spirits, the almost lighthearted atmosphere in the Beecham household a contrast to the heavy, recriminatory cloud that had lain so heavily upon the occupants before she'd gone away for her short sojourn.

Lissa nodded. Indeed, it seemed an answer from her wasn't required as Lady Julia was now occupied with far more interesting company. And indeed, wasn't that the way it was with Lissa. She was below anyone's notice—the drab, dowdily-dressed governess, whose duty was to keep an eye on her wayward charge while her own life slipped by.

"My Lord but you're a sight for sore eyes."

Self-contained she might be, but Lissa was unable to stop her gasp as she glanced up into the face of her own true love. Ralph smiled down at her, the familiar crease lines about his eyes making her want to trace them lovingly. Instead, she shook her head as he begged, "Stand up with me for this one?"

"You know I can't," she whispered, fearful their exchange might be noticed by anyone who mattered. "We're not supposed to know one another, Ralph." She lowered her eyes to the worn hem of her skirts beneath which even more worn slippers peeped. Only a few inches away were Ralph's well-polished shoes, and above that his finely-cut evening trousers. She slid her eyes upward again, thinking what a fine figure he cut and wondering how he dared—or even wanted to—court the unlovely governess she was.

"We're going to know one another all too well before the year is out, Miss Hazlett. I'm going to marry you," he vowed, bowing. "And soon! This waiting is killing me."

"Oh Ralph, it's killing me, too. And here I am, doing absolutely *nothing* that's making any difference at all when I simply want to throw myself into...doing *something*. Anything other than biding my time."

"You've already had one close call, my dearest. Stay safe, that's all I ask."

Lissa sent him a rueful smile. "I think I shall die of staying safe if such a thing is possible. Have no fear, Ralph. There is not the slightest bit of danger that threatens me. I just worry for you."

She glanced across the room to where Lord Debenham was, surprisingly, in the company of his wife. The pair had arrived shortly before, Araminta looking regal in a gown of gold net over a cream underslip. "Go, Ralph, before he sees you talking to me. Oh dear, Miss Lucinda is looking at us. I hope she doesn't ask questions."

She lowered her head, repelled by another sight of her worn dancing slippers, and wondering how she'd have felt had she donned the beautiful pale green confection Kitty had had delivered to her this evening. She'd been sorely tempted, at the same time as knowing it was totally impossible to appear dressed in public in the first stare. Think of the questions she'd be subjected to by Lady Julia and Miss Lucinda. Not to mention the suspicion Lord Beecham would harbor.

"Now there's a handsome couple." Lady Julia was back at Lissa's side, pointing now toward the dance floor. Lissa squinted and felt a curious emotion at the sight of Ralph partnering Lucinda in a quadrille. "The girl looks positively thrilled. Of course, she is not properly out, so I hope she doesn't set her sights on a sixth son when she could do better. Not much, mind you." She looked thoughtful. "Perhaps there's a match in it, after all. He has the name; she has the fortune."

"It's a first dance!" Lissa said with far too much energy, for Lady Julia blinked in surprise before, to her relief, dropping the subject.

"Of course it is, and I'm getting carried away. Goodness but I hope we get that girl fired off before I have to endure a second season."

Lissa was still feeling unaccountably distressed as Lady Julia drifted away. So much so that when she saw Ralph disappear into the passage, she incautiously rose and followed him after whispering to Lucinda that she needed to attend to nature's call.

He turned when he was halfway down the passage having sensed her presence, his delight transparent as he came toward her. "My dear girl!" He broke off, masking his feelings as a gentleman entered the corridor, but as soon as he'd passed, Ralph furtively gripped Lissa's fingertips and gave them a squeeze before dropping them.

"Is everything all right?"

"Oh Ralph, I saw you dancing with Miss Lucinda, and then Lady Julia started speculating out loud about the merits of a possible match between you, since she has a fortune and you —"

"Miss Lucinda Martindale?" He looked as if he'd never heard

anything so outrageous. "And me? Why, I've never met her and we danced but once. Surely Lissa, you can't believe I'd…"

Lissa felt all the fight and energy and optimism she'd ever had drain from her. "Oh Ralph, I'm no good for you. You say you want to marry me, and nothing would make me happier, but the truth is that I have not a penny to my name and, in fact, no name to speak of. There are too many obstacles—"

"*What* are you saying?" He was clearly incredulous. And hurt, too, Lissa realized as he added, "Do you doubt my ability to rise in the world fast enough to enable us to marry before you're too old to hobble up the aisle? Lissa, have patience."

"Oh Ralph, I have that, and I have faith in you in abundance. But…" she was trying not to cry, she who was so brave, "…when I saw you with Miss Lucinda it opened my eyes to how many other eligible young ladies—and their mamas—would be eyeing you. And it made me realize that your family would be so much more amenable to you making a match with them. *Anyone* other than me. My father might be Lord Partingon, but that makes not a jot of difference for he's never acknowledged me, and he won't, and nor would it make any difference if he did for I was born in sin and my crime is too great. No matter what I do, I can never escape that fact. One day, the time might come when you have to choose between your family and me, and I can't bear to be the wedge that—"

She couldn't finish for he'd swiftly dipped his head and stopped her with a very firm, albeit very brief, kiss. There was also a grim determination in his entire attitude, as he canvassed their surroundings before seizing her hand and whisking her through the closest door.

They happened to find themselves in a small, chilly antechamber that was in total darkness, which is perhaps why Lissa completely lost her head, she thought later, and succumbed to Ralph's passionate kiss. If she'd had any consciousness of her surroundings, she knew she'd not have twined her hands behind his neck and pulled him down to her with such single-mindedness, as if to wring from their brief opportunity every last drop of passion.

She didn't care. Neither then nor later, for the flare of feeling and the conflagration of need swept away her despondency, replacing it with fervent determination. This was *so* right. She and Ralph were of one mind, and someday the church would unite them legally as one.

"Oh Ralph, I do love you so very much," she whispered when they drew apart breathlessly.

"Are you now convinced that my heart belongs only to you?"

His tone was back to normal—laconic, slightly amused, and ever so reassuring. His feelings for her had not changed one jot, and nor would they.

She reached up to touch his face, gently contouring the planes of his forehead, nose, and lips. Being unable to see him charged her senses, and she felt a calm sort of happiness bubble up inside her. "One of the things I love so much about you is that you are so entirely dependable, my darling."

"And not likely to be any different, where you're concerned. Now, let me tidy your hair."

"You can't see me in the dark, and besides, I'm wearing a hideous cap. It's a wonder you can bear to have anything to do with such an unprepossessing creature.

"To tell the truth, it's rather a blessing you're required to appear so downtrodden and mousey, I've always thought because you are far and away the beauty of your family."

"Heavens! Kitty is the golden-haired girl and considered one of the most beautiful women in London!"

"Clearly, you want me to elaborate." There was a hint of laughter in his tone. "Kitty is lovely, granted, but I was thinking about Lady Debenham, whom you so closely resemble, and if you were wearing the gown she is tonight and she the hideous bonnet that obscures your beauty, no one would look at her twice, and I'd not get a look in to ask you to dance."

"Hush!" Lissa said worriedly. "My name is never to be linked with hers. Think of the scandal!"

"Scandal? To whom? Why be concerned now, about what will be made public when we wed."

Lissa didn't know what to think about that. Her mind was in a whirl of...she didn't know what. Possibilities, fears, and doubts.

Then Ralph put his arms about her and drew her close for a parting embrace, and all her concerns drained away as she relaxed against his comforting, familiar chest.

"Everything will be all right, Lissa," he soothed, kissing her gently upon the forehead so that she felt the warmth and comfort only he'd ever given her seep all the way down to her toes. "Believe me."

And she did.

ARAMINTA HAD NOT COME SO FAR IN LIFE WITHOUT HAVING HONED AN unsurpassed ability to put on a brave face when all seemed totally wretched. Or rather, *was* wretched. She thought this as she glided through Lady Richmond's ballroom, graciously acknowledging the numerous gestures of esteem sent her way. Ah, but the admiration in the eyes of the gentlemen was balm to her troubled soul, for the events of this evening had left her deeply rattled.

Her secret was dangerously at risk of being exposed, and she had not the first idea what she was going to do about it. Then she was reminded of the next disaster in her life when the Earl of Moncreith murmured, "By Jove, but you've returned to us more beautiful than ever." Of course, he was referring to the fact she'd so recently had a baby, and Araminta felt like dissolving into a puddle of woe and despair right then and there. For in eight months or less she'd be suffering the agonies of childbirth, but even worse, she'd be thickening in just weeks, and then once again she'd become invisible to all these men who looked at her with such interest.

"Lady Debenham, you look ravishing."

It was Lord Ludbridge, as boyishly generous with his praise as he'd ever been. "I was waiting for your husband to claim you, but he appears to be occupied with Lord Smythe and Sir Smithers."

"Plotting revolution or planning whom next to blackmail, no

doubt," Araminta said with a curl of her lip before drawing Teddy into a quieter corner. "Oh, my dearest Teddy, I do hate him so much but what can I do. You're not going to run away with me, are you?"

"Your capacity to shock me never abates, my dear," he said, blinking. "I really can't tell whether you're funning half the time." Two furrows appeared between his brows. "You know I'd do anything for you, but in this instance, I think I must save you from your own impulsiveness."

"Then when do you suggest?" She glanced across at the three men. "I am a prisoner of my husband's desires. I wasn't funning before. I was speculating. You only have to ask your brother to know that my husband is up to his neck in nefarious activities. What happens if he's apprehended and attained? Why, his estate and whatever else he owns would be forfeited to the Crown, and his children could never inherit."

"Why, *then* I should come to your rescue."

"Why not now?"

"Because I would not ruin you." His look became more serious. "I am devoted to ensuring your happiness, and that means ensuring your reputation is not harmed by any possibly rash and impulsive acts on your part."

Araminta gripped his wrist briefly. "Meet me in secret somewhere after this, Teddy. Well, perhaps not tonight because Debenham is here, but tomorrow. Please say you'll do that?"

"Alone?"

"Well, I wasn't suggesting you invite your brother for a midnight picnic. Of course, alone. You've *never* come to me alone though you've suggested often enough you want to." Just the thought made her pulse beat faster.

He swallowed, clearly liking the idea though nervous to say so aloud. "I want to help you, Araminta. But getting you the letter solves nothing."

"No, and I understand it's not enough to help make a case against him, which is good." Araminta lowered her voice. "I need to protect

Debenham if I'm to protect myself. Darling Teddy, if you really want to help me, I need you to find out from your brother exactly what information is held against Debenham, and what they might be following up. Please, will you do that for me? Find out?"

CHAPTER 20

*L*issa was determined not to ask Lucinda about the source of her deep sighs as she brushed out the long locks of her wayward charge. Clearly, the girl was dying to be quizzed, but Lissa was not going to give her the satisfaction.

"Did you enjoy your evening last night?" There, that was as far as she'd go. "Were there any young men who caught your fancy?"

"Lady Julia is dying to marry me off so she can enjoy Lord Beecham's exclusive company. She detests me, have you noticed?"

Lissa had noticed, but she said only, "Lady Julia thinks of little other than herself."

"Exactly, which is why I must be removed. But I'm not going without having my revenge."

"That's rather extreme," Lissa murmured. "Surely making a match that suits you would suffice? You need to find a husband, so if you can do so this season and please your heart, there's no need for revenge."

Lucinda sniffed. "Those excellent pictures you draw, Miss Hazlett. How fast do you sketch?"

Oh, lord. Lissa hadn't expected that. "I don't sketch very often, Miss Lucinda," she demurred.

"Would you, though? If I could get you something you wanted?

Like a few hours to spend with your young man without anyone knowing?"

Lissa stared into the girl's speculative green eyes which immediately danced with delight at supposedly having uncovered Lissa's secret.

"You think I don't notice anyone else around me? I saw the way you looked at that young man and then pretended you didn't care when he asked me to dance."

Lissa hadn't realized she was shaking her head so vehemently, but Lucinda just laughed again. "Really, it's nothing to do with me, so there's no need to look so afraid. I won't tell Lady Julia if that's what you're worried about because I know you're not allowed followers, though of course, you'd know you can't marry a man like that in your situation. And I'm sorry for it, truly I am."

She didn't look particularly sorry, but then she also didn't look as if she was vengefully motivated. She went on, "So now that I've proved I'm rather good at noticing things you'd not expect me to notice, I thought you might consider obliging me with a little game I'm playing that regards Lady Julia and Lord Debenham."

"Lord Debenham? What has he to do with any of this?" Lissa hoped her voice didn't sound as strangled as she feared it did.

"Well, that's the thing. I really don't know." Lucinda frowned. "It's just that I saw him address Lady Julia while they were both in the ballroom in a casual fashion which is nothing to take note of. Only then she looked furious, then afraid, and then she handed him a small package which he put in his pocket before she flounced off. So I wondered what—"

"She handed him a package? How big?" Lissa's mind was buzzing. Money? Jewelry? So Lady Julia was being blackmailed! Here was something at last that she could pass on to Ralph. There were others, but Ralph was becoming increasingly frustrated at not knowing names. Finally, Lissa could tell him about Lady Julia.

"It could have contained bank notes, or it could have contained her diamond earrings," said Lucinda as if she'd been reading her mind. "I'd happily see her hand over every single thing of value she had, but really, I suppose what's more important is why she's afraid of Lord Debenham. I heard her whispering to Lord Beecham the other day, and Lord Debenham's name came up. Neither of them like him. In fact, I think they're both afraid of him. I would be too, for that matter. He looks like the devil. I can't imagine why that Lady Debenham wanted to marry him in the first place, except that of course he's very rich and has a title."

Lissa let her prattle on while she assimilated this information.

"You've not said anything, Miss Hazlett. Will you oblige me by paying close attention to Lady Julia and Lord Beecham? I'm sure you're just as interested, now, to know what might be in the wind. If I can only find out what it is that Lady Julia is so afraid of, perhaps I might find a way of ridding this household of her. You'd like that as much as me, I know."

It was true. Lissa detested the woman. "And if you do that, I'll see that you enjoy a couple of hours free time when I'll pretend you're drilling me in deportment or some other wasted pursuit." She smiled up at Lissa, satisfaction written all over her pretty face. *And it was a pretty face*, Lissa thought with a pang. Lucinda had all the requirements for being a prime catch.

Just the kind of young lady Ralph's parents would be delighted at him snaring.

Nevertheless, all that mattered was that Ralph was as loyal and committed to them marrying as he ever was. And Lissa was nearly bursting with excitement at being able to assist him further in his dealings surrounding Lord Debenham.

So when Lady Julia and Lord Beecham were cozily ensconced in the drawing room listening to Lucinda play the piano—quite nicely, in fact,— Lissa ensured she was discreetly positioned within earshot.

Discretion was her hallmark, as Ralph had remarked. Never once had Lissa given cause for eyebrow-raising through any gesture or remark. She was as beyond notice as the furniture. While Ralph thought her beauty equal to Araminta's—bless him! —Lady Julia clearly didn't perceive Lissa as a threat. Lissa was just the down-trodden governess beneath notice. Why, she'd not recognized Lissa as

Araminta's companion the year prior when they'd chanced upon each other in a glovemaker's on Bond Street.

Now, as Lucinda gently played for her own enjoyment, her fingers running over the keys, and Lissa plied her needle and thread, Lady Julia and Lord Beecham cozied up to one another. If Lissa were lucky, they'd forget she was there.

"You gave him what he asked?" This was Lord Beecham, his voice low, the bristles of his mustache twitching in outrage.

"I did, Beechy darling, and Archie is as grateful as I am for averting scandal."

"Except that it won't avert it, will it, my dear?"

Lady Julia looked distressed. "But it has to. He must be satisfied with that." She smoothed her golden hair and took a deep breath. "Anyway, he can prove nothing. I paid him the money so he'd withdraw publication of his nasty little allegations from the Independent Whig."

"Muckraking newspaper! No one believes a word of what they read it in but it holds such sway! Well, there are whisperings you're not alone. Someone is ferreting out secrets and passing them on to Debenham, who is making hay while the sun shines."

"Are you suggesting we go to the authorities? Beechy, I couldn't possibly."

"I'm suggesting we find our own means of dealing with the matter, once and for all." Lord Beecham looked angry. "He and I have done business together. We've dined and gambled together. He let me believe he was my friend, but I think the time has come to show him I can be as good a friend to him as he is to me."

"Beechy, you look like a man not to be crossed when you bare your teeth like that," Lady Julia tittered. "I can't imagine what you have in mind."

Lissa wondered, too, what he might have in mind, or whether it was all big talk designed to impress his lady love. Lady Julia put her hand up to trace the line of his sideburns. "You are quite magnificent, my lord. I've not met anyone to equal you."

"Not Ledger, certainly. And not that puling ninnyhammer, what was his name—Edgar? Not even Stephen Cranborne." His lip twitched. "Gad's teeth but I could tear his head from his neck every time I see him. Good thing I'm more motivated by the need to get rid of Debenham."

Lissa tried to sink farther into the cushions behind her. What was this about Stephen Cranborne and Lady Julia? Or was Lissa jumping to wild conclusions?

"I'm sure we're not the only ones who'd like to see Debenham at the end of a noose. Alas, securing evidence is likely to see too many of us floundering in the quagmire of what we don't want made public. I think Debenham might just find himself in a sticky situation from which not even he can extricate himself."

Now Lissa knew she really had to make Lucinda honor her promise to let her have a few hours free so she could go and tell Ralph everything about this incendiary conversation.

"WELL, WELL, WHAT HAVE WE HERE?"

Lissa smiled up into Ralph's surprised face as he removed her black cloak, his gaze traveling from the hem of her lovely apple-green muslin to the simple twist of her topknot, so different from the severe style she generally adopted.

Putting his hand under her elbow, he led her deeper into the tiny dwelling where Mrs. Nipkins, who was busy stirring a pot over the fireplace, let out a noise of the greatest appreciation.

"I think you'll agree that I've discovered something very interesting, Ralph." Lissa hugged herself, she was so excited. "Aren't you going to ask me what it is?"

"First I want to feast my eyes on you." He untied the ribbons beneath her chin. "You look even lovelier than you did the night I rescued you from your upturned carriage."

"Well, I've never appeared to such advantage since the night I borrowed Miss Maria Lamont's ball gown, that's true." She grinned. "For more than a year, I've been the mousey governess—"

"Waiting to be revealed for the swan through my clever offices."

"Only it's my clever offices that's going to give you the information you need, which, when added to the letter, will convict Lord Debenham."

"Oh my, Larissa, please sit down. Believe me, I'm all ears and only too ready to cede to you the highest accolades for your clever sleuthing. Truly, you put my poor efforts into the shade. I work for the fellow and have found nothing."

Lissa seated herself in the chair Ralph pulled out and removed her gloves. "Modesty becomes you, Ralph," she said. "I should like to hear accolades rain down on my shoulders. Oh, but Mrs. Nipkins...Ralph! It was quite extraordinary how unguarded Lady Julia and Lord Beecham were as they discussed the fact that Lady Julia is being blackmailed—"

"By Debenham?"

"Yes, but it gets better. Lady Julia and...you'll never guess it...*Mr. Cranborne*. Mr. Stephen Cranborne. Furthermore, Lord Beecham sounded quite threatening. As if he meant to do Lord Debenham harm. But of course, that would be no good as you want to ensure that Debenham gets his comeuppance through official channels. Ralph, did you hear anything I had to say?"

He looked up, his eyes alight. "Every word, my love. I'm still digesting the fact that Stephen Cranborne had dealings with Lady Julia Ledger that Lord Debenham found it worthy to blackmail him over. It doesn't sound like it was a mere liaison."

"You don't think that Lady Julia being married is enough?"

"I do not, and I will have to quiz him on it. He admitted he was being blackmailed, but even I had not the clever cunning and charm to prize the truth out of him. Obviously, when he learns what you've told me it'll be another matter."

"Perhaps that's something I can discover."

"While I don't wish to sound dampening, I think you've learned about as much as you're likely to. Lady Julia isn't going to go into details. Obviously, Beecham knows what the story is. I believe he's besotted with her. No, Stephen Cranborne must make a clean breast of it when I approach him. Likely we'll be able to keep his secret and charge Debenham with three counts of extortion and, with the testimony of Smythe and Buzby, add a charge of high treason. My dear, you've done very well."

"'N 'ow is that sister of yers?" Mrs. Nipkins asked, leaning across to pour them both a cup of tea.

Lissa looked confused. "Lady Debenham?"

"Lordy, no. The sweet-natured one. That famous actress wot's so determined ter get ter the bottom o' all this."

"I don't know that's quite how I'd describe her." Lissa smiled at Ralph, but Mrs. Nipkins clicked her tongue.

"If ever I seen someun wantin' ter do good 'n atone fer her wicked ways—not that they's so wicked in me book as I dunno 'ow else a girl's ter get enough victuals 'n a roof over 'er 'ead if she don't 'ave support —it were 'er."

"She wants to because she thinks it'll somehow make Lord Silverton more kindly disposed toward her, but it's a hopeless situation and sadly, the sooner she realizes it the better."

"You're very uncharitable toward your sister," Ralph remarked, stirring his tea. "Why do you resent her?"

"I...I don't," Lissa defended herself. "I was always the first to see that Kitty was all right. I was the one who ensured she had a clean apron, and a decent pair of shoes. I did her hair and dried her tears. Not Mama. But then Kitty ran away without ever telling anyone anything. The agonized letters I got from Mama were heartrending. Kitty has always thought only of herself, and now she's enjoying the high life."

"She chose her path just as you chose yours. I do think Kitty deserves a bit more sympathy. But let us not stray off the topic. You've been a wonder, my dear. And if I could raise my glass with something stronger, I would."

CHAPTER 21

The season was coming to an end, and Kitty's performance had been lauded in all the gossip sheets and newspapers. She was looking forward to a rest between performances, but worried about the length of time she'd be without income.

Thoughts of Silverton tugged at her, but she forced them away. Within two weeks he'd be married. The thought made her want to weep, but she was a professional. Each night she forced herself to smile and carry on.

The public appreciated her efforts. There were often tokens of regard from all manner of gentlemen that made her fellow actors envious.

Rarely, though, did she receive something as lavish as the bouquet that arrived for her one Thursday afternoon.

Kitty felt the thorns pricking into her as she read the card for the third time. It was an unusually lavish bunch of roses—long-stemmed, with blooms that smelled as if they'd been picked that afternoon.

"Why, they're lovely! But what are you looking like that for?" Jennie asked as she passed by. "Lord Nash wants you back again? Or is Lord Silverton asking you to marry ím, though I don't think you look too joyful about it."

Kitty didn't reply as she put down the bouquet and started to dress. If only it were Lord Nash. She knew how to manage him.

But Lord Debenham? Why would Lord Debenham wish for her company? And with such an offering? Surely he couldn't be thinking...

It was a horrifying thought. No, she didn't want to imagine he thought anything of her other than an accomplished professional. Still, the churning in the pit of her stomach didn't abate. Lord Debenham was not a man to admire anyone or anything publicly without wanting something.

So what did he want of Kitty? And did she have the courage to meet him, as he'd requested?

Was it something to do with the necklace? Did he know of her desire to find incriminating information about him? A tremor of fear ran through her. She wanted nothing to do with the man, and yet he desired to meet her after the performance. Could she somehow slip away before he arrived?

By the time the performance ended, Kitty had bolstered her courage. She'd remembered her duty to her sister and she was ready. Lissa had been the one person in her life on whom she could rely, and clearly, Lissa felt that Kitty had let her down by running off to London. Well, Lissa needed help in finding her heart's desire, and Kitty had been handed an opportunity on a platter. She'd find out exactly what Debenham wanted. Whether he intended to threaten or bully, she would deftly question him so that she had something of value to deliver to Lissa.

Knowing that her sister would be proud of her went some way to mitigating her terror.

However, her training enabled her to hide her fear when Lord Debenham entered her dressing room in the wake of one of the chorus girls who'd brought news that he was here.

She'd been expecting the usual fearsome scowl, something to indicate he was the devil incarnate as she'd always thought him, but instead, he appeared urbane and pleasant humored.

"Divine as always, Miss Bijou. I am a great admirer of yours having seen every performance since you've been in London. It if had been possible, I'd have told you so the night you performed at The Grange."

"I'm flattered, my lord." Kitty made sure she looked as relaxed and at her ease as possible, and with just an enquiring half-smile upon her face. A man like this one thrived on fear. She didn't tell him she was honored by his attention because she was determined not to pander to him. She indicated the hustle and bustle about her with a wave of her hand. "As you can see, I am very busy, but I do have a few moments to spare."

He looked surprised and then burst out laughing. "Why, I had not expected you to be amusing to boot. Beautiful, aware of your attractions, perhaps vain like my wife, but not amusing!" He slapped his thigh as he sank down on the window seat, the only place in the room available to seat himself. "I'd like to take you to supper, Miss Bijou; that's why I'm here."

Kitty could not have been more astonished. "I'm afraid that's not possible, my lord."

"You are already engaged? Of course, I'd realized that was entirely possible—"

"No, no, I'm just very tired, and I have another performance tomorrow."

This didn't go down well, but he recovered quickly and bared his teeth in a rictus of a smile. "You are teasing me, Miss Bijou. I'm unaccustomed to it. For some reason, many people seem to fear me."

"Fear you, my lord?" She raised her eyebrows, glancing at him above the tips of her fingers which she was busy examining as she tried to gauge what this conversation was all about. "And why might that be?"

"You've not heard rumors about me, Miss Bijou?"

"I hear rumors about everybody of consequence, including you, but rumors are worthless unless they're substantiated. Just because I've heard that you've flown to the moon in a pale pink sailing boat doesn't mean it's true."

"I like talking to you, Miss Bijou. By gad, I do! Let me take you Angeline's for champagne and oysters. Surely you are hungry. Surely you'd like to toast tonight's success with the finest champagne. I'm a generous man."

"I'm sure you are, my lord, but really, I do need my sleep though I thank you for your kind offer."

The more she demurred the keener he became. It was quite extraordinary. Eventually, Kitty realized—quite to her surprise—that she'd whipped up the interest of this man in a way she'd not have managed had she agreed to accompany him from the outset. And surely champagne and oysters in a public place would not be dangerous? She'd ensure he drank the lion's share and then he might let his guard down. She might discover something valuable.

They were on their second bottle in a darkened corner of the intimate dining salon and, as Kitty had hoped, Lord Debenham was in an expansive mood.

"Ah, Miss Bijou, it's been a long time since I enjoyed a woman's company this much. We must do it again!"

She shook her head. "I think that would be unwise. You have family commitments, and I work hard to ensure my reputation is free from the insinuation of casual liaisons, if I may speak bluntly."

He looked at her admiringly. "Are you suggesting you'd only be interested in a liaison that was *not* casual?"

"Good lord, sir. I meant nothing of the sort!" Kitty heard her voice as a strangled thread of sound. "I mean that I am not interested in any kind of liaison." With Lord Debenham? The idea was enough to make her run for the hills. "Besides, the gossips say you and your wife are uncommonly fond of each other."

The gossips said anything *but*, however, Kitty was clutching at straws.

He gave a snide laugh. "I can't imagine which gossips those might have been. Have you seen my wife?"

"She is uncommonly beautiful, my lord. The toast of London, I believe."

"Uncommonly vain and self-centered, more like it. Now that she is breeding again she won't want me to touch her. And a man like me needs...affection."

Kitty's gasped. Was he truly suggesting what she thought he was?

"You...know nothing about me, my lord," she managed, her mouth dry.

"Enough to be entranced by the persona I saw on stage, and my favorable impression has been more than bolstered by our little tete-a-tete this evening."

He moved closer toward her across the small table, and carefully laid his large hand upon her small gloved one where it rested beside the single guttering candle.

"I know you were distressed by the defection of your erstwhile protector, Lord Silverton. I know him well, and I abhor such inconstancy." He shook his head, his tone more honeyed but tinged with disgust as he added, "As if his marriage should prevent him maintaining his obligation toward you. Though I daresay he's pinched in the pocket when it comes to looking after the needs of wife and mistress. Which leaves you, Miss Bijou, in very serious need of a protector. I know the pittance paid to artists like you. I know very well that maintenance is impossible without the...ah...assistance of men prepared to be generous. And I am prepared to be very generous, Kitty La Bijou."

He leaned back and looked at her expectantly.

Kitty gathered up her reticule and stood up. "Thank you for a pleasant evening, my lord. I shall, of course, consider your kind and...generous...offer, but now I must return for some much-needed rest."

She didn't wait for his response. How could she when she was quailing like a jelly inside? Only when she turned the key in her front door, which she shut firmly behind her as her heart rate subsided, did she realize she'd gained absolutely nothing of any value whatsoever from him. This should have been a time when she was at her most sophisticated; quizzing him like a consummate professional.

Instead, she'd squandered her opportunity and let everyone down.

ARAMINTA CHECKED HER APPEARANCE ONCE LAST TIME IN THE MIRROR and prepared to meet Teddy. At last, she was about to experience the bliss she so deserved, but which Debenham had denied her through forcing her to marry him. Oh, Teddy had been reluctant when she'd suggested a secret meeting at the ball a few nights previously. Naturally, he was afraid of Debenham. Everyone was. But didn't that spice up the assignation? The secrecy and wickedness of it were half the appeal. Teddy, of course, represented the ideal—safety, unconditional admiration, a title, and grand estate. She had him twisted around her little finger, and although she'd not had confirmation that he'd, in fact, meet her at Madame Mirabeau's salon, she had no doubt he'd be there.

Unlike Debenham. He was so unpredictable. And selfish. When he'd caught her purging her stomach, he'd correctly deduced the reason, but instead of joyful anticipation of the happy event in what she guessed would be a little under eight months, his lip had curled as he'd focused on her mid-region. "I daresay I'd better make the most of my conjugal rights in the next few weeks," he'd said. "You're a bore when you're breeding, Araminta; never wanting me to touch you, as I recall. Well, you can stay in the country this time."

"The Grange?" It's where she'd given birth—or close to—only several months before, and she'd never been more relieved to go home.

"Not this time. I think it's time to unleash your amiable disposition on my family. I have an irascible uncle and uncommonly exacting grandmother in residence at Marsh Manor who deserve to know you better."

Araminta's distress at the idea had only fed his ugly mood. Well, if Araminta had anything to do with it, it wouldn't be long before Debenham had no influence in her life. Somehow she was going to find a way to be with Teddy.

When she told Teddy this, ensconced in a private antechamber at Madame Mirabeau's, he was a little incredulous.

"My dear girl, short of Debenham...er...dying, I don't see how that's possible." He had her sitting upon his lap now. That is, she'd sat herself upon his lap after she'd taken him by the hand and forcefully led him to this room. Madame Mirabeau had private rooms for just this function she'd learned, and she was not the only dissatisfied matron who utilized the weekly Thursday salons for pursuits other than a lively discussion on politics. Araminta didn't know the first thing about politics, and she didn't care to learn, either.

"But that's exactly it, Teddy darling. Debenham has made so many enemies I believe it's quite possible he might...well, come to a sticky end."

"Good God, are you talking about murder?"

Araminta shrugged, not caring that Teddy was clearly quite horrified. But then she thought she'd better appear deeply troubled, at least, so she rustled up a tear to augment a suitably terrified expression and whispered, "Indeed, Teddy, there are people who have expressly threatened Debenham. They think he's done terrible things—"

"Well, my brother is one of those people, and he's trying to find evidence of wrongdoing, which makes this..." he indicated their close proximity "...deuced awkward."

Araminta cupped his face and softly touched her lips to his. She wriggled a little in his lap and was delighted that, despite his words and apparent reluctance, he was highly aroused.

"Awkward for me if Debenham is convicted, for then I'd be humiliated and perhaps left with no support. But Teddy, I'm terrified that Debenham is a target for wrongdoers like...like Lord Smythe and that nasty little shoemaker and grubby pamphleteer, Buzby. They come to the house and pretend to be allies, but the truth is, I think they have ill intentions toward him. I tell him he shouldn't trust them, but I wouldn't be surprised if one of them does something... well, terrible."

"Violence?"

"That wouldn't surprise me at all. But what can I do?" She started to tremble which helped bring on a bout of tears, and Teddy always responded well to tears. That's why she loved him so much. He was so very susceptible and so chivalrous for he drew her to him and kissed away the moisture from her cheeks, which immediately led to a mutual escalation of desire—exactly what Araminta had intended, for if ever she needed an ally, she needed one now, and Teddy answered her every need.

So, soon his hands were roaming over her body—the body that would soon become bloated and disgusting and to which she must introduce him now in all its perfection—though she must do it in the shadows to hide the lingering evidence of recent childbirth.

And when he showed signs of demurring at the last moment, she guided his hands so he could feel the heat between her legs that signaled her desire, and then he was undone. And Araminta helped to make him undone, greedily unbuttoning his trousers, grasping his member which was already rigid, so that he needed little encouragement after that to throw caution to the wind.

Soon they were both naked and writhing with passion in one another's arms, and Araminta could feel the tension and fear ebbing away. What better ally could she have than earnest Lord Ludbridge, brother of the man who posed the greatest threat to Debenham and thus to herself?

KITTY TRIED NOT TO LOOK AS UNCOMFORTABLE AS SHE FELT, BRUSHING out her hair in her dressing room as Lord Debenham sat on a chair nearby, waxing lyrical on the benefits of allying herself to him. She'd been adamant that she wanted none of his generosity; no, she could manage just fine without his help.

And then he said, "You are a stubborn little thing, and it's clear you are nursing a terrible anger toward the man who's wounded you. You'd like to see him brought down, wouldn't you?"

Kitty was about to refute this when he added, "If you want revenge, surely you can see how much I am in a position to help you?" His tone became more honeyed, and he put out his hand to stroke her hair.

"Revenge?" She had to repeat the word for it was such a foreign concept that she would ever desire revenge. Not upon darling Silverton. She was about to use this as an argument to temper Lord Debenham's overtures, which were becoming increasingly unpalatable, when again he interrupted, saying in a low voice, "A little manufactured evidence might well do the trick." He raised an eyebrow. "If your maid had done her job properly, Silverton would be feeling the heat by now—well and truly. But you were in love with him then, weren't you? I didn't realize it—nor how important that little aspect would be in the whole scheme of things, but now I can see how much value we can provide each other—mutually. I can supply a means whereby you see Silverton is toppled from his comfortable perch, while you can safely enjoy the spectacle from the comfort of what I'm prepared to provide you."

After what seemed like an eternity he asked, "Would you like that? To see Silverton brought low and to still enjoy a man's generosity? Or are you too much the romantic, Miss Bijou, and think I should go on bended knee and beg for your favors. I do have my limits."

She held her brush mid-air and gave him a contemplative look. "I'd never thought of such a thing, my lord. Revenge?"

"Never thought of having your revenge? Why, I thought that's what every spurned woman dreamed of."

Suddenly, Kitty laughed. "Revenge!" She said it on a gurgle of amusement, but he took her seriously and laughed with her, and that's when Kitty realized how much power she had over Lord Debenham.

For if he really thought she would seize such an opportunity, then she had all the evidence she needed to pass on to Ralph. She just needed to see how Debenham concocted this plan.

"Come, let us go to supper, Miss La Bijou, and we can mull over the details. Madame Mirabeau's?"

She'd be taking a risk, but she had to if she were going to find a way of helping Silverton escape his nemesis, and help Lissa and Ralph achieve their ends.

So, smiling to cover her fear, she accompanied him in his carriage and issued out into the crisp night air and up the steps to the famous salon where she prayed she'd not see someone she knew.

Lord Debenham ordered champagne once more, and after a few glasses, Kitty was feeling far braver, though far from allowing his

Lordship the license he obviously desired. For when he suggested they repair to one of the private parlors Kitty shook her head. "Not yet, my lord. I am not one to rush into encounters and besides, you have not yet explained how I might find my revenge."

"A woman after my own heart. Hear the bargain first and then decide if the gains are worth it." He leaned across the table and ran a finger lightly down her cheek. "I think the most innocent looking are the most dangerous. I wouldn't want to be in Silverton's shoes for I imagine you've already plotted a fine revenge. So I shall have to persuade you of the merits of my little proposal."

"And what might that be, my lord?"

What on earth might Lord Debenham be concocting? She'd wanted to leap up in outrage, but now she was all ears.

He took a sip, considering. "Surely, my dear, you have run over the possibilities. Losing a lot of money can hurt. I know his Lordship is plumpish in the pocket, but he can't afford to throw away his blunt now that he has the upkeep of a plain wife—yes, it has to be conceded. What Miss Mandelton might offer in terms of pliability and amiability she lacks in looks. Silverton will soon cast his gaze elsewhere, and then he'll have rather large expenses, won't he?"

Kitty considered this. "I don't know how I might achieve *that*. I mean, see that he lost a great deal of money." She looked innocently at him. There, let him suggest something.

Lord Debenham examined the moons of his right hand. "Perhaps during your intimacy with his Lordship, you've learned something he may wish to keep secret, Miss Bijou."

Kitty feigned ignorance. "And if I had, how will that lose him a great deal of money?"

Lord Debenham chuckled. "Ah, you really are either the innocent...or the opposite," he added thoughtfully. "My dear, secrets are worth a great deal of money."

"Blackmail?" Kitty gasped and shook her head. "I couldn't possibly blackmail Lord Silverton. He'd immediately suspect who was responsible for the leak, and then what do you suppose would happen to me?" She needed to appear self-interested and doubtful. Lord

Debenham would be less suspicious than if she eagerly complied with his every suggestion. For now she realized how important it was for Lord Debenham to finally involve her in the trade of secrets with which he was lining his pockets. This was what would implicate him. This is what Lissa and Ralph were after, but it would be Kitty who'd release them all from their burdens. For once, Kitty would be the sister who saved the day.

"Yes, blackmail, my dear Kitty. Tell me what you know about Lord Silverton that he might be willing to pay to withhold. Simple. Pillow talk is the best means of gaining such information."

"Pillow talk? How would you know, my lord?" Kitty angled an impish look at him, and to her surprise, he obliged her like a lamb. But then, men like Debenham loved to brag about their exploits.

"In the golden afterglow of a night of fleshly pleasures, it's astonishing how forthcoming a satisfied man can be."

Kitty frowned, feigning ignorance. "So you've divulged secrets you've regretted in such instances?"

"Lord, girl, what do you think?" His frown was swept away as he chuckled. "You were funning me; I see that now. No, I have girls who are only too willing to offer me the secrets they've discovered when entertaining certain high-placed gentlemen. It's a lucrative pastime, I assure you, and one from which we can both profit, Miss Bijou." He reached across to touch the fur tippet around her neck, then gently caressed her cheek. Kitty closed her eyes, pretending to relish the experience while her insides churned with fear and revulsion.

"You enjoy nice things, don't you, Miss Bijou."

"Oh yes," she whispered, imbuing her words with a breathlessness he might easily mistake for sexual longing.

And being the kind of man he was, he did.

"Well then, tell me what you know about Lord Silverton, and I can make sure you enjoy lots of nice things. Those who fear me do so for a reason, but those who please me know that I can be a very generous man."

Kitty thought wildly. What would satisfy Lord Debenham that she had an axe to grind with Silverton? What did she know of his past exploits that she'd be willing to offer Debenham?

Slowly, she said, "I was very relieved to learn my maid had been unsuccessful in making use of some letters that Mrs. Montgomery—I believe it was—had ordered be secreted in his study. Apparently, they'd been written by him some while ago to a certain prominent MP's wife and had been stolen." She shook her head and added, "But Dorcas confessed and since, at the time, I truly believed Silverton was going to marry me, it was a huge relief to me."

"It wasn't enough, in any case, to make Silverton cough up the blunt. He had less to lose than the lady in question. Think, Miss Bijou." He leaned across the table and looked into Kitty's eyes. "What do you know of Silverton's exploits that would be so embarrassing or terrible that he would be prepared to part with a great deal of money to spare the public. Or is he so snowy-white that not even you, who know him intimately, can come up with anything?"

Kitty thought hard. She bit her lip. Then she reached across the table and said softly, "Silverton is a spy."

Debenham blinked. It was the only indication that her response had made any impact. Then he put his head on one side and looked at her inquiringly.

Kitty thought even more wildly. Of course, Silverton wasn't a spy, but if she chose the most far-fetched reason he might be blackmailed, Debenham would really think it worth demanding ransom to keep it secret.

"A spy for the British government," she whispered. "He is investigating a matter that has confounded the authorities, but I believe he is on the cusp of discovery." She sat back in satisfaction. "I think he might just be willing to pay quite a lot of money to keep *that* secret, don't you think?"

CHAPTER 22

itty reached her home much later than she'd anticipated, and very much excited by her adventures that night. Escaping Lord Debenham's clutches—his attempted kisses and caresses—in a way that hinted she was playing a daring game of cat and mouse was exhausting. It wasn't in Kitty's nature to play such games, but to her surprise, she found she knew, instinctively, what would whip up Lord Debenham's excitement. And at what point she could duck out of the final showdown.

Now, sitting on a chair by her dressing table and removing her stockings while Dorcas brushed out her hair, she began to describe her exploits.

"Yer told Lord Debenham summat he'll want ter blackmail Silverton 'bout? Oh miss, yer dunno 'ow dangerous this is."

To her chagrin, Dorcas hadn't been at all excited by the idea that Kitty was going to play Debenham at his own game, and by proving that he was a blackmailer, ensure he was caught in the act and so put him behind bars.

"It might be dangerous, but I know what I'm doing, Dorcas." Kitty raised her hands for Dorcas to remove the lovely evening gown she wore, followed by her stays and chemise, then donned her night shift and slipped under the covers. "I'll also need your help."

"Me 'elp?" Dorcas almost squealed in fear as she shook her head. "I ain't eva intendin' ter 'ave anyfink ter do wiv Lord Debenham. 'E's the devil, 'e is. 'N yer ought ter keep well away, too. Don't 'ave nuffink ter do wiv 'im, please promise me, miss. Forget yer wild ideas. It'll end badly; I jest know it."

"It'll end with Lissa and Ralph being able to marry at last, and Lord Debenham safely locked away and not harming anyone. No, Dorcas; I'll do my bit by orchestrating a bogus exchange. I'll tell Silverton that I've invented this excuse so that he'll be able to turn up with the funds to give to Debenham, and then those who are lying in wait will arrest Debenham. All I want you to do is to quiz the friends you have at Maggie Montgomery's so that you can find out what secrets they might have told Lord Debenham, and even better, where that pewter box is that's supposed to contain them all. Can you do that for me? It's really important. With that, we'll then have all the other evidence needed to make sure Lord Debenham never causes anyone to lose a fortune to keep their secrets, or end their lives because they don't pay. Surely you understand that?"

"I ain't stupid, if that's wot ye're implyin'."

"No, of course not," Kitty assured her. "I don't want to put you in danger, and I promise I'll make sure the information is only given to Mr. Tunley so he can then build a case, but knowing that all these people's misdemeanors never get into the public arena. It'll all happen in a trice—no dribbling out of information giving Lord Debenham time to question who's behind it. You mustn't worry about you or your friends being in any danger."

"It's yer I'm worried 'bout, miss. Ye're too trustin' 'n I know ye'll not like me ter say it, but if yous pittin' yer wits aginst Lord Debenham, then I'm quakin' in me boots. B'sides, I know wot the girls at Maggie Montgomery's will say. That it ain't worth their while ter be talkin'. They'll never tell yer where to get Debenham's box. They'll tell yer to get it yerself."

~

EACH TIME SILVERTON LOOKED UP AND FOUND OCTAVIA SMILING AT him, his stomach lurched with a vague, deep-seated dread that the time was shortening whereupon he would be gazing at her like this each and every day.

"You're not tired?" he asked. Even in the gloom of the carriage, he could see the dark shadows beneath her eyes. He truly was concerned. "It's been a busy few days for you, Octavia. Your aunt certainly seemed worn out last night. I think she'll be glad when this business is over."

"You mean the business of getting oneself married?"

He gave a short laugh, embarrassed at the way she'd called him up on his phraseology. "Yes, my darling, I do mean that, for it is quite a business, and you are not possessed of boundless energy. You are enjoying yourself, aren't you?"

"London is quite the grand whirl."

He'd heard the pause before her enthusiastic endorsement, and wondered if she were feeling slightly jaded as he certainly would be if every night were a repeat of the same round of merrymaking. Silverton had accompanied her to most events, but diversions such as his collaborations on an investigation instigated by the Home Office relieved the tedium.

And tedious it had been, for with no opportunity to even cast his eyes over Kitty, living the life of the carefree blade about town had been a rather barren business. Although, if he had seen her, he realized, it would only have rubbed salt into the wound. The pain of her departure had not eased as he'd thought it would.

"You really are a country girl at heart, aren't you, my dear?" He patted her hand. "Don't worry; we shall only involve ourselves in this lark for a couple of months of the year."

Her eyes lit up. "You truly would oblige me by spending most of your time in the country? Even though I know you far prefer town?"

"Marriage is a serious business."

"Indeed it is, Silverton!" There was real urgency in her tone. She reached across the small space. "You're not regretting this, are you?"

He was glad of the darkness, for while he could inject the necessary jolliness into his tone, he didn't think he could have done the same for his expression. "When I asked you to marry me, I knew it was the most sensible decision I could possibly have made! Mama adores you. In fact, she quite dotes on you. Always has. My tenants know you better than me for your good work. You are a treasure, Octavia!" He squeezed her little gloved hand and closed his eyes, reminding himself yet again of the need to do what was right for his family rather than for himself.

"You are a kind man, Silverton," she murmured, gently returning the pressure. "And I am a lucky girl. Ah, it looks like I am home. Thank you for a lovely evening."

Wearily, Silverton stepped across the threshold into his dimly-lit townhouse, surrendering his hat and coat. He wouldn't go straight to bed, though it was late and he had an early start with meetings at the Home Office.

"M'lord, you have a visitor waiting for you in the drawing room."

Silverton couldn't have been more surprised—and delighted—at the identity of his unexpected visitor, who leaped up in a rustle of silken skirts as the butler discreetly withdrew.

"Kitty! What are you doing here?" He barely dared hope yet he had to ask the question; the affirmative to which would have made him the happiest man on Earth. For right now, he felt like the loneliest. "Have you come back to me?"

"Oh Silverton, you know I can't do that when you're to be married in a little over a week." She looked truly regretful yet her smile, tinged with sadness, was the most glorious sight he could remember seeing as the last few weeks of London revels blurred across his mind.

"You don't love me quite enough to do that, eh?" It was a low shot but, emboldened by the fact he'd just knocked back more than a few brandies shortly before, he wanted to needle her into some declaration that would hint at the truth of her feelings for him.

"I love you too much to force you into such a conflict with your sense of honor, my dearest."

He was disappointed when she took a step back as he approached, and said softly, "Please don't touch me, Silverton, for you know how susceptible I am to your overtures, and I'm really here for a very noble reason which would be entirely spoiled if it resulted in anything physical between us."

"But the physical between us has always been so mutually satisfying, hasn't it? And we both feel exactly the same about each other as we did—" he paused, then added with difficulty—"before you left me."

"That might be true, but that's not what I've come here to talk about." Her words were truncated on a slow sigh, for Silverton had succeeded in breaching the distance between them and now his fingertips were gently caressing her cheek.

She closed her eyes, but did not move other than to whisper, "It's about Lord Debenham."

"Such a ghastly man, indeed," Silverton murmured, hoping that concurring with what he knew she felt about the man was appropriate under the circumstances. "I hope you'll stay well clear of him." Carefully he drew Kitty into his embrace. He needed to manage this encounter with the greatest skill. Holding the most exquisite woman he'd ever met, the woman he'd made his mistress when he'd wanted so badly to make her his wife, simply reinforced how right she made him feel. She was bright, intelligent, a lively companion, and so very beautiful.

And she was so hell-bent on doing what was right.

Silverton was hell-bent on doing what was right, too, which was why he'd never held his wife-to-be in anything more intimate than a waltz hold for fear it would be the death-knell to his resolve to marry Octavia.

"And what is it about villainous Viscount Debenham that brought you to my townhouse so late at night?"

Kitty twined her arms about his neck and nestled her head against his chest. Her soft sigh of contentment was like a hot needle in his most tender parts, for Kitty was so transparent about her affection for him.

She smiled up at him, biting her lip as a moment of doubt seemed to shadow her features. "I told him you were a spy."

"Dear God! What possessed you to say that?"

She looked surprised at his angry bark before responding with the gentle reminder that, "You, my darling, said that you were as far away as could be imagined from being a traitor *or* a spy when I told you of my Cousin Stephen's warnings about you the first time we met."

She looked dismayed, and Silverton realized his facial features must still be composed into an expression of the horror he was trying to mask. He still couldn't get over what she had said. "That aside, why would you tell Debenham I was a spy?"

Kitty stepped out of his embrace and went to the fireplace to warm herself, or perhaps seek a little distance from Silverton's uncharacteristic ire.

"Don't be angry," she pleaded. "When you hear what I have to say I hope you'll think I've been rather clever."

Just the way she smiled at him made his stomach curdle with longing— rather a contrast to the way it was also churning with foreboding.

"When did you have anything to do with Debenham?" He spoke softly for he was trying very hard not to frighten her with the extent of his fear.

Kitty rested against the mantelpiece, appearing to choose her words as she wrapped a corn-colored ringlet around her finger. "Lord Debenham visited me at the theater and took me out to supper."

"Good God! You went out with him? Alone?"

"Please hear me out, Silverton. It's not what you think."

The idea of his precious Kitty putting herself in danger with such a villain struck terror into his heart. Then he realized that the idea of Kitty being with any man other than himself was what was making his heart behave so erratically. Taking a breath to calm himself, he said in a more level tone, "Of course, I realize I have no claim on you now. I cannot dictate who you see."

"No, you can't. And I know that's not because you don't care." She gazed at him with the deepest sympathy, and he longed to cross the floor and take her in his arms as she added, "I know you still love me, just as I love you. *So* deeply, Silverton. That's why I forced myself to spend time with Debenham because I know that he tried to embarrass you over Lady Kilmore's letters, and I wanted to be the agent for good. It was jealousy on his part, but worse is the fact that my sister, Lissa's beloved, Ralph Tunley, needs to find conclusive evidence of Debenham's wrongdoing if he and Lissa are to marry. It's been his greatest challenge, and now I think I have discovered how to do that."

"*You* think you've discovered a way to do what no one else has managed?"

"There's no need to sound so incredulous." She was clearly hurt but put up her hand to halt his apology. "I'm not pretending to be cleverer than anyone else, it's just that Lord Debenham wants to make me his mistress, and he thinks that because you and I have ended our liaison—I do hate that word—that I harbor ill-will toward you. At first, I was going to refute his assumption that I wanted vengeance against you. You must know that I will go to my grave adoring you," she added as an aside. "But then he said he could help me to harm you, and I just needed to think of some terrible secret you had for which you'd pay a great sum to keep out of the public eye. Naturally, I could think of nothing. You are the most honorable man I know. That's when the idea came to me to tell him you were a spy. And that's why I came here, to warn you that Lord Debenham was going to blackmail you, and that the blackmail note would be the evidence you needed, because all you'd need to do then was turn up with the supposed ransom and instead apprehend him."

This time Silverton did cross the floor, but he only put one hand on her shoulder and with the other, tipped her head up gently.

"Kitty, my dear sweet girl, I do thank you for your desire to help. But the fact is, I really am a spy, and Debenham has obviously had his suspicions for a long time. That's why he tried to publicly embarrass me by using my letters to Lady Kilmore against me. When that didn't work, he's been trying to ascertain if, in fact, I could be looking closely into his affairs and not the friend I profess to be. Second, he would never turn up, personally, to collect a ransom. If he did, we would have arrested him a long time ago."

"You are a spy?" Her mouth dropped open and her knees buckled. He had to clasp her tightly to him to stop her falling. And then, of course, he couldn't let go as he added, "Now I fear that we are both in danger."

"Miss, ye're shakin' sumfink terrible!" Wielding a damp cloth, Dorcas rushed across the room to clean up the spillage caused by Kitty having knocked her powder across her dressing table and over the carpet.

"I've done the most terrible thing," Kitty whispered. Unable to stop her trembling, she lowered herself onto her chair and put her hands to her face. "I've put Silverton in danger..." She heaved in a breath. "Dear Lord, I did not mean to do it, but I have. I told Debenham he was a spy."

"Yer did what!"

Kitty tried not to cry. "I thought it was the last thing he could be, and it seemed such a clever way of enticing Debenham to write him a blackmail note so that then Debenham could be apprehended, but now I see how foolish and naïve I was. Oh, Dorcas!" She reached up to grip her maid's wrist. "I don't know what to do."

Dorcas's face was pinched in reflection of her mistress's distress. "Oh miss, yer was only tryin' to 'elp but lordy, if Lord Debenham finks Silverton is a spy, who knows wot he'll do."

"Who knows, indeed? Why, he might find a way of having him..."This time Kitty did burst into tears. "Suffer some terrible accident," she said over her sobs. "Oh Dorcas, I just have to find a way to protect him."

"I dunno 'ow yer can do that, miss."

"Neither do I, which just means I *have* to find something that will put an end to Debenham's machinations before it's too late for Silverton. Oh, what have I done?"

"Could yer ask Lady Debenham fer 'elp ter do that? She's mortal afeared o' 'er 'usband, yer say."

"She'll protect him to the death, because she knows that if he were sent to prison, his entire estate would be forfeited to the Crown and then what would happen to her and William?"

For a moment, Kitty contemplated using her knowledge about William's true origins as a bargaining tool until she realized that she could never stoop to blackmailing Araminta. Besides, it would taint the child who was an innocent. *Children should never be tainted by the wrongdoing of their parents*, she thought fiercely.

Gravely, Dorcas said, "I fink yer should tell Miss Lissa 'n Mr. Tunley. They can at least advise yer."

"I don't know if I have the courage to admit to such stupidity. And, of course, your friends at Mrs. Montgomery's are too afraid to say anything about what they know of Lord Debenham. Which just proves what a very dangerous man he is."

After a moment of silence, Dorcas said, "I did learn sumfink, miss, that could 'elp. 'Bout Lord Debenham and 'bout what Mr Prism and I was tellin' yer the other day."

Kitty waited with bated breath.

'Me friend, Sal, she said she once paid a visit to 'is Lordship's bedchamber when Miss Araminta were wiv her Mama."

"She what! Sally?"

"Sally weren't 'is regular girl, but Mrs. Montgomery sent 'er ter 'is Lordship one night as a bit of a tryout 'n a surprise. Apparently, Miss Araminta were recoverin' from havin' the babe, 'n 'is Lordship were lonely. Well, Sal were that afraid 'n it's true that 'e were none too nice at the beginnin', but then 'e... well, it turned out 'e didn't mind a bit of entertainin' after all. Sal said she were ever so curious 'bout 'is books 'n papers. She's allus wanted ter learn ter write. Anyways, she were lookin' at 'is desk when 'e came back inter the room after bein' called away 'n shouted sumfink terrible, accusin' 'er of all sorts 'til she cried 'n said she couldn't read. Then 'e locked up 'is papers in a pewter box 'n turned the key, which she saw that he put inter a vase on the mantelpiece afta the lights were out 'n 'e thought she weren't lookin'."

After a pause, Dorcas added, "Reckon I shouldn't 'ave told yer that, miss. If yer ever go ter Lord Debenham's alone, then ye're askin' fer trouble."

Kitty shivered. "He touched my cheek when we were talking, and I had to close my eyes and pretend that the reason I was shivering was because I liked it, rather than that I was feeling like an adder was flicking its tongue over me. Oh Dorcas!" she burst out. "I don't want to spend another second in his company, but what if this is the only way? So it's true that he keeps his secrets in a locked pewter box? Well, it's up to me to find it."

"No, it ain't," Dorcas said firmly. "Yer jest tell yer lovely Lord Silverton wot I jest told yer 'n all will be well. He'll be very 'appy that ye've found out such valuable information."

"It's not valuable until it's in the hands of Lord Silverton or Mr. Tunley. It's worth nothing until then, and meanwhile others—including Silverton—are in danger because I put them there."

"Promise me yer won't do nothin' foolish 'n go ter 'is townhouse alone, miss. It ain't worth it. Lord Silverton loves yer too much to see yer put yerself in danger."

"Does he?" Tearfully Kitty raised her head for an endorsement of what could only make her feel worse. "And I love him so much, which is why I'd do anything to do some good out of the bad I've committed. Poor, poor Silverton. I just want him to be safe and happy."

CHAPTER 23

*A*nother pall of ill feeling hung over the Beecham household. Lissa was conscious of a change between her employer and Lady Julia. Lady Julia still visited just as frequently, but the gaiety that characterized their relationship in the early days had been replaced by a tense wariness.

It was different from the earlier brief lull where Lord Beecham was clearly angry with Lady Julia. Now, it seemed, they were both frightened.

In the evenings, Lissa tried to be as obscure as possible, blending into the dull green wallpaper with her drab clothing as she quietly sewed and Lucinda played the piano.

Lord Beecham and Lady Julia always sat together on the sofa opposite the fireplace, but they were quieter than they used to be.

When they did speak, Lissa strained her ears to catch every word, but usually they spoke of dull, pedestrian matters.

Until one evening she was rewarded as Lady Julia gave a gusty sigh and said in a low voice, "Mr. Cranborne lost a large sum of money to Archie last night."

"So the score is evened since the night of the spiders, eh?" Lord Beecham chuckled, but Lady Julia became agitated.

"Archie is greedy. He says that's barely evened the score because Lord Partington forced him into an impossible wager a little over a year ago when he lost two thousand pounds. Mr. Cranborne won't pay up again. He's only the heir and doesn't have that kind of money. And then what will happen?"

Fascinated, Lissa lowered her head and pricked up her ears even more. Although she'd made no secret of her presence, it seemed they'd forgotten she was there. She was slightly obscured from their view by way of the seating arrangement, but now she was careful to make no noise.

"I wish Debenham were dead!"

The words had resonated at the same time as a resounding chord had signaled Lucinda's finale, but Lissa had not mistaken what she'd heard.

Instantly, she saw Lord Beecham's head twist around to glance at Lissa at the very moment Lucinda announced, "Not a single mistake, Lady Julia. I've worked hard as you've exhorted me to."

Lord Beecham's attention was diverted; he quickly instructed Lucinda to play another piece, and then Lissa heard him mutter, "Don't we all, but I beseech you to never espouse such sentiments in public, my dear. These are dangerous times. He's a dangerous man."

"Surely he has enough enemies that someone will give him what he deserves." She dabbed at her eyes with a small square of linen. "Oh Beechy, I'm so afraid. If Debenham continues to put pressure on Archie what will become of me? Archie's happy this week because he's a thousand pounds plumper in the pocket, but what about next week? What about the future?"

Lord Beecham appeared to deliberate. Then he touched his lips to Lady Julia's brow and murmured, "Matters are in hand, my love. Don't you concern yourself with Debenham. I'll say no more, but rest assured that he will be taken care of."

"HE WILL BE TAKEN CARE OF!" THOSE WERE HIS EXACT WORDS.

Excitedly, Lissa paced the kitchen of Mrs. Nipkins's tiny parlor while Ralph lounged against the scrubbed wooden table. He scratched his chin and said soothingly, "Men often try to sound full of bravado to impress their true loves when they have no intention of doing anything remotely brave. I'm guilty of that. Why, you've been relying on me for more than a year to follow through with something brave or notable in order to rescue you from your life of drudgery. I've failed dismally."

"Don't say such things, Ralph!" Lissa flew across the kitchen and into his arms. "You are patient and clever. That's far more admirable than being brash and foolishly bold. But you really don't think Lord Beecham is planning to do away with Lord Debenham?"

"Would you be relieved if I said no?"

Lissa considered the matter. "I want Lord Debenham to make a mistake so that *you* can be responsible for bringing him to justice. He's an extortionist whose demands have led to the death of more than one, and we're all but certain he was directly involved in the attempt on Lord Castlereagh's life with the help of several associates. *Surely* evidence can be found."

Ralph shrugged. "I fear we may wait in vain for a long time. It's hardly likely that either Beecham is going to bump off Debenham, or that Debenham keeps a neat pile of incriminating evidence in a carefully locked box that would be the answer to all our frustrations."

KITTY WASN'T SURE HOW SHE MIGHT FIND A MEANS TO ORCHESTRATE A tete-a-tete with Lord Debenham that would involve returning to his townhouse, thus presenting her with an opportunity to rummage through his study.

So she was relieved when she breezed into her dressing room at the end of the night's performance to find him seated like a sleek bird of prey upon a striped gilt chair by her dressing table.

"Magnificent performance!" he said, presenting her with another bouquet of roses.

"Why, that must be the third night in a row you've seen me perform!" Kitty fluttered her eyelashes as she swept past him to seat herself in front of her looking glass. She removed the paste ear drops, then unbound her hair from the pearl-encrusted binding which held it in neat order upon the crown of her head. It cascaded in a tumble of curls, and she heard Debenham gasp, though she ignored him as she tried to reach behind to undo the top button of her gown.

"Allow me!" Debenham was on his feet in an instant, his bony fingers deftly undoing the top pearl button.

Coyly, Kitty moved away. "I have my dresser to help me, my lord."

"But she is not here."

"I simply need to call for her and she will attend me."

"Why inconvenience her when you have someone as willing as I on hand?"

"Because I have a reputation to uphold. No man in this theater or anywhere else has seen beyond what is respectable under the circumstances."

"Except Lords Nash and Silverton," Debenham supplied slyly.

"Indeed. Lord Nash would have married me had I gone through with it, and I would have married Lord Silverton if he had desired it. I do not give my favors lightly, my lord."

His hands were in the vicinity of her throat, hovering as if he waited only for her to succumb and allow him access to the other buttons. Kitty clapped her hands and immediately Deborah, her dresser entered. "As soon as Lord Debenham leaves us, I shall require your assistance." She sent Lord Debenham a pointed look but he remained seated.

He made a low noise, a little like a growl. "There is one important matter I wish to discuss." When Deborah made no move to leave, he waved her away, saying, "It is a matter of privacy with Miss Bijou. Please!"

The girl scuttled away and Kitty raised her eyebrows. "You are a man who knows how to get what he wants," she murmured. Just what he clearly liked to hear for his thin lips turned up, accentuating the strong nose beneath the cold gray eyes. It flashed through Kitty's mind to feel desperately sorry for Araminta in that moment, but then her half-sister thrived on danger, so perhaps they were well-matched. Not that having a straying husband made anyone a good match, though Kitty had absolutely no intention of going beyond a necessary caress of the cheek in order to achieve what she had to.

Lord Debenham lowered his hand so it rested on Kitty's shoulder. "Your information about Silverton was much appreciated. Indeed, it was as I had long suspected." His nostrils flared. "Ha! He called me friend. If he'd been an honest enemy, I might have considered dealing with him more kindly."

"What have you done to him?" Kitty thought she'd given herself away in that squeak, but Lord Debenham seemed to think she was his ally.

"I'm sure you'd be most interested, my dear. The man who thought you weren't good enough to marry will soon rue the day he so disrespected you. I, on the other hand, respect you too much to see your future stretch before you in such a state of uncertainty." He gripped her shoulders and drew her to her feet, lowering his head so it was less than an inch away from eye level. "Let us not disturb Deborah. Allow me to assist you to change, and we can discuss the plans I have to aid your future successes from the comfort of your abode."

Kitty forced herself not to move back. "I have no abode currently, my lord, since I moved only yesterday from the townhouse Lord Silverton leased for me." It was suddenly difficult to swallow. She was fairly certain she'd not be caught out in this lie. "I'm currently lodging with friends."

A furrow appeared between his eyes. "Poor Kitty Bijou. Nowhere to go?" With slow, sweeping strokes, he caressed her arm. "I can offer you somewhere to go. For tonight, at least."

"But your wife—"

"She's away. I rarely entertain at home, but I should enjoy the company—and the novelty, Miss Bijou."

Before Kitty had time to answer, he was swinging her around and engaged on undoing the second button before Kitty shrieked her outrage. "No, my lord! I told you my objections before."

"But you will come to me tonight?"

Kitty moved away and began to pace. She truly was conflicted, but her creased forehead must have signaled a different kind of objection, for Lord Debenham clasped her in his arms and tilted up her chin as if he would kiss her, before muttering, "By God, you like to lead a man a merry chase. Come to me tonight, and we shall hammer out the terms by which I can secure you the future you desire, Kitty La Bijou. I am a generous man when my passions are aroused, I assure you."

Kitty managed to only just twist her head away before his cold, unwanted lips might have landed upon hers.

"When we have an arrangement that is pleasing to both parties, I will give you all the license you could wish for, my lord." Smiling, she gained the safety of the door, turning the handle as she called out into the passage for Deborah, before saying sweetly to Lord Debenham, "I shall think about what you propose, my lord."

"And I shall arrange for you to be met at the back entrance."

Kitty allowed him a glimpse of white shoulder as she shrugged. "It could be tempting, my lord, though I make no promises. I do have other offers to consider, you know."

CHAPTER 24

*S*o it had to be tonight.

Kitty literally flew through the streets toward home when the line up of carriages and hackneys suggested a delay. She didn't live far, and besides, if she took a slight detour it would only add another five minutes. She needed to acquaint Lissa with what she was about to do.

Having gained admittance to the Beecham household, she had to wait in the kitchen and bribe the parlor maid who was drinking tea in the servant's kitchen to send a note up to the governess, and she was on the verge of giving up when Lissa appeared.

"You shouldn't have come, Kitty. Not dressed like that," her sister whispered, drawing Kitty away from the curious gaze of her fellow employees. "I do wish you had not!"

"But Lissa, I'm your sister!"

"Yes, and an actress, too! Just look how finely dressed you are, but you cannot be a lady to have come here alone. That's what they will whisper."

"Well, let them whisper all they like. The fact is, you won't be working here much longer, Lissa, because I'm about to go to Lord

Debenham's townhouse and find the locked box where he keeps his secrets."

When Lissa looked at her as if she had taken leave of her senses, Kitty laughed. "It's true! My maid, Dorcas, has a friend who works for Maggie Montgomery, whom Debenham took home, and it's the honest truth. He *does* have a box of secrets, for she saw him lock it up and hide the key."

"You can't do it!"

"I'm going to." Kitty removed her sister's hand from her arm and turned to leave, but when Lissa looked at her as if she were going to either cry or shout, explained, "Lissa, I did a terrible thing earlier. I told Lord Debenham that Silverton was a spy because I truly believed he wasn't, but that it would be a means for him to blackmail Silverton, and then Ralph would have all the information he needed to apprehend Lord Debenham. Then I realized how badly wrong I got it. But now Lord Debenham has invited me back to his home—"

"Dear Lord, Kitty, you've not allowed yourself to become—"

"What kind of a girl do you think I am?" Kitty bristled. "He's done nothing more than try to kiss my cheek and," she lowered her voice, "undo my top button but I refused him both, and now he's wild to have me at his home, which gives me the best opportunity of any of us to actually find out what evil he's been up to."

"No, Kitty! I won't allow it!" Lissa shook her head wildly. "As your older sister, I *forbid* it."

"Don't you understand, Lissa? You have always thought me...quite useless. Well, this time I'm going to prove how useful I can be. I'm going to make sure Silverton comes to no harm, and I'm going to help you and Ralph find the happiness you deserve. And you can't stop me!"

She was out of the door before Lissa could say another word, running as fast as her slippers could carry her over the wet cobbles. But her heart was singing at the same time as it was skittering inside her chest.

Lord Debenham couldn't best *her*. She'd held him off as much as she dared, but tonight she was going to show them all that Kitty La

Bijou wasn't London's most self-centered darling. She wasn't doing this because it would see her achieve her heart's desire, or to rise up in the world. She was doing it because the chance had fallen into her lap to do something that would redress the balance. Lissa had worn her fingers to the bone—and for what? Yet she still looked down at Kitty for forging a life that included freedom and, for a short while, love.

"Dorcas, you've got to help me!" She was out of breath as she let herself into her townhouse, and for the first time, didn't linger with a longing look at all the comfort she would soon lose together with her position of safety as Silverton's mistress.

"I need a sleeping draft. Something strong and fast-acting. What do you know about such things? Where to find them, I mean."

"Lordy, miss, wot are ye on 'bout now? If ye're feelin' poorly yer should go straight ter bed. I'll fetch yer sumfink."

"No! It's not for me. It's for Lord Debenham. He's waiting for me at his townhouse, and I'm going to use this opportunity to get the pewter box your friend Sal told you about."

Dorcas looked as if she were about to fall over. She sat down on the nearest chair and fanned her face with her apron, shaking her head. "No, miss, I won't let yer go. It's too dangerous. The risk is too great."

"The risk is great, but it's worth it if I succeed. I've told Lissa and she'll tell Ralph, and now *you* know so it's not like I'm rushing into some hare-brained scheme. If I can slip a little powder into Lord Debenham's wine—for he knows I'll expect to be properly entertained —then I'll be in no danger at all."

Though she said it brightly, Kitty nevertheless felt a pang of pure terror. But then the excitement that churned in her stomach was bigger than that. For the first time in her life, she was going to be the one to make the rest of her family proud of her.

She put her hands on her hips and faced her maid squarely. "Dorcas, I shouldn't have to say that I do not need your permission. Now, quickly, do I look the part? I don't need to change my gown for I look well enough for what I'm about to do?"

"Wot is that, miss? Murder Lord Debenham or be seduced or murdered by 'im?"

Frustrated now, Kitty brushed past her, rummaging in her wardrobe for her most commodious reticule.

"Ye're really goin' inter the dragon's lair, miss?" Dorcas sounded on the verge of tears.

"I'm going to visit Mrs. Mobbs along the way. I'll ask her for a sleeping draft without revealing the nature of my mission. She's used to my visits." She did not need to put into words the fact that Kitty got her regular supplies of Queen Anne's Lace seeds to prevent conception.

ARAMINTA RAN HER PALM THE LENGTH OF TEDDY'S NAKED THIGH AND sighed. "If only it could be like this every night, Teddy dearest," she murmured. She truly didn't think she'd ever been happier.

The clandestine nature of their assignation had infused everything with an excitement that made up for what might have been lacking in Teddy's performance. Of course, he wasn't used to women, and he'd been so eager and adored her so very much so it was only natural that things might have seemed a little...rushed.

She glanced across to see him staring at the ceiling, a look of wonder on his face as he turned and met her eyes. "You are... exquisite!" he breathed. The most exquisite woman I've encountered in my entire life."

He rolled onto his side and held her to him and Araminta closed her eyes, enjoying the feel of his chest, lightly dusted with fair hair, damp from their exertion and so dependable. Not like Debenham's arrack-infused torso, coarsely coated with black hair, that was not dependable at all. Excitement was all very well, and her heart was still running a little fast at the risks she was taking, for there was no telling what Debenham would do if he discovered she was being unfaithful.

There was no telling what he'd do if he discovered he'd been cuckolded so, she reasoned, this was far less serious a crime, and since she was clearly already pregnant again, it was almost no crime at all.

"Oh Teddy, I wish we could be together like this all the time," she said in a burst of feeling. Yes, danger and excitement were all very well, but her life was so dreadfully chaotic and uncertain, and Debenham could fly into a temper and do something dreadful if he learned of her misdemeanors.

"I wish to God my timing had been different, and I'd never left you a year ago. Then you'd be married to me," he muttered, holding her as if she were the most precious creature he wanted to protect forever. That's what she wanted. To be loved and nurtured, indulged and protected. Just when she hoped he might suggest they run away together to a far-distant land, where he had an endless supply of money and a handsome residence waiting for them, and where she could start afresh with no blemished reputation, he said, "Alas, we dare only risk such pleasures when your husband is away."

Araminta had told Teddy that Debenham was up north shooting. She knew her darling would have refused to be alone with her if he'd known Debenham was in London, but time was running out. Araminta badly needed to secure Teddy's affections at the earliest juncture. There'd only be a few weeks—six, at best—before her pregnancy started to show and Teddy would be repulsed and refuse to make love to her, since he seemed a stickler for propriety, even when it came to matters of the flesh.

"But don't you want us to be together always?" she prompted.

"Of course, I do. But I don't know how we can possibly do that."

"We could if Debenham died."

She felt him go rigid, and to ameliorate the shock, laughed and said, "Well, it's true. Debenham is perfectly vile to me, and I don't love him at all. He's quite likely to drink himself into an early death, or have someone come after him since I know he blackmails people so one of them is bound to take revenge. No need to look so shocked."

Teddy raised himself onto one elbow and stared into her eyes. "You seriously wouldn't grieve if your husband...were no longer around?"

Araminta shrugged. "I've been called heartless, but I don't believe in pretending something I don't. I'm not pretending when I say I adore you, Teddy. Why should I have to pretend I'd mourn my husband since he tricked me into marriage and is cruel to me?" She stroked his neck. "I only feel safe with you, Teddy darling."

"My dearest, you seriously mean that? That you adore me and want to be with me forever?"

"Of course, I do!"

"And you'd be prepared to suffer privation and scandal?"

"Well, I wouldn't have to if I were widowed."

"But if Debenham were found guilty of gross wrongdoing, then you'd be placed in an intolerable position. His estate would be forfeited and he'd go to prison, or worse, and you'd be neither wife nor widow."

"Well, that's not going to happen," Araminta said lightly. "But if I were widowed..." She let the idea take root in Teddy's mind. Really, the way Debenham carried on she couldn't see him outlasting her. As for the alternative, she certainly *wasn't* prepared to suffer privation and scandal, which meant she certainly wasn't going to let Debenham stupidly walk himself into danger.

"I probably shouldn't tell you this, darling—"

There was such an ominous edge to his tone, Araminta's happy contemplation of Debenham's demise was replaced by sudden, all-enveloping dread.

"What is it, Teddy?" She rolled onto her stomach and flung a leg over him, as if to cement him there and force out the truth for he suddenly looked evasive.

"I really shouldn't say it, dearest." He held her more tightly to him. "I will look after you. Whatever happens."

"Look after me! That's what I want. I want to be your wife! You asked me a year ago but...but then you raced off on your foolish quest to help someone else you hadn't seen in years, and look what happened to me. And now I've made the greatest sacrifice a woman could make. Look at me! Look what I've risked to be with you."

"Hush! Everything will be all right; I promise you," he soothed. "We'll find a way out of whatever trouble might arise."

"You haven't had reason to suspect that Debenham knows about us?"

"Dear Lord, I'd be quaking in my boots if I thought he suspected anything. But with Ralph keeping such an eye on him, I feel safe in reassuring you on that score."

Araminta started to breathe easy again.

"And Silverton has the matter in hand. Now there's a chap I trust. He and Tunley are well on the way to making up a case that'll get Debenham out of our hair, eh. Spencean, blackmailer. You said it yourself. Thought you'd be happy to be reassured, though I shouldn't have come out with it like that. Ralph wouldn't be at all pleased, but you mustn't fear the future, my angel. Like I said, I'll look after you. We'll go abroad, perhaps. Find a little place—"

"What are you talking about?" Araminta sat up and shook back her glossy dark hair as she stared at him. "Debenham isn't about to be...?" She couldn't say the words. All her worst nightmares were closing in on her. She thought of her reduced dress allowance. Debenham could be generous. Even if he was floating in the River Tick he always managed to find a way. If it came from some of the demands he made for secrets, that only served the victim right for having secrets in the first place.

Teddy, looking concerned now, sat up also and tried to comfort her. "You won't say anything to him, will you?"

"About what, Teddy?" She tried to keep the panic out of her voice.

"They are organizing a search warrant to search his townhouse tomorrow night, but you must promise you won't say a word. I wasn't supposed to say anything, but I heard Ralph and Silverton talking when they thought I wasn't attending. Anyway, they know how I feel about you and that whatever happened to Debenham you'd be in safe hands. With me, that is." He seemed oblivious to the turmoil in her breast as he smiled and tenderly stroked her brow. "Debenham's heir will be provided for. Everything will be for the better. You've married a bad chap, but that's not your fault. It's a good thing

I'm around, dear heart. Truth is, I'd never have gotten this far—he gave a short laugh as he indicated their nakedness with a nod" —had I not known what was in the offing. Now, I daresay we should talk practicalities."

"Practicalities? What do you mean?" Araminta felt ill. Debenham was going to be apprehended? Dear God, she needed to warn him— fast! She was not going to be left stranded, pregnant, and without the financial support of a husband who was at least duty bound to provide for her. Teddy was a love, but he'd already proved unreliable. If he'd only succumbed to her charms and taken ownership of that wretched baby a year ago, they'd have been blissfully joined as husband and wife.

But that hadn't happened. Araminta had had to make a bold and daring plan to get her life on track, and now it looked like—thanks to the information Teddy had just provided her—she was going to have to do it again.

"How, exactly, is this going to happen?"

He looked evasive. "I really shouldn't tell you, my darling. It's a very important investigation, and I only mentioned it to forewarn you so that you were prepared. Having ascertained the ill-will you bear your husband for his appalling treatment of you, and the fact that you are so distressed that he has been operating outside the law, I'd hoped to reassure you that whatever happens, you can rely on me to look after you."

"So, you say this is going to take place tomorrow? Is there no more warning than that?"

"No, I heard that…well, I really shouldn't say, but because a certain young lady had ascertained the whereabouts of a great deal of incriminating documents and other material, and had announced plans of laying her hands on them, my brother had felt compelled to act at the earliest, even though the investigation has been ongoing for some time."

"A certain young lady? Dear God. Connected with my husband?"

"Dearest, these are things I'd meant to keep from you so as to save you distress. You already know the kind of man your husband is. It serves no purpose to paint him even blacker. Where are you going? I thought you were staying?"

Araminta gathered her shawl about her and tried to hide her urgency as she smiled at him. "I know I said I should stay, Teddy, but the bliss I've just experienced has made me feel anxious about poor William, who is cutting a tooth and needs his mama. You know how I dote on him."

"Really?"

"I think one can't help a mother's instinct. I hardly see Hetty these days; she's forever with her baby." She knew she was prattling, but it helped to discuss inane and unimportant matters when her fingers were shaking so badly, and time was of the essence. "Please help me with my fastenings? Thank you, darling." She stroked his cheek before seizing her pelisse and rapidly doing up the buttons in the front. "And now for my hair. Untangle it for me, please, and I'll fashion it into a semblance of order which will be perfectly acceptable beneath my bonnet. There...how do I look?"

"Like a goddess. Some women would take hours to look as you've managed before I have time to...click my fingers."

Araminta thought this a very pretty compliment and bent to kiss Teddy, feeling much more charitable toward him than she had when he'd said such dreadful things about privation and no dress allowance and losing her reputation. None of those things were going to happen to her, and furthermore, she was going to get her man. Yes, she was going to enjoy a blissful and worry-free union with Teddy, who would love and indulge her, but she was not going to do it wearing last season's castoffs as the wife of a traitor and living in penury.

She snaked her arm around the back of his neck and rubbed her body against his, pleased at the instant response she received. Teddy was like soft clay in her hands, and that's what she needed him to be if she were to find the happiness she deserved.

"Who is this young lady? Please tell me, Teddy, for you know how I hate being the last to know, and of course, by tomorrow it'll be all over and...and I will be yours forever."

He pursed his lips. "I suppose it's all right to tell you since you are sisters..."

"Hetty?" She jerked forward as fury bubbled up inside. "Why, she pretended her argument with Debenham was in the past. I know she hates him, but she pretended so well during my birthday." Her brain raced. "No, it can't be Hetty. Surely Sir Aubrey is behind it!"

"No, neither. Please, darling!" Concerned, Teddy tried to cool her anger by holding her to his chest, but Araminta would not be comforted. The knowledge that someone who would do Debenham harm, that might in turn damage Araminta, was beyond bearable.

"Dear Lord, Lissa? Lissa is the traitor? That mousey, mealy-mouthed—"

"No! Not Lissa—"

Perplexed, Araminta stared. "Then who? I have no other sisters."

"My dear, did you not know?" Teddy pushed back her dark hair and regarded her with a look of concern and uncertainty. "Ralph mentioned it once. I was sure you knew..."

CHAPTER 25

"**My** dear, has anyone told you how exquisitely diamonds and rubies become you?" Kitty fingered the necklace Debenham was admiring, and which she was going to have to sell before long if she were to pay her rent and purred, "Many."

"I believe it sets off your fine coloring better even than it did my wife's."

"Yes, Lord Nash told me it had once belonged to Lady Debenham," said Kitty. "In fact, had it not been for this very necklace I may have married Lord Nash."

In response to his enquiring look, she added, "I learned he'd acquired his so-called wedding gift to me from a brothel he regularly frequented. How he came to discover it there, I do not know. There's no telling what items of value one will surrender if the bargain is good enough."

"Everything has its price, eh, Miss Bijou?" Debenham patted the sofa onto which he'd just lowered himself. "And what is yours?"

Kitty raised her eyebrows. "Surely such important negotiations are conducted over the finest champagne?"

"Of course." Debenham leaned forward and pulled on the bell rope, his summons answered by a young footman to whom he dispensed the requisite orders. Once the door had closed behind the lackey he moved his hand to Kitty's, trailing it up her arm to fondle her neck.

"You have very soft skin, Kitty La Bijou. And quite a reputation. In fact, you are beyond rubies, I'm told."

"And who tells you that?" Kitty was feeling distinctly uncomfortable at the close proximity, and the sudden fear that her plan may not yield the results for which she was hoping. The footman had returned and uncorked the bottle before discreetly withdrawing. Kitty glanced over her shoulder to see the light, fizzing liquid in the glasses, and her chest constricted as she wondered how she could dispense the contents of the vial of powder she'd obtained from Mrs. Mobbs. A distraction, of course; she was an actress. She could do that.

A shout of anger from his Lordship was not what she'd been expecting. She startled as he rose and snatched up the bottle.

"This is not what I would have for such an occasion!" For a moment Kitty thought he was angry with *her*.

"I wouldn't foist this on my worst enemy. My pardons, Miss Bijou. I shall procure something more suitable." In a moment, he was out of the door and Kitty was suddenly alone in his private sitting room. Just through those double doors was his bedchamber. The bedchamber Dorcas had described where he kept the box. Lord, was this the God-given opportunity for which she'd dreamed? And without her having to suffer any more of his caresses?

His footsteps suggested he'd hurried to the end of the passage. She might have a few seconds, or she might have longer. Battling the conflict between desire for the right outcome and necessary caution, she rose and pushed open the doors to a large, spacious bedchamber decorated in blue and gold. Rich carpets added an air of sumptuousness, but also promised good sound protection. A small adjoining anteroom suggested the possibility of a study.

Kitty paused on the threshold. Dare she risk it in the time available? The box could be anywhere, and she had literally seconds. It was madness even to begin to look when any moment his Lordship would return. Then how could she explain herself?

She was about to slip back to Debenham's private sitting room when through the partly open door, she caught a glimpse of the escritoire that might have been described by Sally. There was little time, but surely time enough to dart across to investigate?

The escritoire was closed, but the key was still in the door. Kitty opened it and within seconds was pulling out a small pewter box and, without even checking its contents, rushing to the mantelpiece. There was the vase that had been described. She dipped her hand in and, to her astonishment, felt the key at the bottom. Even as she ran Kitty was trying the key which, to her incredulity, fitted. She reached the sitting room just as she heard voices from farther up the passage. She'd not been gone more than a minute so accurate had Sally's instructions been, but if she ran fast enough, she might even make it out into the corridor and around the corner before Lord Debenham returned.

ARAMINTA ARRIVED AT THE TOP OF THE STAIRS JUST AS SHE SAW Debenham approaching. He halted when he saw her, and his face went rigid. His lip twitched. Clearly, he was far from pleased to see her. She wondered what plans of his she might have derailed, and didn't care. He'd be very pleased with her when she told him what she'd learned.

"You were staying with your sister, you told me." His tone was curt, and his eyes glittered, reflecting the candle sconce above his head. "What are you doing here?"

"I missed you too much, my darling." She didn't expect him to believe her, but she made a good show of accompanying her words with a long, soulful look as she rested against the balustrade at the top of the staircase, and put her hands to her burning cheeks. She could still feel Teddy's hot kisses branded there. He was her future, and she wasn't going to let Debenham near her if she could help it.

But Debenham was too valuable to have been thrown to the wolves, much as she'd have loved to have done the pushing herself.

"Well, you've completely turned my plans for this evening upside down," he grumbled. "Now you'll expect me to entertain you when I had other plans."

"Such as entertaining a rather fetching actress?" His expletive made her laugh. "Don't think ferreting out information is your preserve, darling. I'm rather good at that. Always have been, and it's what I learned tonight that had me rushing over here with rather more haste than I might have otherwise done."

"Jealousy?"

"I would prefer to think you had a shred of loyalty toward your wife, but I gave up on that hope long ago. I am resigned to the fact that loyalty is a foreign concept to you, so no, it was not jealousy that brought me here."

He laughed. "Concern? Love or desire?" He looked anxious to leave. Raising his eyebrows, he added with heavy cynicism, "It must have been a particularly strong emotion to have caused you to act so out of character."

"Well..." She drew out the word, so he could see she had something important to say. "You are my husband, and if I learn of a plot that endangers your financial interests through your likely arrest for treason, I have a vested interest in acquainting you of such a dastardly plan."

"Oh, so you'd not mourn if I hanged, but you are concerned with how your financial interests would be affected."

"Precisely."

He chuckled. "My dear, my secrets are under lock and key. Not even you know how to ferret them out of me or indeed where they may possibly be."

His supreme arrogance irritated Araminta. She closed the distance between them and ran her fingers up his sleeve. "*I* may not, but word has it there's someone who's going to make a good job of trying."

He snorted.

"A little birdie told me that someone, in fact, does know where you keep your secrets under lock and key."

He regarded her lazily beneath his hooded eyes, his silence

spurring her on. Yes, she'd tell him, but she'd draw it out. Make him wait.

"In fact, a certain person who is not at all the kind of creature I'd associate with and who, in fact, you shouldn't either—except that I know how susceptible you are to a pretty face." While her words sounded as if they were coated in butter, there was a jagged edge to Araminta's fury. How had she remained in ignorance for so long that Kitty La Bijou was her sister? All this time the girl had pretended ignorance, but she must be filled with spite and envy that Araminta had what she'd been denied. Miss Bijou must have been carefully plotting to bring to fruition her evil plan—the total destruction of Araminta's life.

"For God's sake, Araminta, stop talking in riddles and get to the point. Yes, I'm interested if there is something to suggest a threat against me, though doubtless your only motivation in forewarning me is to save your own skin."

"Precisely, darling, which is why you should listen to me and why I am, in this instance, so very valuable to you. All right." She rolled her eyes. "I believe you've made arrangements to entertain Miss Kitty La Bijou after tomorrow night's performance, and I have it on good authority that she has an ulterior motive for agreeing so readily to your charms."

Just saying the name brought the acid to her mouth, but she went on sweetly, "She is very jealous of me and has been telling terrible lies about me, did you know. But worse is the fact that she knows about a certain box—" Araminta stopped and called after him as her husband turned on his heel and tore up the passage. She didn't think she'd ever seen Debenham run in his life.

Kitty slipped out of Lord Debenham's bedchamber with literally a split second to spare before the sound of his footsteps around the next bend alerted her to the fact he was on the warpath. She couldn't believe it. She had it. The pewter box was in her hands, and it had been so simple.

But how to continue to avoid detection? Surely someone would challenge a strange young lady in an evening gown?

Kitty kept to the back stairs where the lighting was dim, and the corridors were empty. If she could successfully weave her way through the catacombs of Lord Debenham's spacious London townhouse, she should eventually find her way to the basement and so to the welcoming outdoors.

When she did manage this, blinking in the moonlight at the top of the stairs that led from the coal delivery access, she set her footsteps for north.

She couldn't go home to her lodgings. While she'd pretended she no longer had the right to live there, it would be the first place Lord Debenham would seek her out as he undoubtedly would do. If the box she had in her arms contained the secrets of which he was suspected, he'd kill to keep her from handing them over. She had to be swift and canny.

She couldn't go to Lissa. Not at this late hour.

She thought of Ralph, but again, he might not be there whereas Silverton was close by. Close enough so she could seek his help and his advice.

She told herself that her decision to seek him out first had nothing to do with wanting to show him how clever she, alone, had been; that it had nothing to do with the fact she loved him to distraction—still.

None of this was evident when she was admitted to his drawing room, and he faced her from the other side of the sofa with an expression of mild perplexity, for they had parted—for good, it would have appeared, not long ago. And his marriage was in just days.

"Silverton." She simply breathed the word. She was delirious with her cleverness. Then she carefully laid the box on the low table and waited for realization to sink in or curiosity to get the better of him.

He received her alone in his drawing room where it appeared he'd been playing cards. There was no one opposite him at the small walnut table, and when he glanced up after she was announced, a gamut of emotions flickered across his face. Then he rose, and flicking just the barest of glances toward the box, stepped forward and placed his hands on Kitty's shoulders. "I don't believe it."

"Silverton...are you not you proud of me?" His worried frown had not been swept away by delight.

"You put yourself in grave, grave danger." Kitty did not like the hint of suspicion in his tone when he asked, "What did you have to do to get this?"

She shook her head. "He hasn't touched me if that's what you're worried about. In fact, it was all astonishingly easy. Dorcas had been supplied the exact location by a friend who'd been to Debenham's house, and then when he invited me into his bedchamber—" she glanced down and blushed, "I had a vial of powder that Mrs. Mobbs had given me to put in his drink."

"Dear Lord, Kitty, I don't believe it."

He turned back to the box and finding the lid locked, was instantly supplied the key by Kitty, who said, "I knew exactly where that was, too. Open it, Silverton. I want to see what it contains."

"A treasure trove," he murmured.

It was as if Debenham was proudly keeping an inventory of each evil extortion attempt and other felonies in which he'd been involved. Indeed, here was all the evidence they needed to convict him of a multitude of crimes, including the blackest of all—treason. Beneath the list of those whose secrets he'd ferreted out, and those who'd paid to have their scandals suppressed from threatened publication, were his notes from three years earlier on how he and his associates intended to bring down Parliament following their attempt on Lord Castlereagh's life.

"Dear Lord, not only is so much in his handwriting, he's signed all manner of incriminating correspondence," breathed Silverton. Carefully closing the lid, he rose and drew Kitty into his embrace, but when she moved her head slightly, he kissed her on the top of her head.

"You have done what no one in the Home Office has managed in more than two years. You are a ...." He put her away from him and stared with wonder into her face. Kitty's heart hitched, and it took all her willpower not to throw her arms around his neck and hug and kiss him rapturously, for excitement—and pride—were fast flowing through her veins.

"Say it, Silverton," she murmured. "I want to hear what you think I am."

"I've always known what you are," he said with more energy this time though he didn't move his head closer. "You are the most courageous, beautiful, astonishing young woman I have ever met." His eyes glowed as he lowered his voice. "If we existed within the pages of a romance, we would get our happily ever after."

"It's too late now." She moved but did not entirely pull away. "You are not going to abandon your worthy bride at the altar, throw me astride your white charger, and gallop into the sunset to where a priest is waiting to preside over our holy vows."

"It doesn't mean I wish I couldn't."

She smiled. She felt the familiar tug at her heartstrings; the pain in the back of her throat as she fought the tears. "The inevitable is too hard to resist. There's too much of everything to fight. Our marriage would simply not be accepted. I'd be shunned, and possibly, so would our children...our female children, certainly. I wanted respectability through marriage, but I wanted love more. And now I can't have either."

"Where are you going?"

She turned at the door and looked over her shoulder. "Home," she said simply. "I've achieved my greatest wish—to deliver to you what you wanted above all else."

In two strides he was at her side. He restrained her with a hand upon her shoulder. "That's not what I wanted above all." He glanced back at the box on the table, then again at her, his look full of meaning.

"But we know it can't be."

Reluctantly, he nodded. "But you can't go home."

"I realized that, of course. It's the first place Debenham will look. After here, of course. No, Mrs. Mobbs has a bed for me."

"Kitty, I can't let you go. It's too dangerous."

"I certainly can't stay here." She put her hand on the doorknob. "Not with your mother in residence." She pulled away, more firmly this time. "Good night, Silverton. I'll slip out the servant's entrance."

"I'll take you." But when Kitty protested strongly, he finally persuaded her to accept an escort of one of his servants, and wearily Kitty made her way through the streets in a hackney, suddenly exhausted. She'd proved herself, and now she felt she could sleep for a year.

SHE DIDN'T SLEEP MORE THAN AN HOUR, IT SEEMED, FOR MRS. MOBBS was soon rousing her urgently.

"I gotta get yer out 'o 'ere, Miss Kitty," she whispered. "'I dunno 'ow but 'is Lordship seems ter fink yer 'ere and 'ere ain't where yer can be if that's wot 'e wants, is it?"

In a panic, Kitty threw back the covers of the bed she was sharing with some other newly-arrived maid to town and stood, disoriented, in the middle of the room while Mrs. Mobbs bundled her discarded dress into a bag.

"Out the back, 'urry!" she whispered. "I'll keep 'im talkin' in the parlor. Take the first hackney yer can get. It don't matter where yer go, yer just can't be 'ere."

With her mind in a whirl, Kitty dashed out of the back door and into the cobbled laneway. She could hear Mrs. Mobbs raising her voice cheerily in greeting for but a second, before a passing hackney caught her attention and she darted in front of it, rapping on the door to make it slow.

"Just drive! As far as you can get away from here, and don't stop!" she cried out, handing the jarvey a coin before leaping inside.

Only when they were well on the road and had put considerable distance behind them, did Kitty's heart finally start to slow down and she felt she could relax.

Where could she possibly go? she wondered. Was her home in the village a possibility? But no, she hadn't the money to go such a distance in a hired hackney, if it were even possible.

The jarvey had taken her at her word and was simply continuing, so Kitty relaxed back in the squabs and closed her eyes while her mind churned over the enormity of what had occurred.

Perhaps a lodging house on the outskirts would suffice. But at this hour? She'd be mistaken for a prostitute and refused admittance, even if she could pay.

For the moment though it was easier just to do nothing while the hired equipage rumbled through the streets. Kitty thought of the danger she'd just escaped and wondered what might be in store for her. She should have let Silverton take charge, but had wanted to prove that she'd not done this to gain his gratitude. She'd done it as much for herself as for him. And Lissa.

She must have dozed off, for suddenly the hackney was slowing. She looked out of the window and saw they were beyond the outskirts of London and that the river illuminated on her right was unfamiliar. The rank odor of rotting detritus wafted through the cracks in the door, and she held her nose at the stench while her stomach heaved.

Suddenly, she was frightened. The silence was unnatural. Not the hustle and bustle of London, but the eerie quiet of some country hamlet.

Where was she? This did not seem right. How long had they been driving? What instructions did the jarvey think he was following?

Then a more insidious question filtered into her adrenaline-flooded brain.

Whose instructions was he following?

She rapped on the roof to gain the driver's attention, but he did not falter though he must have heard. The track they were following twisted and turned as it contoured the hedgerows by the river. Kitty had never been this far east of the city. She knew of no one who lived here.

The carriage lurched as it hit a deep rut, and Kitty was flung against the side, hitting her head and heightening her fear.

Last night, she'd been a guest at Debenham's townhouse. She'd thought she'd been so fortunate and clever in achieving her aims with virtually no physical contact with Debenham. Then she'd fled to see Lord Silverton and to hand him the information he needed, before slipping away to the least likely place Debenham might find her—Mrs. Mobbs's.

How then was she a prisoner? For that's what she felt she was at this moment, thundering over the muddy roads toward who knew what.

She grabbed the doorknob, but the vehicle was traveling too fast to make it an option to throw herself out, even if she were able to fling open the door which seemed unyielding, even as she tried.

Dear God, if Lord Debenham were behind what seemed increasingly like an abduction, what might be the outcome?

Finally, the carriage slowed in front of a tidy little house on the banks of the river. It looked to be a mill with its large waterwheel slowly turning the sluggish water. Dawn limned the horizon, giving just enough moonlight to make out the eerie outline. Kitty hoped she might seize the chance to leave and run before the carriage came to a halt, but she heard a gate close behind them at the same time as a large, burly, balding man in a hessian apron and leather gaiters emerged at the top of the mill's steps. He advanced purposefully toward the carriage, opening the door as it stopped, and shouting a few words to the jarvey before he thrust in a meaty hand and hauled Kitty out and onto the dew-covered grass.

"Welcome, Miss Kitty," he greeted her, seizing her hand and pulling her up the steps. She was no match for him she quickly realized, and to struggle was pointless. He was *so* very much larger.

And he smelled. Of flour, but also of something stale and rank that made her eyes water.

"Who are you?" she managed as she stumbled over the threshold of the enormous, wooden-floored storeroom into which he pushed her. "What do you want of me?"

He ignored her, dragging her toward the open window from

where she could see only a wide expanse of river, mudflats and reeds with, in the distance, a scattering of humble dwellings.

"Yer'll 'ave to stay 'ere awhile. I got me orders, and I ain't one ter disoblige when there's so very much at stake ter line me pockets."

Kitty rubbed her wrist where his grip had been vice-like. Her skin was red and sore.

"I have a performance to put on tonight," she told him. Not that she expected that to hold much sway. "Do you know who I am? An actress. People will recognize me. Miss me. They'll come looking for me. You don't want to be accused of... of taking me against my will. And if you don't release me, that's what you'll be guilty of."

But he was already at the door. "I don't care who yer are, miss. Fact is, I'm bein' paid ter keep yer 'ere until further orders. Yer won't get far." He nodded toward the open window, with its deadly plunge to the ground, then opened the door, brandishing the key to show her he was about to lock her in. "I dunno what ye've done 'n, like I said, I don't care. I got a family ter look after, 'n a few coins ter keep yer contained so that yer can answer fer what yer done ain't a big deal ter me." He smiled, not unpleasantly, but with a frightening vacancy and lack of empathy. "I'll send me daughter up wiv a plate 'o victuals 'n a loaf 'o bread. That'll keep yer until I know what we're ter do wiv yer."

"Please, stop!" Kitty ran across the room, but he'd already closed the door firmly behind him and made no response when she banged loudly. "Who has ordered me to be detained here?"

When there was no answer, she ran to the window on the side opposite the river and saw him crossing a muddy courtyard where a few hens pecked at the ground. Even though she shouted through the window, he did not heed her as he mounted the steps to a ramshackle cottage where he was greeted at the door by a dirty-faced toddler before he went inside.

CHAPTER 26

"I know I married a tyrant, a blackmailer, a philanderer, and a gambler, but I didn't know I'd married a fool!" Araminta made no secret of her disgust as she glared across the table at Debenham in what would probably be their last drink together.

Alone in the library, he'd just admitted to entertaining that fancy trollop whom she thought had been her friend, but whom she realized had set out to ruin them both.

Araminta drained her glass then slammed it upon the table. "So you have conveniently supplied in one little box every damning secret you ever had to hide. You have nowhere to go, and very soon you will be behind bars. You will be attainted. Your estate confiscated. You will hang, and I will be left with nothing. Not even a noble husband to mourn. Your son will be a penniless nobody, while I will be vilified, and your memory will be blackened forever more. That's how it is, isn't it, Debenham? There is no other way."

He looked ashen, even in the soft candlelight. Vanquished. There was no other word for it.

Her rage was like a ribbon of white-hot fire chasing through her veins. "And all for the dubious delights of a common little actress. You allowed her into your bedchamber; you allowed her access to your secrets. And as a result of your stupidity, you will be known as a traitor. You will be attainted. Yes, let me say that word again! *Attainted*! All the lands and estates of a traitor are forever forfeited to the Crown. And the second consequence? Corruption of blood; an attainted person can neither inherit property, nor transmit it to his or her descendants. Do you have any ideas on how to save our skins?"

For the first time, it seemed he had no cutting words either.

"So you are simply preparing to die?"

He couldn't look at her, and his voice shook. "I shan't let them just take me without a fight."

"So you'll run away."

He shrugged. "What else can I do?"

Araminta raised her eyes heavenward. "I always knew you were a coward, Debenham. After all, it's the only way you got me to marry you. By coercing me, for you couldn't have had me if I'd been allowed to make the decision for myself before you seduced me so thoroughly."

The clock ticked loudly in the silence. Araminta was unmoved by the quaver in his voice. "I'll be gone before the morning. You can take whatever valuables you can store away so that you and William won't be completely destitute…" His voice cracked. "I shall miss the boy."

"And me? Shall you miss me? For I certainly shan't miss you, Debenham."

To her surprise, her husband put his hand across the table and rested it upon hers, almost tenderly. "I will miss your fire and spirit." He raised his eyes to hers. "I've always admired that."

"Even while you've tried to vanquish it?"

"I've always enjoyed a challenge."

"But now you can see there is nothing left for you. You've ruined yourself, and you've ruined your wife and son."

A small sob escaped him. "If I didn't have William, I wouldn't care so much about what happens after I'm gone. But to think that my son will bear the stain of ignominy…that he will be denied what is due to him—the noble title of Debenham and the rich estates that go with it."

Araminta drummed her fingers upon the table. There had to be a solution. Some way to salvage something of what Debenham had thrown away.

Time seemed to slip away before her very eyes, the hopelessness like a wave that threatened to wash her away.

"I have an idea, Debenham," she said slowly, as the fire from the second brandy she'd just consumed rather rapidly spread a welcome warmth through her belly, infusing her with inspiration. She leaned closer to him, trembling as it gained a life of its own. "There is some risk to yourself, but I can't see any other way."

He didn't respond. Hope had truly left him, but Araminta was on the cusp of it. She'd always managed to come up with a cunning plan, and this surely was her best yet. "You're a strong swimmer and you can surely dodge a water wheel. Now here's my plan which I'm the first to admit is not perfect. It's just that I can't see any other way of ensuring that William's future and fortune remains intact."

WHILE THE MORNING FIRE CRACKLED IN THE GRATE, A SLEEP-DEPRIVED Silverton and a burning-with-enthusiasm Ralph Tunley focused their attention on the engraved pewter box that sat on the table in front of them.

Stephen Cranborne paced the room behind him, every now and again glancing across at the box, framed by the yellow curtains at his sash windows. "Without a doubt, gentlemen, we have what we need to put our man away for a very long time."

Silverton wasn't surprised at the lack of enthusiasm in Cranborne's tone. What he was surprised at was the degree to which Cranborne's activities had been documented by Debenham and used against him.

Stephen Cranborne straightened and ran his hand through his light brown hair. He looked older suddenly. And very cornered, as well he might.

"No need to look at me like that," Cranborne darted a sideways look at Tunley. "You're thinking more than just that I'd be a thousand plumper in the pocket if I'd confessed my sins to you when you first intimated your suspicions."

Silverton's sins were not the only ones clearly outlined in the oblong pewter box. Cranborne had been named as the father to the child most likely to inherit Sir Archie Ledger's estate. In the biggest shock of all, he'd also been labeled Lady Partington's lover.

Only Ralph was lily-white compared with Silverton and Cranborne, not to mention a raft of society's notables whose various affairs and misdemeanors were carefully tallied in the lists Debenham had compiled.

Of course, the elephant in the room was to whom the box should be delivered—to Sir Edward alone? And with its full complement of secrets?

The early morning sun was filtering across the floor, and the question still had not been addressed, when a loud knocking at the door came as a relief. The question could be delayed while a matter of apparent urgency needed attention. Even if it was only a question concerning dinner.

They all turned, and Ralph was the first to step forward as Miss Hazlett flew into the room. Silverton hadn't seen the young governess for some time, and then she'd been dressed in drab serge with her hair severely restrained beneath her bonnet. Now, she'd clearly not taken the time to properly dress her lustrous dark locks, which had come undone from their bindings and cascaded down the shoulders of her hastily-buttoned pelisse. Indeed, the top two buttons were not fastened. Miss Hazlett was a young lady of such restraint Silverton wondered what could have prompted such a departure from her usual careful toilette.

"Lissa?" Clearly, Tunley thought the same, but with more alarm judging by his tone.

"Kitty sent this!" she cried, coming to a stop before him in the center of the room and thrusting a piece of parchment at him. "Oh Ralph, she's been taken. I went to your lodgings, and Mrs. Nipkins sent me here. I beg your pardon, gentlemen, but this is a matter of urgency. Lord Debenham is holding my sister against her will. She's sent a message to that effect, and beneath it, his Lordship has written that he's prepared to negotiate in return for her release."

"Kitty? They've taken Kitty?" Silverton felt the air sucked from his lungs as he repeated, "Debenham wants to *negotiate?*"

"There's nothing he can negotiate over," said Cranborne with a frown. "We have all the evidence we need for a case against him."

"He says he has nothing to lose, and he'll simply take Kitty with him when he goes. That he's going to jump into the river, and that if you don't entertain his demands, he'll...he'll kill her."

It was true. Debenham didn't have anything to lose. He knew that all the evidence needed to see him hang was there in that little pewter box. He was also vengeful, and he'd know that no court would consider Kitty's life important enough to haggle with. Besides, there wasn't time.

"I'll go." The others had said nothing, but it had taken Silverton no time at all to come to the conclusion that he'd do whatever was physically within his power to secure Kitty from Debenham. Remorse hung heavily upon him. "I knew I shouldn't have let her go when she gave me the box last night. Thank God she's all right for the moment, is all I can say. I'll go now."

They all went. However, the others traveled by carriage while Silverton went on horseback once he'd changed into riding clothes.

It was less than an hour to the hamlet named, but he was bone-weary by the time he arrived, for the roads had been half washed away by a recent deluge.

The address had not been familiar to him, and now he found himself before a large flour mill. He had no idea why Debenham might have chosen such a location, except that it was remote. Kitty would not be overheard by curious neighbors.

He saw her from the window before he'd even come to a halt, and his heart seemed to double in size when she smiled her relief; her face a faint and far-off mirage that gave him hope. "Silverton!" She'd barely managed to utter his name before she was abruptly torn from the window, and Silverton threw himself off his horse and ran to the door of the mill.

Kitty was in danger because of him. She'd taken an enormous risk, and it was up to Silverton alone to extricate her from whatever threat was hanging over her head. Debenham had everything to lose, but he was clearly not going to go out without a fight. If Silverton had only thought the thing through better, he ought to have known that he should have put a constant watch over Kitty until Debenham had been brought to justice. What a fool he'd been to have underestimated the importance of everything that had happened in the past twenty-four hours, not least the danger to Kitty. As if she'd not already put herself in mortal danger through her brave act—of folly, some might say—to entice Debenham to his home.

The sound of squelching boots across the courtyard made him turn from his hammering on the mill door, and the miller nodded his head in greeting.

"I eard as 'ow there'd be someun ter fetch the lass." He was an enormous fellow with huge meaty fists and a bullet-shaped head poking out of his rough clothing. While he looked menacing, his tone was conversational. "Brother, mayhap? She's done a grave wrong, I 'eard. Stole sumfink that wasn't 'ers. You 'ere to give it back fer 'er return?"

Silverton looked about him. He had to raise his voice above the fast-running river and the clank and creak of the waterwheel nearby. Recent heavy rains had caused a veritable cascade. He wondered why Debenham had chosen this, of all places, to entice Silverton.

And what he had in mind.

It didn't matter. Silverton just needed to get Kitty out of here, safe and sound.

"That's what Lord Debenham told you? I need to see Miss Bijou now."

The miller opened his mouth to reply but stopped at a sound behind him.

"Ah, Silverton, so it was you all along."

Silverton jerked his head around at the familiar caramel tones as Debenham came into view. As sartorially elegant as ever, his high shirt points seemed to hold up his long neck, almost serpent-like neck it seemed, given that his eyes glittered amber in the morning light.

"I wondered whom Miss Bijou would summon to her rescue. Fool that I was, I believed you were the last for whom she harbored any fondness after you gave her your congé the moment you announced your betrothal to worthy Miss Mandelton."

"Miss Bijou knows I will always look to her interests and not only in this instance when she has delivered to me exactly what you know will see you rot in prison."

Debenham looked regretful. "I do curse my stupidity in making it so easy for you, having successfully obfuscated matters for so long. But there it is. You have me, and I could either offer to go peacefully now and accept the inevitable or make you a proposal."

"You're not in a position to make proposals."

"I think I am considering I hold in my hands the life of the woman you apparently love. I had not known that, Silverton. I thought she was a passing fancy. Very lovely, she is, I do agree. I'd hoped to secure her charms myself, but it appears she desires only you. You can imagine I do not hold her in such high esteem having now realized she is the very creature who has ruined me. I would wish her dead. I may be headed that way thanks to her, and I should rather like to take her with me since I have nothing to lose by it. Do I?"

Silverton's blood ran cold. "Very soon you will be overrun by sheer force of numbers."

"As I expected. But also as I expected you have come ahead of the pack. You wanted to talk to me because of secrets you wish not to be broadcast. You see, there is room for negotiation."

"I need to see that Kitty is unhurt."

"Of course. Let us go upstairs and meet the girl, shall we? Hear what she has to say." Genially, Lord Debenham invited him inside. It was cold, the temperature having dropped as the rainclouds became more oppressive. The thick walls of the building kept the warmth out and the chilled air in and Silverton shivered, despite his woolen coat.

Yet it was like the sun had burst upon him when the top-story door was opened, and Kitty rose at their entrance, standing in a shaft of light from the window like a sun queen, her hair burnished gold, looking even more beautiful if possible, though he quickly saw the strain in her face when he advanced.

"Kitty!" he cried, hurrying across the floor to take her in his arms. Her warmth and willingness to be embraced were the balm he needed to assuage his guilt. "I am responsible for this," he muttered. "Dear God, forgive me. Has he mistreated you?"

She shook her head. "No, but the guarantees he wants you to make are impossible." Clearly, she was trying to hold back her fear. They both knew how vulnerable she was. Evidence that would see Debenham swing was in Government hands now, and Debenham was a vengeful man. He'd have no compunction in killing Kitty for no other purpose than revenge against her and Silverton.

"Enough!" Debenham brought out an elegant silver blade at the same time as he gripped Kitty's wrist and jerked her out of Silverton's embrace and into his. With a smile, he drew her back toward the window. "We can both go now if you choose," he said, indicating the drop to the churning river below while the paddles pounded their deadly rhythm.

Kitty's gasp raked across Silverton's conscience as if Debenham's blade had already done its work.

"I'm a ruined man and this woman is the cause. She has delivered me to you like a lion to the slaughter, and I want my revenge. Only my complete exoneration will save her."

The bleak horror in Kitty's eyes reflected Silverton's.

"The box is out of my hands. You know that, Debenham. But you are no murderer. Not in cold blood. Not even you could do that."

"I think I am capable of rather a lot when my life is hanging in the balance. It would give me a great deal of satisfaction, in fact, to take Miss Bijou with me to the grave since I was unable to take her to bed." He chuckled. "I want what you had, Silverton. And which you threw away."

A little piece of Silverton seemed to crack and disintegrate. Yes, he had thrown it away. Thrown away his chance of true happiness, by sacrificing Kitty at the altar of respectability and family expectations.

And now he would be all but responsible for throwing away her very life.

Very slowly, he stepped forward. The blade was sitting almost gently against the soft white skin of Kitty's throat. It was a small and deadly knife. Just one neat thrust was all that was needed to end Kitty's life, and here Silverton was, bargaining Debenham's life for hers. He'd never felt more powerless. With the box and its secrets out of Silverton's hands, how could he possibly give promises Debenham knew he was in no position to keep? Secrets he may well not, as far as Debenham was concerned.

"I can bargain for your life if you promise not to harm Kitty. I'm in a position to do that." Silverton hoped the dread in his voice wasn't as clear to Debenham as it was to him. Debenham had always fed on fear and dread. Silverton had not had a huge respect for Lady Debenham, but he remembered feeling pity for her on occasion.

"And how can you do that, Silverton?" It was a sneer, and indeed, how could Silverton? He had connections and influence, but he had no means of effecting an outcome any more than Debenham right at this moment.

"You've just admitted you have secrets that could send you to the gallows, and that now we have those secrets, there's nothing for you to fight for. What about the little honor you have left? Would you simply snuff out the life of a young woman on the cusp of everything ahead of her because you can, and you want vengeance? Put her aside and fight me, man to man. You have the knife, and I have nothing. I'm prepared to take you on at such a disadvantage if you just let Miss Bijou go."

To Silverton's surprise, Debenham laughed as he pushed Kitty aside, in the same moment as he lunged for Silverton. "I've been wanting to do this for a long time," he muttered. "False friend, you are, Silverton. I don't believe false friends deserve to live." The knife sliced through the air by the side of Silverton's ear and he ducked, immediately feeling the sting.

"Silverton!" Kitty cried, foolishly entering the fray before Silverton pushed her away at the same time as a trickle of blood obscured the vision in his right eye.

"That didn't take long!" Debenham crowed. "I have the advantage, don't you see? You want to both die? I can arrange that. It would be my pleasure!" There was shrill satisfaction in his laughter as he leaped with surprising agility in a man so tall toward Silverton, slicing the knife once more at throat level. Silverton jumped aside in time, only to see Debenham thrust and parry then lunge toward Kitty. He seemed fueled by blood lust, and Silverton realized he really did want to do Kitty the gravest ill. It hadn't been empty talk or a means of simply bringing Silverton to the bargaining table. He would kill Kitty if he could.

The imperative now was to draw him away from her. Kitty didn't deserve any of this. If Silverton hadn't been so fixated on behaving as society demanded, she'd be flourishing as she deserved.

"It's me you want. You'd kill a defenseless girl?" he taunted, drawing Debenham to the window. Silverton settled himself on the deep window ledge; the drop below to the river long and fatal. But if he could only entice Debenham closer, he might succeed.

Debenham's face broke into a parody of a smile as he paused a moment, assessing his target. Silverton could see the workings of his mind as Debenham prepared to launch himself forward. So this was it. Debenham had made his choice—that he would not be taken alive, but that he'd take Silverton with him. Silverton had made himself a target, to be bowled over by the momentum of Silverton's rush toward the ultimate freedom—death by waterwheel.

Kitty's shrill cry and Debenham's bloodcurdling scream of vengeance were, he imagined, the last sounds he would hear before oblivion. He was conscious of the blur of rage and hatred on Debenham's face as the man barreled forward; of the heavy body blow that dislodged Silverton from his position—the two of them locked in combat at that great height. The resounding cry of defeat that echoed in the silence. And then Silverton was clinging to the harsh stone, his hands struggling to find purchase while his feet scrabbled in the stone, mercifully finding a chink in the sheer surface of the wall.

Incredibly, he was alive, and there was Kitty's face, beautiful and terrified, staring down at him.

And if this were the last vision he ever had, he believed he would be a happy man.

But it was not. Kitty's screams had alerted the miller who now appeared, and whose meaty grasp was what saved Silverton, though without Kitty, he'd never enjoyed the cathartic sense of knowing finally what he was prepared to compromise and what he was not.

CHAPTER 27

*A*raminta knew she looked fetching in black. Of course, having to wear it for a full year was going to be tedious, but there would be compensations.

Teddy, for one. She was almost rather glad she was breeding for, it meant she need not worry about inconveniently producing a child at the wrong time. There'd been no risk when Teddy had come to console her the night before when all hell had broken loose about Debenham's death at the flour mill.

What a shock that had been, but what a fool her husband had been. A fool to have been so incautious as to have been caught, most of all.

As Teddy had held her in his arms and made tender, careful love to her, Araminta had wanted to scream and scratch and give herself up to her joyful enthusiasm. It just hadn't been quite the right time to show such abandon, she felt.

There was one major niggling concern, however, and that was that she had no idea if Debenham could be tried in absentia. His body had not been recovered—which was hardly surprising in view of the plan they'd concocted—but she'd heard vague stories about seven years having to elapse before he'd be considered officially dead.

So where did that put Araminta?

She'd poured out her fears to Teddy, who hadn't been much help except that he'd sworn he'd love and protect her for all that time, if necessary.

Well, that was very comforting and helpful, but it wasn't enough. Araminta needed iron-clad guarantees. She needed to know her husband's estate would not be confiscated, that William would carry his title, and that Araminta would be free to remarry when her year of mourning was over. She needed to know that Debenham's dirty little secrets wouldn't be aired for all the world to snigger over, and that she would be just as well-regarded in society's loving embrace as she had before Debenham's death.

And if securing all those guarantees required just a little more planning, then so be it. Araminta didn't have time to waste while the wheels of the law slowly turned up answers in drip-like fashion.

Which was why, the very day following her husband's tragic demise, she appeared in the most becoming widow's weeds she could find, to present herself to Lord Silverton and Messrs. Cranborne and Tunley. Oh, she was very clever in having gathered together these three unlikely men in the one place.

Solemnly, they all offered their condolences upon her recent loss, before inviting her to sit at the large oval table in Lord Silverton's palatial dining room. Araminta was surprised and quite envious to discover it was larger than her own dining room table.

"No doubt you are aware of why I am here," she said in the low, respectful tones of one recently bereaved.

Lord Silverton and Mr. Cranborne muttered their assent but Mr. Tunley said with creased brow, "I own that I am in the dark, Lady Debenham, unless it is to petition us to minimize the extent of your husband's list of ills, which will obviously soon become public."

Araminta sighed. "When those become known, I hope I shall gain more public sympathy, rather than less. Surely, I have made it clear since my marriage that I was a less-than-willing participant in that holy union? Mr. Tunley, has your brother not told you how Lord Debenham tricked me into marriage, blackmailing me into attesting I visited him at his supper house, so he could avoid being incriminated for meeting with his two compatriots in a case that would attach him to certain misdemeanors of which I had no knowledge of that time? My husband was a wicked man, and neither our son nor I deserve to suffer for his crimes and bear the stain of his wickedness after his death. Especially when I was so unwilling to marry him in the first instance."

There were murmurs of sympathy at this, but only the very forthright Mr. Tunley appeared to take any active role in the conversation, for he said with irritating officiousness, "You have my sympathies, Lady Debenham, but I do not see what we can do to alleviate your suffering. The law is the law."

"And you have the evidence to support the fact that Debenham was involved in a litany of crimes. I know that," she said crisply. "You have obviously seen the inventory of his misdemeanors which he so helpfully compiled for you before Miss Bijou stole the box which contained them."

"And thus proved herself a heroine to this country," countered Silverton.

Araminta bowed her head. "I am sure she is very deserving of your accolades. She inveigled herself into my husband's affections. I wish I'd been able to do the same. I was, however, canny enough to keep myself apprised of his activities in order to protect myself, should I need to. And now the time has come when I am able to congratulate myself on the fact I took such precautions. I do not know if you have surrendered the full contents of that box to the Home Office, gentlemen. You received it only yesterday morning, and the drama involving my husband took much of your attention through the following hours, so I suspect you might still be discussing what you will do with...every piece of information it contains. Such as the fact that you, Mr. Cranborne, are named as the father of Lady Julia's son, who is touted to succeed his father due to the ill health of his remaining brother. In addition to that fact, there are also signed witness statements attesting to the fact you've taken advantage of the goodwill of my father, Lord Partington, to trade upon...the access it gives you to..." she paused delicately, "...my mother, Lady Partington."

Saying the words made the bile churn in her belly, but she retained the sweetness of her smile. She'd no more smear her mother's name in the mud than her own—they were one and the same to an extent—but she had to show how much she knew and to make them very, very frightened.

"And you, Mr. Tunley; you are desirous of a match with my half-sister, Larissa. But how will a lowly governess be received in society? I might choose to blackball her, which I am quite in a position to do, given my well-known friendship with Countess de Lieven, one of Almack's Lady Patronesses." She paused for effect. "And you, Lord Silverton, have lost your heart to an actress. Yet you are compelled to marry a woman you do not love and one, in fact, who does not love you."

Silverton's choked response was just what she was after. "You had not guessed? Why, Miss Mandelton was pouring out her heart to me only the other day saying that honor must dictate her actions. She is so very attached to your mother, who dotes on her and who desires this union between the two of you, and while Miss Mandelton does not actively rail against marrying a man for whom she feels only the fondness a girl would feel for her brother, she told me she is prepared to sacrifice her happiness for the duty she feels toward your mother whom she esteems above all others."

"Sacrifice her happiness to marry me?!" Silverton repeated. "Just to please my mother?"

Araminta smiled. "Yes, those were her very words, and I was impressed by her quiet dignity. She will make you an excellent wife, and I'm sure will be agreeable in all things, but is this what you really want in a wife—a pliant, dutiful creature reluctantly agreeing to marriage because she wants to please your mother? Of course, the vibrant Kitty La Bijou could only be an encumbrance. Certainly, it's not without precedent that an actress has married into the hallowed echelons of the aristocracy. Common Emma Hamilton secured the hand of Lord Hamilton and was lucky to be accepted. She had created a stir and society was intrigued. I can imagine society would regard Miss Bijou as a heroine just as easily as they would shun her. We all know how very fickle are the arbiters of social acceptance. Goodness, to think that securing a voucher to Almacks can give that signal of social acceptance that can make one's past simply disappear. Something I could very easily persuade the countess to arrange."

There was a very long pause after this. They did not interrupt as they let her make her point. Yes, Araminta smiled at Lord Silverton, Mr. Tunley, and Mr. Cranborne and felt the power go to her head. "I suspect that *only* the three of you have thus far witnessed with your very eyes the blackmail threats and recordings my husband made of your various peccadilloes, Mr. Cranborne. I suspect you are very undecided as to what should be done with the incriminating material. Let me help you make your decision. Remove the evidence that incriminates you, Mr. Cranborne, and you remove the damage that would be done in the event of a potential or more probable leak. Your reputation and that of my mother, and also Lady Julia, will be removed. Where's the harm? My husband is dead."

She gave a little sob and dabbed at her eyes with the corner of a piece of fine linen. "He is where he would be had he faced the law which might have seen him at the end of a noose. I know how much you would like that evidence removed. I certainly shall say nothing of it. But I would ask only one thing in return. Remove the evidence that might see Lord Debenham convicted in absentia of those crimes which would see him attainted, and you have my pledge that I will use my considerable influence with the Countess de Lieven to ensure that Larissa Hazlett, my half-sister, will be acknowledged, both by her noble father, and by each one of the six esteemed Patronesses of Almacks."

She sent Silverton a considered look. "I shall do the same for Kitty La Bijou. It was a shock to discover her true identity, and under different circumstances, I admit I would have done all in my power to have her blackballed for life and never ever accepted by society. She is beautiful and too great a threat, and the gossip could only be damaging to me. But I intend to turn the attention into something novel.

"I'm clever at turning a situation to advantage, and I will do so in the case of my two half-sisters, the women you, gentlemen, would marry if only you could be assured of their happiness, and yours, through the acceptance of society and the acceptance of your respective families. Leave the tactful negotiating to me. If you only remove those pieces of evidence that would otherwise see my husband forfeit his land and estates, then I will remain in a position of sufficient influence to do all this that I have pledged is within my power."

CHAPTER 28

"No one could have made a more beautiful bride, Lady Silverton. I am so very happy for you." Miss Mandelton's pleasure was clearly genuine as she pressed Kitty's hand and raked her bridal attire with glittering eyes.

Tears welled in Kitty's own eyes and she blinked rapidly. "It could have been you," she responded, stricken, and was almost cut off by the rejoinder.

"But I'm so glad it's not! I'm so glad I realized before it was too late that Silverton didn't love me. To be married to a man whose heart belonged to another would surely have been like living a slow death until I was put in my grave."

Laughter and chatter echoed all around them, and a great joyfulness filled Kitty from her toes upward. "You cannot imagine how tormented I was when I met you, Miss Mandelton, and realized that you were to be married to Silverton." There wasn't much time for confidences with the church bells pealing, and guests waiting to congratulate the pair of them, but Kitty wanted to take her opportunity while she could. Silverton was a little to one side, beaming as the Duke of Albion pumped his hand in between casting furtive admiring glances in Kitty's direction.

Kitty put her head closer to Miss Mandelton's. "I relinquished any claim I might have had to Silverton as soon as I realized he'd made you an offer. I knew I could never marry him. I was not respectable enough."

"But now you are. And you deserve to be marrying the man you love because you are the heroine of the country. You risked your life to bring a dangerous criminal to justice."

"I'm sure you overstate it, Miss Mandelton," Kitty said modestly.

"Indeed I do not! The news sheets and gossip sheets have no room to discuss anything else—and with good reason. The safety of our country is due to you, for was there no limit to the evils perpetrated by that traitor, Lord Debenham. First, he was cruelly responsible for blackmailing a poor innocent into becoming his wife over that incident at Vauxhall Gardens. Poor Lady Araminta—I believe she balks at using the name Debenham, synonymous as it has become with perfidy—didn't know what else to do other than agree she'd been in Lord Debenham's supper room when really he was plotting with two other villains. And as a result of her name being tarnished, she was forced to marry the man!"

Kitty blinked. Miss Mandelton obviously relished scandal more than Kitty would have supposed.

"Yes, marry the very man who would have murdered you as revenge for the fact that you were clever enough to discover the evidence that would convict him."

Kitty thought it wise that Miss Mandelton didn't go into too much detail over how Kitty had discovered this evidence.

Miss Mandelton suddenly became diffident. She lowered her voice and gripped Kitty's hand. "I...hoped we could be friends. I mean, that I could call on you when I'm in London, and that you'd call on me when Silverton and you repair to the country at the end of the season. I know his mother took a little while to come around to the idea that he wasn't marrying me after all, but I've thoroughly persuaded her of the fact I would have been dreadfully unhappy married to someone I regarded more like a brother, and you with your publicly lauded gifts are in the position to advance not only his prospects, but his happiness so much more than I could ever have done."

"Oh, Miss Mandelton." Kitty squeezed her fingertips. "Nothing could make me happier. I would love that."

"Kitty."

It was her sister. The four of them were together today at Kitty and Lissa's joint wedding, but Kitty recognized it as the voice of the sister who'd always been more like a mother to her. The sister she loved more than any other. The sister whom she'd sought to make proud. Lissa.

Smiling, she turned, and her heart swelled to see that Lissa's normally serious expression was joyous. But then Lissa had done little else other than smile since Mr. Tunley had apparently proposed in the most heartfelt terms, on bended knee, with a family ring his romantically minded favorite aunt had bequeathed him for the purpose.

"Ralph wants to introduce you to Sir Edward," she murmured, nodding her regrets at Miss Mandelton for taking Kitty away. "He's been extolling your virtues, Kitty—and your bravery." She pressed her lips together as she and Kitty stood facing each other, alone for the moment. "I'm ashamed to admit that I didn't give you the credit you deserved for forging ahead and doing what you believed in—both to advance your own happiness and then for what you saw as the common good."

"The common good? You make it sound so noble, Lissa, when the truth is that I did it for *you*."

"Me?" Lissa looked taken aback.

"I wanted you to be able to marry Ralph. After everything you've ever done for me—being the mother I never had, keeping me in line when I was little and needed it, reading me stories, mending my clothes, making sure I went to sleep on a laugh and not in tears. All those things I've never told you, but which I only realized was the foundation of my happiness after I'd run away to London. When I made my name on the London stage, I couldn't bear to think you were ashamed of me, and that was the reason you didn't make contact. I had no idea you were doing what you do best—working quietly and without fuss to achieve a good end. I wanted to repay you in the best way I could, and because I thought I had nothing of importance left to lose since I'd lost Silverton and your respect— or so I thought."

"Oh Kitty, you really thought all that?" Impulsively, Kitty leaned forward and kissed her sister on both cheeks. "In truth, I'm far showier than you'd imagine. I wanted to be the one to shower us all in glory and so enable Ralph to wed me."

"But it was your sketchings that brought all of this into the open and alerted the government to the nature of Lord Debenham's wickedness. Without your talent, none of us would be here." Kitty indicated the petal-strewn cobbles that surrounded St Margaret's and the rarefied, finely-dressed crowd distinguished by a more than respectable smattering of England's Upper Ten Thousand. She smiled over her shoulder as she saw Ralph and her beloved new husband advancing toward her. "Let's just say that finding happiness today has been a family affair."

Thankfully, Kitty was about to slide into obscurity, safeguarded from the hubbub by Silverton's protective bulk, when a stately figure in half-mourning stepped in front of her.

"Kitty, the Countess de Lieven wishes me to introduce you to her." It was Araminta, wearing her widow's weeds over her pregnant belly like a badge of honor. "And you too, Lissa, though she's more interested in the extraordinary circumstances in which society can so readily embrace someone who's made their living on the stage. Not that she said it in so many words. She's a stickler for convention but loves knowing that she can confer the right to be accepted or not— just by her endorsement. Rather a lucky coincidence she was on more than passing good terms with Papa, which of course made it rather difficult to refuse to acknowledge you after Papa publicly accepted you."

Papa. *Their* Papa. Not so many months before he'd stood in this very church and declared to Nash and the small gathering of wedding guests—though he might have declared it to the world—that Kitty was not a suitable match for Lord Nash, and could never consider herself on an equal footing with respectable society because of the sin in which she'd been born.

The perpetual sin to which *he'd* consigned her.

It was astonishing how courting the favor of a handful of the right people could influence society as a whole.

It seemed Araminta had turned the ignominy of Debenham's end to her own advantage, making herself a victim and her sisters heroines who had saved society as they knew it from the chaos her husband would have imposed had he his way.

Silverton rolled his eyes as he took in the last of this speech. "Go on, take her away to meet the countess, but I would like to spend *some* time with my wife on our wedding day." He smiled fondly at Kitty, who gave his hands a quick squeeze, pulling him down for a daring kiss on the cheek.

Lissa had assumed her look of polite disinterest that Kitty had come to realize hid so much of what she was feeling. "I can do quite well without making the acquaintance of Countess de Lieven," she said airily, though she changed her tune when Ralph said, in the fond and jocular way Kitty had noticed swayed Lissa every time.

"Come, my dear, it never hurts to court the good offices of those who are in a position to advance us all. I quite like the bland fare served at Almacks, but I'd much rather be able to sample it in your company."

So Kitty followed her vain and self-important sister to the influential Countess de Lieven, and exchanged a smile with her beloved and down-to-earth one along the way, noting that all the while Ralph's brother hovered not so far away.

She put her head close to Lissa's, and whispered, "Do you suppose Araminta will lose interest in poor Lord Ludbridge before her mourning period is officially over?"

Lissa shook her head. "I think Teddy's slavish devotion is far more to her taste—when she needs someone dependable—than the dangerous charms of anyone more exciting. No, I believe I shall soon find myself bound even closer to our sister than you before the year is out."

And so, after the public endorsement conferred upon the two hitherto unacknowledged Partington 'bastards', Kitty and Lissa returned to their adoring husbands who whisked them into two separate carriages, at last, to take them to the palatial new residences they could now occupy as fully accepted members of the haut ton. And there they enjoyed what every bride in love looks forward to with such anticipation—learning how to please and be pleased by their husbands in the marital chamber.

And Araminta, fueled with the success of having secured her own future through elevating the half-sisters she'd once despised, happily went home alone then waited with genuine anticipation for the secret visit of her darling Teddy, which would occur at the same dependable time of eleven p.m.

She thought it rather a good feeling to be known for doing a worthy service, as she signed the monthly letter of credit her supposedly-dead husband relied upon to keep up a modicum of his wicked old ways in whatever den of vice he'd chosen to inhabit on the Continent as the price for keeping his life. He'd been lucky, but perhaps clever, too, in dodging the deadly blades of the water wheel before he'd swum to freedom.

Thank the good lord that with Debenham considered dead, Araminta could hold his estates in trust for young William. He would never be able to return home unless he was prepared to accept his sentence of death.

And if perchance the Thames or the sea disgorged some unrecognisable corpse, Araminta would find a way to identify it as her husband.

Meanwhile, Araminta was rather looking forward to the novelty of being known for her goodness and charity, acknowledged as the architect of her sisters' acceptance by respectable society.

Thus transformed, a whole new world beckoned.

EPILOGUE

Sybil felt surprisingly emotional as she gazed at her two daughters, who were chatting on the steps of the church in the few minutes before the christening of Araminta's twin daughters, Arabella and Theodosia.

As usual, Araminta cut a dashing figure, her gown of heavy mourning a distinct contrast to her animation. Sybil thought the veiled adoration on Lord Ludbridge's face as he waited for her a few steps farther up was hardly surprising. Most men behaved like moths to a flame when Araminta smiled in their direction. Lord Ludbridge had been loyal when Araminta had needed him, and no doubt held high hopes he'd be repaid when Araminta's twelve months of mourning was over. Meanwhile, Hetty was looking lovelier and more serene than Sybil had ever seen her. Marriage clearly agreed with her.

It was hard to imagine that Araminta was now a mother of three—and a widow within two years of her marriage. So much had happened since Debenham's terrible death. The truth was that he'd not been mourned. His crimes were abominable—those that were publicly acknowledged. Stephen had told her there were many others that would not be aired in the public arena since he was not alive to defend himself.

As a widow, Araminta had garnered far more public sympathy than Sybil would have expected, given the litany of Debenham's misdeeds. However, her eldest daughter seemed to have a gift for turning a situation to her advantage, and influential members of society were publicly lauding her as a heroine for having survived the trials to which Debenham had no doubt subjected her.

Astonishingly, Araminta had chosen as the godmothers of her infants, former actress Kitty La Bijou, now Lady Silverton, and one-time governess Larissa Hazlett, now Mrs. Ralph Tunley. Sybil had been surprised at how painful she'd found the experience when Lord Partington had acknowledged the two young women as his daughters not long after Debenham's broken body had been identified, washed out to sea several months after his death.

She'd been equally surprised at how short-lived her angst had been after she had realized Kitty was the young girl she'd comforted during Araminta's birthday ball and to whom she'd taken an instant liking. Sybil had been touched to learn that the words of wisdom she'd imparted during their exchange had led to Kitty renouncing Lord Silverton as her lover. And now she'd married him.

That would not have been possible had Kitty not acted with honor, and followed through with her painful and noble act in leaving Lord Silverton completely unencumbered to wed the deserving Miss Octavia Mandelton, whom Araminta had reported was on surprisingly friendly terms with Kitty and who'd declared herself far happier living quietly in the country.

Then there was Lissa, whom Sybil remembered had come to the house several years before supposedly seeking funds for a village school she'd wanted to set up. Sybil remembered the revulsion and anger that had surged through her veins when she'd realized the identity of the girl.

Now she understood how the girl had suffered through no fault of her own. Humphrey had condemned her and her sister to live life as outcasts, just as he'd condemned Sybil to a cold and passionless marriage.

When Sybil saw how deeply the girl loved her new husband,

charming and genial Mr. Ralph Tunley, and her determination to make the world a better place, it gladdened Sybil's heart to know that sometimes truly deserving people were blessed with happiness.

The revelation that Kitty and Lissa were Lord Partington's illegitimate daughters had been regaled with spurious glee in all manner of muckraking newspapers, as well as respectable news sheets. However, it had also been reported they'd played major roles in bringing to light Lord Debenham's part in terrorizing the ton with his propensity to reveal their secrets, so Humphrey, Lord Partington, his wife and both legitimate and illegitimate daughters had withstood the scandal. In fact, they'd grown stronger.

She turned as her hand was surreptitiously seized for a quick squeeze before it was almost instantly released. Stephen had just passed by to join the two sisters, but now he hesitated, then took a few steps toward Sybil as if to address her in the fond but distant manner disinterested onlookers would expect, given the nature of their formal relationship. Theirs was one pairing that would not be condoned were it to be revealed, yet its foundation of honest and enduring love gave it the stability to satisfy Sybil. For twenty years, she'd survived a marriage without love. Stephen's love was a blessing she did not take for granted and never would. It imbued each day with a sense of wonder and enchantment. Their child, Celia, would grow up in the belief that Humphrey, Lord Partington, was her father, yet knowing the love of both her real parents. Sometimes such compromises had to be made for the happiness of all.

Sybil stepped a little to the side as the attention turned to the squalling infants, now being borne by Kitty and Lissa into the church in the wake of Araminta and Hetty.

"You must be very proud of your daughters," Stephen said. "And your granddaughters, though Lord knows you barely look old enough to be a mother, let alone a grandmother."

Sybil rolled her eyes, unable to keep the affection out of her tone as she replied. "Yes, both of them. Araminta truly has distinguished herself by her dignity as a young widow."

"I can only admire the manner in which she's refused to be tainted by her husband's sins." Stephen's tone was wry. "In fact, I am full of admiration for the way in which she's turned Debenham's villainy to her advantage. But now, Hetty is beckoning to us. She's blooming, isn't she? Sir Aubrey has been a better match than I expected. Well, no secrets between them. That helps."

Sybil hesitated as she slowed her progress up the church steps. She glanced about her to ensure they were not overheard. "I wasn't going to say anything before, Stephen, but as there are no secrets between *us*, I will tell you about Hetty's concerns..." she cleared her throat, then added in a hurried whisper, "...regarding the paternity of a child she believes was fathered by Sir Aubrey."

She wasn't surprised at Stephen's sudden intake of breath. He sent a furtive glance over her shoulder before looking her in the eye. "Did Debenham apprise her of his suspicions?" he asked. "How would she suspect? But of course, it was the hair, wasn't it?"

"Yes, a child she saw at a fair. The adopted son of a farmer and his wife. He had the Banks' swathe of white hair amidst the dark. Well, suffice to say that Hetty has chosen to say nothing to Sir Aubrey as the age of the child confirms any liaison occurred prior to his marriage to Hetty. However, Hetty is sponsoring the child in secret." She felt a great pride in her daughter, as she added, "Like Araminta, she has chosen family unity as her life's greatest goal."

Gently, Stephen traced the contour of Sybil's cheek. "Yes, it is wonderful that Araminta has embraced family unity, though I run the risk of displeasing you if I suggest that might be more from the strategic advantage it currently confers on her." They were alone now on the church steps, the rest of the party having just passed through the doors. Very gently, he cupped her face and kissed her lips. "But you, Sybil my love, always see the best in people. You saw it in me when I was despairing for myself. You are my redeemer, and you make me better than I could ever have been had I not met you." He dropped his hands, offering Sybil his arm instead to lead her into the church. With a smile, he added, "Araminta is the best she could hope to be for having you as her mother, and I hope she will continue to make you proud." Gently he caged her hand with his and gave it a squeeze. "It's because of your strength, endurance, and mother's love that today is such a joyful day. You deserve every happiness."

They'd reached the top step now, and were about to pass through the large double doors to play their part in that holy ceremony that would anoint babies Arabella and Theodosia and give them validity in the eyes of the Christian Church. Stephen hesitated, his expression grave but his eyes bright with fervor as he lightly held Sybil's hands. "And just know that I will always be here for you, Sybil darling, through the years ahead, come what may. For family unity is everything."

The End

AFTERWORD

I hope you enjoyed the final book in this first series of four very different sisters from different walks of life.

It was wonderful to be able to provide Kitty and Lissa with happy endings however Araminta's lost son is another story -in another series soon to come.

I happen to be one of three sisters but the sibling rivalry between Araminta, Hetty, Lissa and Kitty is purely fictional as I've been blessed with two warm and supportive sisters. Apart from the odd bit of hair pulling and a well-remembered case of stomach-biting that we love to rib our youngest sister about, nothing but harmony has reigned amongst us.

If you'd like to read more of my stories, you can find me at www.beverleyoakley.com.

Happy reading!

ABOUT THE AUTHOR

Beverley was seventeen when she bundled up her first 500+ page romance and sent it to a publisher. Rejection followed swiftly. Drowning one's heroine on the last page, she was informed, was not in line with the expectations of romance readers.

So Beverley became a journalist.

After a whirlwind romance with a handsome Norwegian bush pilot she met in Botswana's beautiful Okavango Delta, Beverley discovered what real romance was all about, saved her heroine from a watery grave in her next manuscript and published her first romance in 2009.

Since then, she's written more than fifteen sizzling historical romances laced with mystery and intrigue under the name Beverley Oakley.

She also writes psychological historical mysteries, and Colonial-Africa-set romantic suspense, as Beverley Eikli.

With an inspiring view of a Gothic nineteenth-century insane asylum across the road, Beverley lives north of Melbourne with her gorgeous husband, two lovely daughters and a rambunctious Rhodesian Ridgeback called Mombo, named after the safari lodge where she and her husband met.

You can read more at www.beverleyoakley.com

www.beverleyoakley.com
www.beverleyoakley.com
beverley.oakley@gmail.com

www.ingramcontent.com/pod-product-compliance
Lightning Source LLC
Chambersburg PA
CBHW030637110726
47901CB00002B/475